Mystery at the Hidden Harbor

An Ethel Thomas Detective Story

By Cortland FitzSimmons

Originally published in 1938

Mystery at the Hidden Habor

© 2015 Resurrected Press
www.ResurrectedPress.com

Published by Resurrected Press

This classic book was handcrafted by Resurrected Press. Resurrected Press is dedicated to bringing high quality classic books back to the readers who enjoy them. These are not scanned versions of the originals, but, rather, quality checked and edited books meant to be enjoyed!

Please visit ResurrectedPress.com to view our entire catalogue, and like us on Facebook at Facebook.com/ResurrectedPress to stay updated!

ISBN 13: 978-1-943403-09-7

Printed in the United States of America

Resurrected Press Books in *The Chief Inspector Pointer Mystery* Series

RESURRECTED PRESS CLASSIC MYSTERY CATALOGUE

Journeys into Mystery
Travel and Mystery in a More Elegant Time

The Edwardian Detectives
Literary Sleuths of the Edwardian Era

Gems of Mystery
Lost Jewels from a More Elegant Age

Anne Austin
One Drop of Blood
The Black Pigeon
Murder at Bridge

E. C. Bentley
Trent's Last Case: The Woman in Black

Ernest Bramah
Max Carrados Resurrected:
The Detective Stories of Max Carrados

Agatha Christie
The Secret Adversary
The Mysterious Affair at Styles

Octavus Roy Cohen
Midnight

Freeman Wills Croft
The Ponson Case
The Pit Prop Syndicate

The Uttermost Farthing: A Savant's Vendetta

Arthur Griffiths
The Passenger From Calais
The Rome Express

Fergus Hume
The Mystery of a Hansom Cab
The Green Mummy
The Silent House
The Secret Passage

Edgar Jepson
The Loudwater Mystery

A. E. W. Mason
At the Villa Rose

A. A. Milne
The Red House Mystery

Baroness Emma Orczy
The Old Man in the Corner

Edgar Allan Poe
The Detective Stories of Edgar Allan Poe

Arthur J. Rees
The Hampstead Mystery
The Shrieking Pit
The Hand In The Dark
The Moon Rock
The Mystery of the Downs

Mary Roberts Rinehart
Sight Unseen and The Confession

Dorothy L. Sayers

Whose Body?

Sir William Magnay
The Hunt Ball Mystery

Mabel and Paul Thorne
The Sheridan Road Mystery

Louis Tracy
The Strange Case of Mortimer Fenley
The Albert Gate Mystery
The Bartlett Mystery
The Postmaster's Daughter
The House of Peril
The Sandling Case: What Would You Have Done?

Charles Edmonds Walk
The Paternoster Ruby

John R. Watson
The Mystery of the Downs
The Hampstead Mystery

Edgar Wallace
The Daffodil Mystery
The Crimson Circle

Carolyn Wells
Vicky Van
The Man Who Fell Through the Earth
In the Onyx Lobby
Raspberry Jam
The Clue
The Room with the Tassels
The Vanishing of Betty Varian
The Mystery Girl
The White Alley
The Curved Blades

Anybody but Anne
The Bride of a Moment
Faulkner's Folly
The Diamond Pin
The Gold Bag
The Mystery of the Sycamore
The Come Back

Raoul Whitfield
Death in a Bowl

And much more!
Visit ResurrectedPress.com
for our complete catalogue

LIKE us on Facebook for upcoming release
announcements!

Facebook.com/ResurrectedPress

FOREWORD

Cortland Fitzsimmons was best known for a series of mystery novels involving sports and other forms of popular culture. It was his novel *70,000 Witnesses: a Football Mystery,* that brought his talents to the attention of Hollywood when the novel was made into a film. This was followed several years later by *Death on the Diamond: A Baseball Mystery* which was also made into a movie. Other mysteries involved professional ice hockey, a dance band, and a stage magician. These mysteries were well written, fast paced, and entertaining, and one suspects, at least after the success of *70,000 Witnesses,* were written with the potential for adapting them to film in mind.

As successful and popular as these mysteries were, Fitzsimmons' best work as a mystery writer may be four mysteries involving Ethel Thomas. It's hard to imagine a more unlikely detective. A seventy-five year old spinster at the time of the first mystery in which she figures, *The Whispering Window,* Thomas is a wealthy, unconventional member of New York's social elite. With the exception that she seems to know everything about everyone that matters, she bears almost no resemblance to that other famous female sleuth, Agatha Christie's Jane Marple. Whereas the latter confined most of her activities to a small English village, Thomas occupies a much larger village, the island of Manhattan. And rather than being prim and fussy, Thomas is not adverse to the occasional cocktail or whiskey and soda and fully enjoys an active social life with her many friends of a much younger age.

Considering that she was born about the time of the Civil War, Ethel Thomas has adapted remarkably well to the twentieth century. Telephones and radios no longer amaze her, she takes automobiles and airplanes in stride, and she has reveled in the changing fashions. A woman who was at her prime during the "Gay Nineties," she has made herself at home amidst the jazz and cocktail parties of the "Roaring Twenties" and the "Thirties." Shrewdness as a businesswoman has allowed her to weather the Depression with only minor concessions. And through it all she has kept her sense of humor and proclivity for making wry observations about the world around her.

The setting for *Mystery at Hidden Harbor* is a perfect one for murder mystery; a private island just off the shore of Long Island, cut off from the mainland by a storm that washes away the only bridge and disrupts electricity and telephones as well, and murder is what happens when Henry Baldwin, an outsider who has bought his way into the close knit community of Hidden Harbor but who is disliked by almost everyone on the island, is found dead at the Club House. There are plenty of suspects as Miss Thomas soon discovers, unfortunately, most of them are old friends and she must race to solve the mystery before the police arrive and arrest one of them.

Fitzsimmons does an excellent job of portraying the various residents of the island, both those that keep summer homes and boats on the island and the year round "granters," so called because they were granted land for cottages when the island was privatized. The Depression hasn't been kind to many of the residents, a number of whom have lost their wealth and have retreated to Hidden Harbor as a sanctuary of last resort. Relations between the granters and the members are tense at times, but, like any insular group, they find themselves drawing together when faced with an outside threat.

Fitzsimmons portrayal of his narrator, a spry spinster younger than her years, whose acerbic comments enliven the novel is just as wonderful. Few male authors have created a female character as engaging and as entertaining as his Ethel Thomas. The problem is that she only appears in four books.

As with all of his works, *Mystery at the Hidden Harbor* is well paced and entertaining, a joy to read for anyone who likes their murders with a touch of humor. That Fitzsimmons was a screenwriter during the 1930's is clearly evident in the way he structures his novels.

During the dozen or so years that mark his career, Cortland Fitzsimmons was both a successful author and screenwriter with over a dozen novels and as many movie scripts to his credit, including at least four film adaptations of his own novels. Yet today, he is relatively unknown. It is therefore with great pleasure that Resurrected Press offers this new edition of *Mystery at the Hidden Harbor*.

About the Author

Cortland Fitzsimmons was born in Brooklyn, New York (possibly Queens) on June 19, 1893 and died July 25, 1949 in Los Angeles, California. After attending New York University and The City College of New York, he worked for some time as a salesman for several book distributors and publishers before turning to writing full time in 1934. Most of his works as a writer were mysteries, a number of which were based on sports themes such as *70,000 Witnesses: A Football Mystery*, *Crimson Ice: A Hockey Mystery*, and *Death on a Diamond: A Baseball Mystery*. A number of his novels were made into films and he moved to Los Angeles to work as a screenwriter. His last book was a cookbook that he co-wrote with his wife Muriel Simpson *You Can Cook If You Can Read*.

Greg Fowlkes
Editor-In-Chief
Resurrected Press
www.ResurrectedPress.com
Facebook.com/ResurrectedPress

CHAPTER ONE

LOOKING BACK ON what happened at Hidden Harbor those two days I honestly think I felt a tension in the air as we crossed the low bridge and stopped at the gate where our ex-ferryman, Willie Pole, a fish-eyed grouch, protected our tight little island community from the influx of sightseers and other non-members.

I say our island because for years I owned one of the cottages near the yacht club and only sold it because I felt I was getting too old to be bothered with a summer place which meant a great deal of extra work for the servants and they, like myself, are not getting any younger.

Under normal conditions I would have refused Abbie Abernathy's invitation to "rough it" down there. But I wasn't normal the day she arrived from Detroit. It was frightfully hot in town and I was bored with myself and the placid routine of my life.

I went with my eyes open. I knew Abbie spent her time at the Harbor in the loft of the old boat-shed which she shared with her cousin Peter Randall. I knew they did for themselves. Abbie warned me that the place would probably be filthy. She said Peter had never been one to leave a clean place behind him. I was in the mood for adventure and accepted her invitation gladly, although she insists I must have sensed what was coming, but that, of course, is sheer nonsense. If people don't stop expecting murders just because I happen to be on the scene I'll be forced to spend the rest of my life in solitude.

We drove out in Abbie's car much to the disgust of my chauffeur Malcolm. He doesn't trust me in any car except my old Lincoln with him at the wheel.

It was at the gate that I had what we call a premonition for lack of a more exact term. I believe in hunches, intuitions, and premonitions and I am not willing to accept them as mere coincidences. It may have been the miracle of Willie Pole's speaking at all which gave me the first impression of something unusual. In all the years I had been going to Hidden Harbor I had never heard him say more than a grudging Yes or No in answer to a direct question. After he had looked us over with that dead-pan scrutiny of his he hesitated for a moment as he said, "'Lo, Miss Thomas." I was amazed and my face must have shown it, for he sort of blew himself up for the effort and said, as his hand tugged at the rope which would open the gate, "The *Albatross* ought to get in today."

That was my first conversation with Willie. Fragmentary though it was I knew that it carried a meaning far beyond the uttered words. Of course the *Albatross* would be in unless she had met with further trouble.

As the gate slammed shut behind us Abbie laughed. "Well, Ethel, you would be the one to make Willie break his silence. I wonder just what he meant?"

I was puzzled by that myself. I had been out of touch with the Harbor and Harbor gossip while Abbie had been away in the midlands.

"Perhaps," she suggested, "it is just a further mark of the disapproval which I have always felt lurked somewhere in the recesses of that expressive dead-pan of his. Funny he should include you in it."

"In what?" I asked, too absorbed to follow her line of thought.

"Willie knows, as he knows everything else that goes on at the island, that we are going to stay in the boat-shed. That sentence, as colorless in itself as the face that gave it birth, is probably Willie's hint that a divorced, woman and an old maid ought not stay alone in a shack with an unmarried man even if he is my cousin and you are old enough to be his grandmother."

"Rubbish!" I replied. "Willie might not approve of our morals, but he wouldn't be interested enough in them or us to voice an opinion no matter how guarded. It wasn't the excitement of seeing me nor was it the fact of the *Albatross'* expected arrival. In his way I think he was telling me to keep my eyes open, but for what? Everybody has known for several days that she was safe and struggling into port under her own power."

"True," she replied. "I read it myself out in Detroit. There is something else going on, Ethel. Something here which we have missed but, whatever it is, I'm sure it's connected with the *Albatross*." She pulled up in front of the community store, explaining that it would be necessary to supplement Pete's skimpy larder.

"Here's our chance to learn what is going on," I said as I nudged her to look at the store porch where Nora Baylis was breezing out of the door with that side-twist motion of hers which is interesting to watch. There isn't a normal door wide enough for her to get through beam end to.

"Well, Abbie!" she called. "And you too, Miss Thomas. Trust you to come down on an exciting day! We expect the *Albatross*, you know!"

I felt Abbie tighten up beside me, closing like a clam. I might have chatted with Nora, for I was dying with curiosity, if she hadn't greeted us the way she did. It was the inflection in her voice which brought us down to her level that I resented.

"So Willie told me," I replied coolly and not too graciously as Abbie slid from under the wheel on her side and I struggled with at least three gadgets on the door before I could let myself out.

"Willie!" she shrilled. Her amazement was genuine. "Well, it just goes to show how we all feel when even Willie breaks out and talks. But then you have a way with you where men are concerned." She actually smirked at me, pleased with the dig she had managed to put over so nicely. I don't believe she had enjoyed anything so much since her last baby. She's one of those women who enjoy childbirth. You know the kind I mean.

I smirked back and moved up the steps behind Abbie. I resented that "all" of Nora's, for although she had married to Bill Baylis I didn't feel that she was any part of the real community. She was about as seagoing as a steam-roller, turning green around the gills the way she did the moment a boat went outside the harbor bar. Nora was one of those accidents the depression brought to Hidden Harbor. Bill Baylis, like every one else, was caught in a jam. When it became a question of giving up everything he loved, mostly boats, he married Nora and brought her and her money to the Harbor. It was quite a price to pay for a couple of boats and a few lazy afternoons on the Sound, but he didn't seem to mind and Nora loved it all. I wish you could see her house; she did it over in anchors, life preservers and fish-nets. There now, I'm getting catty.

The depression had done a number of things to Hidden Harbor. It certainly made a wreck of Abbie s life, but it is just as well the crash came for her when it did. If the depression had been delayed she'd have gone on living in a fool's paradise for several years longer and then would have wakened to find that everything had gone, worthless husband, money and youth. At least she had some youth left. She was twenty-seven and though the experience had made her bitter I felt she was getting over it rather nicely. At least she put her shoulder to the wheel and was beginning to accomplish things. There was a time when I thought she wanted to die because Tim Abernathy ran out on her. She had vowed to me that she would never marry again, but I didn't believe her. Abbie is the marrying kind. Abernathy was her second husband.

I had offered her a home and money. She refused both. She said if I could make a reputation as a detective at my age there was a place in the world for her. She found it as a special investigator and I must admit, right here and now, that she did more than half the work on the Hidden Harbor Case and would have found the murderer herself if I hadn't been able to put the pieces together when and how I did.

I was thinking about the difference in women as I followed Abbie across the porch. There was Nora and there was Abbie, as far apart as the Poles. Nora's baby voice jerked my attention back to her. "What do you suppose will happen?" she called as she pressed her too-wide hips through the narrow door of her sport roadster.

I took a deep annoyed breath, ready for a sharp retort when Abbie laughed and said, "Hold everything!" I did.

In the store Martin Jones greeted us from behind his immaculate counter. "Well, Miss Thomas," he cried with a warm glow in his voice, "and Abbie, too," he continued, being a diplomat at heart. "I suppose you've been worried about Pete," he went on as he blinked his turtle-eyes and stretched his long neck to get a better view of Nora sweeping out of the parking space. He bit his lip painfully as she sideswiped the privet hedge at the entrance.

He was a funny little man, short and stubby with a long stringy neck and a chisel-sharp face surmounted by a ridiculous halo of frizzy white hair.

His remark about Pete Randall was a peg on which I had hoped we would be able to hang further conversation and perhaps a little gossip. I know Abbie was just as curious as I was.

When she said, "Naturally, but Jerry Carter always manages to come through," something flickered over his eyes telling me that conversational gossip would be difficult.

I've never known any one, particularly a man, as tight-lipped about gossip as Martin Jones. Perhaps that is one of the reasons he has been running the store for so many years. If ever a man was in a position to know things and gossip he was. The store was and always has been a clearing-house for talk. I've often felt sorry for his wife. Imagine being married to a man who is full of nice juicy stories about people you know and yet you're not able to get a word out of him.

"He's a good captain," he said. "None better in this harbor."

That was perfectly true. Jerry Carter was a good captain and a fine young man as well. Yes, you've guessed it, he is one of my pets though I hadn't been seeing much of him due to my activities with murders. I saw Abbie shrug expressively.

She had told me that morning over breakfast that good men were as scarce as radium and just as valuable. I was a little surprised at the warmth in her voice as she said, "I don't know of any one else who could have weathered such a storm. I guess he had his luck with him."

Once more I saw that protective curtain flicker over Martin's eyes, only this time there was a curious expression about his sharp little mouth that seemed to belie her statement about luck.

"What will you have today, Abbie?" he asked, shutting off the conversational stream.

"Six cans of beans," she answered absently.

"Don't you think Pete will be a little tired of beans?" he asked, breaking into his cackling laugh.

"I hadn't thought of that. . . Why, they've probably been eating beans for weeks!" she cried, looking at me a little helplessly.

I may not know how to cook, but I know how to order food. I took a quick glance at his shelves and recognized many of the things with which I was familiar at Charles'.

While I looked at the stock he rattled on, "Well, there's nice canned chicken and this here canned fricassee they tell me is good though I haven't tried any of it myself yet. The canned ham is always good, and Pete likes tongue quite well. He buys one of these jars now and again."

I knew what that meant. When Pete had money he bought tongue; when he was broke he probably ate canned beans and spaghetti.

I studied the instructions on the can of fricasseed chicken. The directions sounded simple enough. "We'll take two cans of this," I said, "a large ham, a glass jar of the tongue, two pounds of bacon, four cans of cream of mushroom soup, a pound of butter, a pint of cream. . . ." I raced on, determined that Pete's larder should be well stocked for once. My cook would have had a fit if she had heard me, but Martin was delighted with the size of the order as he scribbled the items on the back of a paper bag.

"How about eggs?" I nodded. "Want to take anything with you now?" he asked.

"Yes," I answered promptly, "some information. Abbie has been away nearly as long as the *Albatross* and I've been out of touch with the Harbor for months. Something has happened here or is about to happen and we'd like to know what it is. Willie broke his vow of silence down at the gate, Nora nearly bubbled over when we met her outside, and you seem determined to keep us in the dark. Come on, Martin, be a good fellow and tell us why the arrival of the *Albatross* is causing, so much additional excitement."

He looked at us speculatively for a long moment, then turned to Abbie and asked, "Where you been?"

She told him about her trip to Detroit.

"Didn't you read the papers?" he asked us both.

"Naturally we followed the reports about the *Albatross*," I replied.

"And you ain't heard nothing else about the Harbor?" he demanded cautiously.

"Not a thing, Martin," Abbie cried. "Don't be so aggravating."

"Well, I never thought either of you was much of a hand for gossip and I think you ought to know, since you're good friends of both parties. People around here ain't been talking about anything else for so long we kinda forgit that some folks might not know." He leaned forward to say with lowered voice, "Mary Verity married Henry Baldwin last week."

"Don't tease us!" Abbie cried.

"I ain't teasing you. I don't blame you for not believing it, when her and Jerry was supposed to be married on Labor Day. I couldn't seem to get it through my own head for a spell, but it's true. She's living up there in the Taylor house with him right now."

"Are you sure, Martin?" Abbie asked.

"You know Mary wouldn't live in sin," he snapped. "Now you know why everybody's so interested in the arrival of the *Albatross*. Jerry don't know nothing about it. His radio has been out of commission or I expect Art Tobias would have sent him the news. It might be a ticklish kind of a situation when Jerry finds out. I understand some of the women have been trying to decide who should tell him. As near as I can make out, Mary has decided to tell him herself, which, of course, is the decent thing to do, but it's going to be pretty hard for both of them if she does. People like Nora Baylis are just waiting to see them youngsters suffer. Mary's down to the club, I saw her go, so I guess she's going through with it. Don't you tell anybody I told you all this," he admonished. "You've made me break one of my rules. I'll send the groceries right over."

"We'll keep your secret," Abbie promised thoughtfully.

"Are you going to be at the club when she gets in?" he asked.

"I don't believe so," Abbie answered. "There'll be enough people down there to see the show."

"I know, but if you and Miss Thomas were to go and sort of be on her side it might buck her up. She thinks a lot of you, Mary does, and this thing hasn't been easy for her, with people dying to know why and not daring to ask." There was a softness in his eyes as he spoke, a gentleness that I had only half suspected.

"We'll go," I promised as I followed Abbie out to the car.

"Mary Verity married to Henry Baldwin! It's incredible!" Abbie echoed my thoughts as we settled in the car. "You know, Ethel, when a girl like Mary and a man like Jerry Carter are in love it makes you believe, in your secret heart, that there is such thing as romance in the world. And now . . . Damn!" she exploded as she slammed on her brake, throwing me forward toward the windshield.

We came within an inch of crashing into Stella Ketcham, who was swinging out of the shore road as Abbie tried to turn in. Stella was at fault. Like so many other people driving cars, she seems to assume that she is the only person using the roads. Abbie was boiling as she eased her car ahead, forcing Stella to back up out of our, way. Stella backed up, all right, but she smiled with sweet resignation implying that it was Abbie's fault. When she saw me she called flippantly, "Hello, Miss Thomas! Down for a murder?"

"Some one after your scalp at last, or were you trying to get ours a moment ago?" I replied.

Stella is what I call poison sweet. Tall, dark and definitely handsome, she knows how to wear clothes and always manages to look well even in beach pajamas. She has charm until you feel the nettles under that misleading surface. I've never known any one, young or old, who can so sweetly and irrevocably put you in the wrong. She is a master of the art of innuendo and implied criticism. She can say the simplest things in the meanest way of any person, under heaven or earth and the awful part of it is, that you can't take exception to what she says without a lot of explanation and floundering that finally seems to make you guilty.

"Aren't you going to the Club?" she asked as our cars drew abreast.

"Maybe later," Abbie replied, "after I get the shack cleaned up."

"Pete wouldn't know whether it was clean or dirty." She arched her brows. "Perhaps you haven't heard that he spends most of his time up at the Taylor house."

"No. I'm too busy for gossip," Abbie snapped and then asked with the illogical curiosity of our sex, "What's up there?"

"Now, Abbie, you know perfectly well that Henry Baldwin has a lovely niece with plenty of money." What she didn't say was that Pete Randall was a long, lanky, harum-scarum marine architect who frittered away his time tinkering with the Club boats instead of getting out in the world and making money.

"Other people have been known to marry for money," Abbie said without trying to pull her punch, for that was exactly why Stella married Ketcham even though we all knew he had a leg and a half in his grave.

"You ought to know," Stella came right back with one of her poison-sweet smiles and verbally dumped Tim Abernathy right in Abbie's lap.

I was tempted to fire a shot in Stella's direction but the glint in Abbie's eyes assured me that she was able to take care of herself. "Well, Stella, better to have loved and lost, you know," Abbie jabbed right back at her.

Stella took it without a flicker of an eyelid. She knew perfectly well what Abbie meant. She'd been crazy about Jerry even when her husband was alive. As a matter of fact, it was Stella who introduced Jerry to Hidden Harbor. After Ketcham's death she did everything known to man to bag him, but without success.

"I wonder if that's what Jerry will think when he hears about his paragon Mary?" she asked brazenly.

As our car shot forward Abbie said, "I don't know why I react the way I do to her. I hate bitchy people. Most of the time I think I'm easy to get along with and rather a decent person in a crowd, but women like Stella and some men make me just plain unadulterated cussed."

"It's a good sign," I assured her. "You have spirit."

My thoughts drifted to Jerry Carter. Poor lad! He was going to be in for a hard time. As we turned off the road that led down to the boat-house and Pete's rather primitive quarters in the loft above, I could see the parking space in back of the Club. Practically everybody's car was there. I tried to tell myself that they would have been there in any case because the home-coming of the *Albatross* was an event in itself, but I knew that most of them were down there to see what would happen when Mary and Jerry met.

I didn't know then, why Mary had done what seemed to be a heartless thing, but I knew her well enough as a young girl to realize that whatever her reason she had believed it sound. I never for a moment thought that she had stopped loving Jerry. No one who had ever seen them together would have believed that.

No wonder the community was all agog. Jerry was coming home glad to be alive, thinking of Mary probably as each wave slipped past the bow of the battered *Albatross*. There was a little catch in my throat as I thought of those two. What a pity the spectacular trip of the *Albatross* made Jerry's homecoming such a public event. But, then, if young men will go gallivanting about in the Atlantic in boats better suited to sailing in the Sound they must expect things to happen.

"How could she do it?" Abbie asked as she parked and began tugging at the luggage.

There was no answer to that. We were at the rear of the old boat-shed, which smelled pungently of cedar shavings, pitch and varnish. Far off on the horizon I caught a glimpse of something low which might possibly be the *Albatross*. I began to feel excited myself and took hold of Abbie's arm to point out toward the slow-moving spot.

Born and raised on Long Island, there was salt in Abbie's blood. She'd never have been part of Hidden Harbor if that were not true.

"I think you're right," she said after a long squint of her lovely dark eyes. "She's come through beautifully, hasn't she?"

That speech of hers was typical of Hidden Harborites, boats first, other considerations afterward.

Never having been a real boat-man myself I could think of more important things. If that were the *Albatross*, what would Jerry do when he heard the news? He was so hot-headed and impetuous. It would be hard for him to realize that Mary was no longer his. There would be a hurt look in his wide friendly eyes that would change the contours of his face. Then he would quite probably pop off into a rage as he had done that day when the truck ran over and killed his dog. Of course, it hadn't been the driver's fault, but Jerry hadn't stopped to consider that. All he knew was that his dog was dead and the truck and the driver had been the means of that death. That little scene had been terrifying until Jerry's wild rage had been controlled by my chauffeur and several other men. I didn't like the present prospect. I was trying to think of some way of preventing a scene as I climbed the wooden steps behind Abbie.

"The place is a mess as usual," she said as she went about opening windows to let in some fresh clean air. It wasn't exactly musty, but it had an old smell, of dead tobacco, damp wood ashes and men's clothing.

She was really very efficient. She put a kettle of water on the stove to take care of some soiled dishes that Pete had left standing in the sink. I enjoyed puttering along with her as we aired the beds, swept and dusted. It was an easy place to clean. I've often thought I'd like to be in a little cottage doing my own work.

As we cleaned I kept my eye on that growing spot out on the Sound. Abbie located a pair of binoculars and after a long careful look said "It's the *Albatross*, all right. They've rigged a temporary mast to help their motor."

A little later when I looked out of the front window, I saw Judge Verity, Mary's father, wandering aimlessly along the tide edge poking at odds and ends of refuse with the end of his cane. He must have been feeling pretty bad about the situation, because he and Jerry were the best of friends and between them they ran the Club, invested the community money and generally took care of things so that Hidden Harbor was a paying proposition.

"If she had married any man but Baldwin!" Abbie paused once to exclaim. "Jerry has opposed Baldwin at every turn. He didn't want him in Hidden Harbor in the first place, and hasn't made things easy for him since he bought Archie Taylor's place and a right to the community privileges."

"Why did people let him in?" I demanded.

"Because we were all broke. Archie Taylor was caught in a bad jam and had to let most everything go. Baldwin wanted Taylor's house badly and offered Archie a pre-depression price for it. I don't suppose Jerry and the others felt that they could hurt Archie by keeping Baldwin out."

I was thinking of the power of money as she went on, "Baldwin didn't help matters much. He just moved in on us, and because he honestly believes in his business ability he tried to run us and everything about the Harbor. No one doubted his ability as a business man, but since we had been running the community well enough in the past we didn't feel that we needed a change. Jerry was the one who expressed that feeling for all of us. While as individuals we couldn't boast about the way we had handled our private affairs, the Club seemed to be sailing under pretty fair weather and we wanted to leave well enough alone."

The rattling lid of the boiling teakettle reminded her that there were dishes to be done before we could go down to the Club. We had a cup of tea while she washed and I wiped. I was enjoying myself no end.

In another half-hour we were on the Club porch, with the rest of them, excited and eager. Mary was sitting by herself at the end of the long piazza. While I stopped to chat with old acquaintances who eyed me speculatively as if they were sure that my presence was an omen of things to come, Abbie passed on to be with Mary.

When I finally joined them Mary looked up quickly and said as her hand trembled in mine, "I'm glad you and Abbie came."

"We'll help you if we can," I promised as I settled into a willow rocker beside her.

"I know that," she replied warmly, as her gentian-blue eyes followed every movement of the slowly approaching boat which was about a quarter of a mile off the spit and heading for the narrow channel at the end of the bar.

Unhappiness blurred the freshness of her beauty as she sat there pretending indifference to the sly glances cast in her direction. It took stamina to face that battery of wondering eyes when she knew that they were feeling that she had let them and Jerry down.

Baldwin came and went, looking a little ridiculous in his blue coat, white trousers and yachtsman's cap. He was a clubhouse admiral if ever I saw one. I doubt he could handle a pair of oars decently, but I'd never seen him in a boat so I didn't rightfully know. Mary smiled at him once or twice as he fussed over her. There was a drained look in her eyes when she glanced in his direction that made my heart ache, because I realized she was determined to go through with this unreasonable marriage of hers.

Actually I don't suppose he was so bad as men go; I've seen worse. He was definitely the successful business type, blustery and dictatorial. He looked forty-five or more; his eyes were a little too hard and calculating for friendship, and he was beginning to develop a middle-aged contour—a trifle too pudgy above the waistline. His jowls were beginning to sag and his face was a bit bloated.

From the Sound beyond the rocky wooded backbone of the island a deafening roar grew to booming proportions. I looked aloft expecting to see a plane, but the sky was clear and blue, empty except for a few wheeling seagulls. In another moment a high-powered sea-sled shot into view beyond the point, throwing lacy billows of spray away from her plunging bow. She raced ahead of the *Albatross*, reduced speed, swung in a wide circle and drew up abeam of the limping yacht.

"Reporters," Abbie announced with annoyance. "I suppose they were bound to come," Mary sighed hopelessly.

"They just arrived in time," I said, forgetting how distasteful they might be to Mary. Reporters are always exciting to me, though I must admit that there are times when they are a nuisance.

"They usually do," Abbie complained as she leaned forward to watch the two boats.

Five minutes later the wind-swept, wind-wrecked *Albatross*, her auxiliary motor chugging fitfully as if each exhaust would be its last, limped through the channel in the wake of the sea-sled. The yacht was a mess, mast gone, decks swept clear of superstructure; it was a wonder she had made port at all. She had been unreported for three anxious weeks after the North Atlantic gale had carried her far off her course. And now after six weeks she was limping home.

As the boat chugged into safe waters I fancied I could see Jerry squinting at the shore. He looked like a Norse god badly in need of a hair-cut as he stood at the wheel in a brief pair of trunks, his erect, bronzed body gleaming in the sun.

There was a welcoming cheer from the crowd on the porch. Then Pete Randall limped forward over the battered deck, boat-hook in hand to pick up the bobbing, mooring-block. Abbie and I had stood up, excited. It is thrilling to realize that two men had battled with the fiercest elements of nature and had won. I was hoping that Jerry would comport himself as well with the disappointments of the civilization to which he was returning. Our eyes were on the stripped boat when I felt a hand on my arm. It was Mary, her eyes blurred by tears, standing between us.

"I can't do it." She fought to control the sobs. "Not here in front of all these people. I'd funk it horribly. I'd cry. I'd probably throw my arms about him and sob." She bit her lips to keep the tears back.

"You've got to face him sooner or later," I warned, believing the hard way is often the easiest in the long run.

"But not now, not here with Henry Baldwin looking on. If I see him at all it must be alone and I don't believe that's going to be possible," she ended hopelessly.

"You mean Baldwin?" I asked as I realized he was watching us with a sadistic gleam in his eyes. As she nodded, I said, "We may be able to fix that."

Jerry was poking his long lean legs into an old pair of trousers as a dingey approached the *Albatross* to bring them ashore.

"If you could only tell him before he learns it from the others. I don't want them to see and enjoy his suffering." Her eyes filled with tears that trickled down her cheeks.

"Okay, I'll do it," Abbie promised. "I don't know how at the moment, but it will be done."

Mary held back the sobs which were choking her. She turned and fled down the porch, colliding with three chairs before she stumbled down the steps toward the parking space.

There was an abrupt weighted silence as Mary made her exit. A moment later as the roar of her car announced her frantic departure general conversation broke out.

"She couldn't face him, after all, and no wonder!" I heard Nora Baylis say with relish. "Do you suppose he knows?" she asked, looking toward the water and Jerry stepping into the dingey.

"Certainly not! I wonder how the incomparable Jerry is going to take it!" Stella Ketcham threw that into the jumble of comments.

Just then I noticed Del Baldwin, Henry Baldwin's niece, skip down the pier toward the float. Her curly, chestnut hair billowed in the light breeze. She was a cute child, small and vivacious, with sweet eyes that were all aglow as she waved to Pete Randall.

Others began to follow Del toward the float. I glanced at Abbie, who stood considering ways and means of getting the news to Jerry. The sea-sled with reporters and camera-men eased up just beyond the float to get good pictures of Jerry as he stepped ashore. Abbie snapped her fingers, her mouth smoothed to an even line as she started forward.

I trotted down the pier in Abbie's wake as she bumped and jostled her way to the edge of the float. I didn't know what her plan was, but I was determined not to miss it. I could see Jerry's unbelieving eyes searching the group on the float. Then I was conscious of Abbie leaning forward, too far forward for safety, but I understood because she had whispered, "Give me a little push if you can do it without being too obvious." She was shrilling cries of getting to Pete.

I swung round, teetered and bumped into her. Poised as she was on the float's edge, she lost her balance. Her arms flailed the air for a moment before she hit the water with a resounding slap, doing what the boys call a belly-whopper.

She was an excellent swimmer and I was wondering how she would manage it when I saw her big straw hat float away as she sank out of sight. She was down for a long time. I peered anxiously as air bubbles floated up.

When she came to the surface she gasped, looked up at the dingey with a piteous glance, threshed the water with her arms and proceeded to sink again. I knew she was shamming but I saw Pete and Jerry exchange unbelieving glances. The next moment Jerry's trousers were falling about his ankles. Abbie's plan was working. Jerry, his body a bronze arc, went overboard after her.

They were several feet away from the float when they appeared together. I saw her say something into his ear as he treaded water and held her up. Then her arms circled his neck and she tried to climb on top of him. They sank out of sight. When they came up again Abbie was behaving as a rescued woman should. The dingey was beside them as Jerry towed her to the float and boosted her up to eager outstretched hands ready to help.

Abbie's performance had taken the edge off Jerry's home-coming. Of course she didn't have any more water in her lungs than a stuffed owl but she had to go through with the motions of having been rescued. She let them work over her for a few minutes.

Jerry said, "The fall must have knocked the wind out of her." Good old Jerry! That was fast thinking after the body blow she had given him.

Abbie squirmed then and tried to sit up. "Take it easy," Jerry cautioned, going on with the deception.

"Move aside!" I commanded, going into action. "Let her rest! She'll be all right. Go away, all of you!"

Jerry grinned at me. Pete stood with his arm around Del Baldwin gaping down at Abbie curiously.

"Should we send for a doctor?" Nora Baylis' birdie voice floated over the shoulders of the ring formed about us

"I'm all right. Just leave me alone!" Abbie cried petulantly and rolled over on her stomach, burying her head in her arms.

"She's more fish than chicken, anyhow," I heard Stella remark. "Strange, isn't it, how some women always manage to steal the star's performance." That was a double-edged dig, but I paid no attention to it and Abbie pretended not to hear.

"Come on!" Jerry suggested to the group. "Abbie's probably more self-conscious than anything right now." His voice sounded steady enough as he stepped across Abbie's body, little runnels of water streaking down his legs.

That was the signal for the belated cries of "Welcome home!" and general chatter about the *Albatross* as their voices faded away up the pier.

I gazed out at the boats in the harbor, wondering what would happen to Jerry and Mary. Abbie did not move. We were like that for several moments when I turned round and gazed into a pair of shrewd gray eyes which at the moment were supposed to be hard-boiled and cynical. He was sitting on the float a few feet away from me. He was a sparsely built young man, with a straight nose, flaming red hair, and an expression in those gray eyes that was full of question-marks.

"Home-coming Hero of *Albatross* Rescues Ex-society Matron," he said in headline quotes.

Abbie rolled over and glared. "Dave Walsh!" she cried. "Can't you forget you're a reporter?" She gave him what I believe is known as a dirty look while I studied his baggy tweed suit, dark blue tie and inevitable pencil stub tucked behind his ear.

"Not when get-her-man Abernathy does a flop at this exclusive watering-place and the super-sleuth Ethel Thomas is on hand knowing all about it. Come on, Abbie, tell a fellow why you're here in the first place, why you fell overboard, why you pretended to drown when you can probably out-swim any ten men including myself and I was my college champion?"

"And you never got over it," Abbie accused.

"What's the dope, Miss Thomas?" He appealed to me. "I'm Dave Walsh of the press. Abbie should have introduced us but she's all wet and, I think, a little annoyed with me. Don't tell her I told you that, though," he mocked as a grin wiped away all the cynical hard-boiled concentrated effort of his eyes.

"Believe it or not, David, my boy," Abbie said curtly, "I belong here. So does Miss Thomas. We're part of the community and we're fussy about the people who get in here. I once owned yonder mansion. That was before the depression took the family fortunes and the ex-husband.

As for my present condition I was leaning too far out trying to call to my cousin Pete Randall when Miss Thomas accidentally bumped into me. My foot slipped. I lost my balance and fell flat, which knocked the wind out of me. I became panicky and you should know that more people die from fright in the water than from any other cause—or don't you?" she ended.

I looked with renewed interest at the young man, glad that some one was able to bring out that old bantering spirit of Abbie's.

He moved his head up and down like some wise old bird and said, "So that's why you hung on to the young Adonis' neck and whispered something in his ear that took all the heart out of him. Try again!" he jeered.

The sea-sled came back alongside and rubbed the bumper at the edge of the float. "Come on, Dave," a bored voice begged.

"I'm staying down for the afternoon with my friend Abbie Abernathy," he announced. "Go ahead. I'll be in by train."

There was a roar, the sea sled moved away from the float, her underwater exhaust gurgling and chuckling back at us.

"Even the boat is giving you the ha-ha," he teased.

"So nice of you to stay down," Abbie said scornfully as she rose to her feet.

"I'm delighted, nice of you to ask me," he replied as he fell into step, helped me courteously but not too obviously up the ramp with a light touch of my arm.

"You're wasting your time, Dave; there is no story here except the arrival of the *Albatross*," she protested.

"Where you and Miss Thomas happen to be, there is a story," he answered doggedly, no doubt remembering the time Abbie tricked him away from the Vanderventer house.

"Young man," I said as severely as I could manage, because I found myself liking him immensely, "don't you think you're a little presumptuous?"

"It's no use, Ethel. You can't insult him or make him see reason. We'll just have to put up with him." She turned to Dave. "Have it your way. Our humble home, such as it is, is at your disposal for the afternoon and no longer."

"Fair enough," he agreed.

Further conversation between them was cut short as we reached the pier-head and the group clustered there. They parted to let us pass through.

"Are you all right, darling?" Nora chirped, beaming at Dave with those saucer-eyes of hers.

"Fine now except for being a little wet," Abbie replied and kept right on going, leaving a trail of seawater behind her.

"Wetter than usual," I heard Stella say over the squishing of Abbie's sodden shoes. There was a laugh at Abbie's expense.

"The tall slinky dame is a great pal of Abbie's, isn't she?" Dave remarked as we moved toward the car.

"We're all pals here," Abbie answered.

"What were they expecting to happen?" he asked as he slid under the wheel after helping us into the car. "Whatever it was, you disappointed them."

"The *Albatross*," she replied, still annoyed by his persistency.

"Huh!" he scoffed.

"Trust him to smell a story a mile away," she said to me. "Mr. Walsh should have been a great fortune-teller, a soothsayer or a sand-diviner. He has occult powers. Sees into the future."

"Don't you believe her," he denied "I see what I see. There was something connected with the *Albatross*, something she spoiled by that belly-whopper of hers. Do you think she'll tell little Davie or will he have to find it out for himself?"

"He's as relentless as Fate, with a nose like a blood-bound's and the stickiness of treacle," she advised me. "There is nothing we can do that would stop him except perhaps appeal to his sense of decency if it isn't too entirely submerged by his long career as an ace newshound. What do you think?"

"There's some good in every man," I replied with a wink at the appreciative Dave.

"Pull up there," she ordered, pointing to a sheltered spot at the edge of the road. "We'll try."

"But you ought to get into dry clothes," he protested with nice personal interest in her comfort. I like that in a man.

"I've been wet most of my life," she answered, "so don't worry. And, besides, Jerry is at our place and I can't tell you in front of him."

"Did any one ever tell you that you are a remarkable woman?" he asked with a nice glow in his eyes.

"Too many," she replied tersely. "I always suspect their motives."

"It's too bad you've coated yourself with such a crusty protective shell, Abbie. It blinds you to the charm of a fellow like myself. You're so sure we're all a bad lot that some day you're going to walk past the right man and not even see him. You're going to miss a lot. Isn't that right, Miss Thomas?"

"I forgot to tell you that he is also conceited and something of a Don Juan," she advised me. To him she said, "I'll risk the unhappiness. I'm doing all right by myself, thank you; but I didn't stop here to bring on a damp, backhanded proposal, or was it a proposition?"

He was nice in his funny way as he shrugged and said, "Lady's option is my motto."

"Then we'll skip it. You want to know what's in the air down here and I'm going to tell you, but if you print one word of it I'll get even with you if it's the last thing I do. Is that understood?" she demanded.

"You heard her threaten me," he said. "But I'll run the risk."

She told him quickly all we knew of the situation.

"It's Sunday magazine stuff," he scoffed rather contemptuously; "more in the line of sob-sister stuff."

"Then you won't print it?"

"I don't know yet," he evaded. "Tell me something about Hidden Harbor itself. You've got something here. Who started it? How was it developed and all the rest of it?"

"Why are you so interested?" she asked.

"It's such a swell place for a murder," he replied thoughtfully.

His remark gave me a turn; I knew exactly what he meant. He afterward told me that all he had seen and heard up to that point seemed to be forming in a pattern for murder.

"The Harbor was started by my grandfather, old Josh Randall," Abbie began. "I can remember him as a gaunt sharp-eyed old man when I was just a little girl. He ran a fleet of schooners out of the Harbor to New York in the old days before Long Islanders became railroad-minded. He carried bricks, coal, lumber and general supplies. He owned the entire island. When business began to go bad he turned the cove into a yacht harbor for the wealthy men who were beginning to buy up the North Shore for summer estates. The rich yachtsmen liked the sheltered cove. Through the years the popularity of the place grew. My father incorporated the island and sold shares to the people who wanted to settle on the land because of their boats.

"Before he did that, however, he gave grants to all the old families who had worked for my grandfather and lived on the island. With the exception of the 'granters,' who keep to themselves socially and mingle with the rest of us only as workmen, the island is a private community, a place for people who love the water and all that it implies." She paused a moment and added, "You see we're as boaty as the hunting and riding crowd are horsy, only we think we smell cleaner."

"Which of course," he said, "is a matter of opinion. Now I myself rather like the smell of a horse and the feel of one between my legs."

"But you can't compare that to the tang of the, sea in your nostrils and the salt spray on your face as you run with the wind or beat your way to port," she countered.

"I wouldn't know about that," he said a little wistfully; I thought.

Abbie shivered in the freshening breeze. Without another word he slipped the car into gear and drove on toward the shed.

"Don't let Jerry know you know about Mary," Abbie warned him in a whisper as we left the car.

We climbed the stairs and shoved the door open. We found Pete fussing over the oil stove. Jerry sat in the open loft door gazing out across the cove, looking for all the world like an old man of the sea. There was something pathetic about the drooping slope of his fine young shoulders under his old jersey.

I sniffed incredibly and glanced at Pete. Of all things, he was warming a skilletful of canned beans.

CHAPTER TWO

ABBIE WENT OFF TO change into dry clothes. Dave lent Pete a hand in the scullery, while I hesitated before speaking to Jerry. There's nothing as pathetic as a man in trouble. Theirs is the battered helplessness of a small boy, a frustration which only a woman—mother, wife or sweetheart—can remedy. I decided against speaking to him then: he seemed to be so busy thinking.

I went into the room that Abbie and I would share together. There was a comfortable bunk built into each corner. I sat on one of them. "Jerry's taking it pretty hard," I said.

"I know," she said. "Poor kid! I feel so sorry for him. We've got to help. You know, Ethel, sometimes I stand off, take a good look at myself and have a nice quiet laugh at my own expense. I'm susceptible as hell to men. I suppose in spite of the shell into which I believe I have withdrawn, I'm so damned full of maternal instinct that I'll always be a fool over men, but not fool enough, I hope, to ever marry again."

"I don't suppose the things young Walsh has been saying to you has anything to do with your mood," I teased.

"How do you like him?" she countered.

"Very much. He's a good-un," I replied. Further conversation was interrupted by Pete's cheery call of "Come and get it!"

Pete, who was probably thinking of Del Baldwin, was the only one to eat normally. I certainly was not a bit hungry. I had made Abbie stop for hot-dogs on the way down. Jerry was not interested in food at all. Dave spent most of his time watching Abbie, who tried not to stare too speculatively at Jerry.

Abbie was the one to bring the dreary meal to an end. "Ethel and I are going to walk home with Jerry while you boys do the dishes," she announced as she left the table.

Jerry and I followed her down the steps and out to the old ways in front of the shed. We three sat on the stringer for a long time listening to the voice, of the harbor. The incoming tide gurgled and lapped at the piles. Some terns wheeled and screeched over the cove. Once or twice there was a plop as one of them dove for a fish. Behind us land birds chattered in the tangled patch of wild-cherry and scrub oak; the sun, filtering through the huge old willow, made sparkling patterns on the dark-green, scum-stained water as a killie broke its smooth surface, sending tiny ripples toward the shore.

Jerry reached down for a handful of pebbles and tossed them into the water one by one. "I guess I'll go away," he said, finally breaking the silence which had hung between us.

"It's a good idea," Abbie agreed, "only it doesn't help much in the long-run. You can't run away from yourself and your thoughts or the memories that keep tugging at you, pulling you back," she stated with conviction.

"It'll make it easier for her," he said.

"I suppose it will," she replied, "but you have your life to consider, Jerry."

"Why did she do it?" he cried desperately, throwing his philosophical calm after the last of the pebbles. "I've got to find out."

"Wait a minute, Jerry," I cautioned. Then I told him what Mary had said to us there on the club porch before she had rushed away.

"Then he's determined to keep us apart unless he is there to gloat over us, is that it?" he demanded. As we made no reply he growled, "I'll see him in hell first!"

"Easy, Jerry," I said. "We're resourceful people, we'll find a way."

"I've got to see her, talk to her," he insisted, standing up. "I'm not going to let him—You don't think she loves him, do you?" he asked as the possibility dawned on him.

"Certainly not!" Abbie cried.

"Let us manage the thing for you," I suggested "Perhaps tonight, at the dinner which is planned to celebrate your home-coming."

"Not in front of everybody," he objected. "I couldn't! Besides, I don't believe she'll come to the dinner."

"I hope not," Abbie said. "There are too many people who would get a kick out of seeing you both suffer. We'll think of some way to get you two together, alone. Ethel's good at managing things. Let us think about it. Until we do, please, for heaven's sake, do nothing foolish to make things worse."

"Foolish!" he scoffed. "I have murder in my heart right now."

"Then take it out of your heart," I ordered. "What a mess that would be! After all, we're supposed to be civilized."

"Are we? I'm not so sure after the past three weeks. Pete and I were got to the point where we were pretty elemental."

A crunching footstep made us all turn round It was Dave and I was sure by the narrowing of his eyes that he had heard Jerry's remark.

"Could you give me a taste of that sea-tang and salt-spray you were so poetic about a little while ago?" he asked, with what was supposed to be a casual and disarming smile.

"Take my little catboat if you like," Jerry suggested.

In spite of the pinched quality of his usually wide blue eyes and the grim line of his set jaw, he was a handsome creature standing there facing us. His sunburned, light-brown hair, still damp from his recent ducking, clung to the nape of his straight tanned neck in tight little ringlets. His head was well shaped and properly poised. He swung round to look across the cove, a Leander seeking his Hero. I felt a tug at my heart. For a second I had a vision of those broad shoulders and strong arms swimming out toward the setting sun until weariness ended it all. No! He was built of sterner stuff. He might commit murder in a heated moment or fight in a way of which I might not approve, but he'd never quit.

He pulled his belt a notch tighter across his flat stomach to keep the baggy trousers from slipping over his lean flanks. "I'd better go home," he said. "Phoebe probably has high blood-pressure by now. See you later," he threw back over his shoulder as he sloshed indifferently through the rising water lapping the shore.

"Who's Phoebe? A possible antidote?" Dave asked.

"She's his housekeeper. He's an orphan bachelor," Abbie explained.

"Who doesn't know his own luck," he said cynically with a smile that belied the words.

"Because he's a simple soul, a Babbitt to you," she retorted.

"He's taking it pretty hard, isn't he?" he commented as he settled beside me.

"Maybe you would too, if you had any feeling outside of type and printer's ink," she accused.

"You know, I like it here," he said, ignoring her retort. "It grows on you, doesn't it?"

"Take a good look, because I'm going to take you out in Jerry's boat and drown you," Abbie announced. "It's the only way to keep him from printing the story," she said. "Come on!"

"It's going to be a wonderful death." He winked at me. "Pair Found in Love-pact Suicide."

"You're drowning alone," she corrected.

"Too bad, too bad! It'll spoil a good headline."

"Can't you be human, Dave?" she begged. "Can't you see that that kid is eating his heart out? Can't you forget that he's a human interest story trudging along the shore, hurt and bewildered. . . . Don't you believe people have a God-given right to their private lives?" she demanded.

"Not murderers," he countered. "Am I right, Miss Ethel? When you get a case do you stop to consider that perhaps the murderer had good and sufficient reason for what he did? Do you ever say to yourself, 'Ethel, be a human being'? You do not! You get that lovely nose of yours on the trail and you stick to it, win, lose or draw, until you reach a conclusion."

He had me there and he knew it, but I said, "I think I'm about to change. If and when your body is ever found, I'll forget all the things I've heard today."

"Then you don't like me? Too bad. I'd been counting on you."

"There are murders and murders," I laughed.

"Particularly if you happen to like and are interested in the murderer," he accused, more than half-serious. "Now just suppose, for argument's sake, that Baldwin was found murdered this afternoon, you wouldn't think for a moment that our friend Jerry did it, would you?"

"Of course not! He's not the type," I replied.

"But it would make a wow of a story," he teased. "That's where I would come in."

"I'm beginning to believe I really will drown you," Abbie warned "You're just the type who would kill Baldwin because of the situation Jerry is in and then let yourself go on the story you would be able to write about the grief-stricken youth who killed for love."

"Abbie!" he cried. "You've got something there! I think I'll stick around for a day or two. Pete offered to put me up, being as how I'm such a good friend of yours."

"Tell Ethel where to ship the body," she advised as she moved away.

She pulled a dingey up to the shore and indicated the stern seat for him.

"Let me row," he suggested.

"No, thanks! You're the one who is to be drowned."

They stayed out for the balance of the afternoon. I watched them through the glasses from the loft door. He knew absolutely nothing about a boat. When she told me about it, she said she had no idea people could be so dumb, but then she admitted that she was that way about chess, so I guess things sort of even up.

After they cleared the cove and were out on the bay, he said he'd like to try his hand at sailing. Abbie gave him the tiller, stick and told him to keep the boat headed for the sandy bluff on the opposite shore.

Dave liked sailing and did fairly well at first until he began making a few experiments. He managed to get himself tangled in the sheet-rope so that Abbie had to take over again.

"I like horses better," he said, "though this smell is nice. Now, suppose you give me a little of that spray."

"Okay. Let down the centerboard," she instructed.

He looked at her blankly for a moment until she pointed to the pin which held it in place. He released it with a push. The water sloshed up into his face.

"How do you like it?" Abbie laughed.

He gave her a damp grin.

"Look out!" she called. "I'm coming about!"

She supposed he'd know enough to duck, but he didn't and the boom swinging over hit him a vicious crack on the side of the head. He staggered, looked at her with unbelieving eyes, tripped over his own clumsy feet and went overboard with a splash.

Abbie was busy for the next few minutes. She let go the sheet-rope and was ready for him when he came up. He had said he could swim, but she didn't know whether he could or not. When he came spluttering to the surface, there was a quizzical look in his eyes which made her laugh. She tossed him a life ring and tugged him in. He could swim, all right, but he was groggy from the blow on his head. He was panting and gasping when he floundered aboard and flopped in the cockpit at her feet.

"Did you do that on purpose?" he asked, looking up at her puzzled.

"Don't be a fool," she snapped. "I'd miss your indirect proposals. You're my only attendant swain."

"Thanks." He explored the growing lump with gentle fingers.

"You'll probably find a pair of trunks and some dry clothes in the starboard locker. Take those things off," she ordered.

"Aye, Aye, Captain," he said, rose to his knees, moved forward and banged his head on the cabin.

He fished some things out of the locker and then turned round to glance at her somewhat apprehensively. Any changing he might do had to be done under her nose, so to speak.

"Go on, change. I won't look at you," she promised. She didn't, either, because on the shore two figures caught her eyes.

Hidden Harbor, originally known as Parson's Island, is more square than round if you include the cove, point and sandspits which are all parts of the island formation now. The north and west sides are high bluffs, a part of the moraine left by the glacier which formed the ridge along the north shore of Long Island, Parson's Island, Fisher's, Block, Martha's Vineyard, Nantucket and parts of Cape Cod.

The high solid back of the island is in the northwest corner and tapers down to the south and east in an arc which forms the cove. There is a long rocky arm jutting into the Sound in a northeasterly direction. Through the centuries wind and tide have piled a sandspit along the easterly end of the island, nearly blocking the cove except for the narrow channel at its southern end. The southeast corner, tipped with sand, juts out from dark-green meadows on the bay side, making the protection of the cove complete.

While Dave was changing his clothes, Abbie was watching the two figures moving in and out of the low growth on the southeast point. At first she thought it was Jerry and Mary, but as she drew closer she realized that it was Henry Baldwin and Stella Ketcham who were strolling back toward the Club through the wild beach plum bushes that line the low ridge.

Dave crawled out from the cabin, a wary eye on the boom as he stood near her. She had rather expected him to be a scrawny duplicate of Mahatma Ghandi, but she was agreeably surprised. He was well if sparsely built and had nice straight legs supporting an excellently proportioned body.

As they sailed into the narrow inlet, Abbie was busy lowering the sail with the willing but clumsy help of Dave. As they drifted through the channel on the tide, Abbie stood on the rear deck, the tiller stick between her ankles.

"What are you looking for?" he asked.

"I just thought I saw something that might be interesting," she replied. She was busy for the next few minutes paddling up to the mooring, which Dave finally managed to catch, making a wet and sloppy job of it. After they had furled and covered the sail and had things shipshape, she took him into the Club float and up to the bar for a drink.

As they crossed the Club veranda she saw Baldwin enter the lounge by the south door. He was alone.

Abbie had a drink with Dave after introducing him to Weeks the steward. They smoked a cigarette before she started back to the shed. She gave him carte blanche at the bar, telling him to stay away until we had had time to dress for the evening.

"You're going to look funny in Pete's clothes," she said with a chuckle, 'but here nobody cares how they look except, of course, the women, and they always make a great to-do of dressing for the Saturday night dances and special parties."

"I'll take those," he said quickly as she gathered his wet things from the chair where he had dropped them.

"You wouldn't know what to do with them if you did," she scoffed and left him there to grow chummy with Weeks.

As she went along the porch she could smell the clam chowder and fried chicken being prepared for Jerry's welcome home dinner. At the end of the porch the sound of men's voices raised in heated argument pulled her up. "We'll see about that!" she heard a man shout in hot anger. She stepped from the end of the porch just as the screen door into the side entrance slammed shut with a vicious bang. Baldwin stood there looking at the door as the bang echoed between them.

"Good-evening," she muttered.

"Do you think so?" he asked sulkily as she hurried away.

I was nearly dressed when she arrived at the shed. I finished quickly to be out of her way.

"I would forget to take out my dress," she complained as she puttered about. "I'm glad I brought this new black crepe with the silver collar, though, wrinkled as it is."

"Your sudden interest in clothes has nothing to do with Dave, has it?" I asked innocently. Then I remembered her threat. "Did you succeed in drowning him?"

It was then she explained about the boom. After that I left her.

When she came out ready for the evening, she really looked stunning.

"You're charming, my dear!" I cried with enthusiasm.

"I'm a fool, Ethel. I'm definitely and irrevocably through with men, but if you see me getting gaga over Dave pull me up short, will you?" she begged.

I nodded. They were an amusing couple. It would be fun to watch their romance develop.

Men who go down to the sea in ships, even our little group who play at it, are sticklers for time. Supper-dances and special dinners are served at eight, which is supposed to give all members plenty of time to get in, bathe and be ready. There is never any variation from that rule. At eight bells exactly (we are very nautical) the first course is served and if you are late you miss part of your dinner. It's a good rule and keeps the help satisfied and contented because they are able to plan their own time and amusements.

I sat in the loft door while Abbie went through Pete's clothes trying to find something suitable for Dave to wear. She had just finished when he came clumping up the stairs with Pete.

"I'm glad you're here," Pete said. "I've just seen Jerry and he's desperate. Mary refuses to see him and his dander is rising. Can you girls help him?"

"We'll see," Abbie promised as she joined me.

I adore the late twilights at Hidden Harbor. At that moment the falling sun glinted on the sand banks across the bay, casting an orange blanket over the water.

It seemed but a few minutes before the boys were ready to start back to the Club.

The entire island was at the dinner—that is, every one but Mary. It was one of those things, a few speeches of welcome and then a description of the adventure by Jerry, who is an excellent raconteur and made me feel the lashing of the howling wind and the rush of waves that swept and pounded over his boat. His descriptions were vivid and colorful but his heart wasn't in it.

When the dinner was over, the party began to go stale. A few people turned on the radio and danced, but the rest of us took the sure way of reviving a dying party and went into the bar. After all, a drink or two is the only thing that can lift that kind of party. There was good-natured chatter, a few stories and we were, beginning to feel better when Baldwin came in. It was Jerry's round. We had had several and Jerry, who had eaten nothing during the dinner and probably nothing at all during the day, was beginning to be a little high.

I held my breath for a moment, but nothing happened. Baldwin offered to buy the next round, but Pete, who was getting expansive, insisted that it was his turn. Baldwin hated to be blocked in any way but he gave in under the weight of Pete's insistence, but he did throw Pete a glance which seemed to say, "How do you expect to pay for it?"

It made us all a little uncomfortable. I don't know why it should, unless we were thinking that Jerry might start a row. He stood against the bar-getting glummer and glummer.

Baldwin bought the following round without any argument and proposed a toast to the home-coming heroes. Jerry refused to drink. He didn't say anything, but he pushed his glass aside distastefully and ignored the whole proceeding.

A row might have started if an attendant had not called Baldwin to the telephone. It was shortly after that that he startled us all by suggesting that we transfer the party to his house and carry on the celebration there.

It was a difficult moment. We stood there, all of us, not knowing what to say or do. Conversation ceased, and the air grew tensely weighted as complete silence greeted Baldwin's proposal. It was Jerry, who was not nearly as drunk as I had suspected, who accepted the invitation, saying a little too pointedly, I thought, "I think, it's a swell idea, Ballwin. I missed a chance to kiss your bride, you know."

That was throwing the gauntlet at Baldwin, all right. Jerry shouldn't have said it, but then I don't know what I would have done under similar circumstances. Baldwin's eyes flared at the implications of the remark. Just as he was about to retort, Pete stepped into the gap and proposed a toast to the welcoming committee before we left.

"The going's getting good," Dave whispered in my ear.

"I don t like it," I replied turning away.

"Aren't you going to the party?" he asked, chagrined.

"I suppose so. Wild horses couldn't keep the rest of them away. It's going to be tough on Mary. I'm going to call her and give her some warning.

I slipped into the telephone-booth and told Mary what to expect within the next half-hour. She gasped with surprise. "Please come," she begged, "and bring Abbie. I'll need all the moral support I can get."

That settled it. I'd go. When I left the booth Jerry signaled me from one of the writing-desks in the lounge. In front of him there was a hurried scrawl. "You've got to help me," he said. "She won't see me. This can't go on. Will you get this note to her so that she will know how I feel when she sees me up there?" He handed it to me just as it was.

"I'll try," I promised as I started to fold it. "Read it. I want you to know what you are doing. You might change your mind."

That was a fair thing to do. I read:

Mary darling,

I don't know why you've done this awful thing and I don't care. You belong to me. You can't be happy; neither can I. Tonight during the party I'm going to take you away. Be ready. I'll love you always.

JERRY

I guess I get sentimental as I grow older. There was a mist before my eyes as I said, "You can't play Lochinvar." I was trying to prepare him for Mary's refusal. I knew and he should have known that she would refuse. She might decide to go to Reno, do anything publicly and aboveboard, but I knew she wouldn't agree to a flight by night.

"If you don't want to do it, I'll get some one else," he said tersely.

"I'm glad to do it, but don't be disappointed if she refuses," I warned.

"She can't refuse. Go now before Baldwin or the rest of us can get there," he urged.

"Bring Dave along," Abbie instructed Pete as she led me toward the parking lot. Baldwin was there ahead of us. He was into his car, and away before we could get started. Abbie waited long enough to sight a cigarette and take a few puffs before she started her motor. Since he had gone first she wanted him to have plenty of time to get there and be out of our way.

I looked back at the Club. Stella Ketcham was moving out from the porch clinging to Dave's arm and chatting with him in her bright animated way. I nudged Abbie. "Look!"

"I'll spike that little game," she vowed and raced the car out toward the road. As we reached the fork that led on up the hill, Baldwin's car shot out of the parking lot in front of the store and tore up the hill.

"Now, what do you suppose he was doing in there?" Abbie asked as she went into second gear and ground slowly up the grade. We could see Baldwin's lights as he circled ahead of us on the curves.

The Taylor house bought by Baldwin is the show place of the island and stands at the very top of the bluff. It is reached by a tortuous road that snakes its way up the hill. Just below the house there is an artesian well from which we get our water supply. The overflow trickles down the hill, making a small gurgling brook which empties into the cove near the old boat-shed.

When we finally arrived at the house and parked, Baldwin was out of sight. A houseman opened the door. We asked for Mary. He said she was with Mr. Baldwin and would be down shortly. We were determined that she should have the note. Abbie asked for Mary's maid, Clara.

We went up to one of the guest-rooms and waited for Clara. When she came, we gave her the note and cautioned her to slip it to Mary when Baldwin was not present.

"Yes, ma'am," she said. "It's awful, Miss. Abbie. It just breaks my heart, it does, to see her cry like she does." Her white eyes were wise in her round ebony face. She slipped from the room and down the hall, a tall dark column of devotion to Mary.

That accomplished, we went down to the huge living-room, which runs across. the entire front of the house, with a three-way view of the cove, and the bay beyond, the Sound and the long narrow inlet running to the mainland. It was a lovely room, built for happy carefree living. There was a great stone fireplace in one wall, between two large plate-glass windows, so that in the, early spring and late fall you could sit in front of the fire and enjoy the magnificent view. A small library snuggled under and at the left of the stairs. A large airy dining-room occupied the right rear end of the house. The kitchen and service quarters were built against the hill beneath the living-room.

The staff were hustling about getting ready for the influx of guests under the direction of Mrs. Dunn, Baldwin's rather gaunt housekeeper, who in turn was aided by Sidney Venter, Baldwin's nephew-secretary.

Mrs. Dunn intrigued me. She was a dark woman. Her deep olive skin seemed positively dingy under her deep-shadowed eyes, so black and piercing. Over her tight mouth, which at the moment was all efficiency, there was a faint line of hair. I know such women are supposed to be beautiful and she probably was a great beauty in her younger days, but I've always thought such women ought to shave. I turned to look at Abbie. Her grandmother, old Abbie Randall, was one of those hairy women. Thank fortune Abbie had not inherited the beard.

Sidney Venter was just a young man. I had met him any number of times at the Club, in and about the island, without remembering a single thing about him. He was of average height and nicely put together, wore clothes well played a fair game of tennis, swam adequately and could handle a boat in a half-hearted way.

He followed Mrs. Dunn about or carried out her short terse instructions intelligently and efficiently but left no mark of himself on anything that he did. I wondered about him as I watched him work. He took direction beautifully with silent understanding and yet gave out absolutely nothing. I decided I that he was terribly inhibited or else had been completely cowed by Baldwin for so long that he had lost the habit of expressing himself in any way. Del and Sidney were cousins and as opposite as the two poles. There were times when I thought him interested in Del, but I never saw any outward manifestation of it. When Mrs. Dunn gave him her keys and told him to have the liquor brought out he accepted them with a faint smile, swung on his heel and disappeared into the library.

I had been in the house hundreds of times when Archie Taylor owned it. I knew where Sidney Venter was going unless Baldwin had thought of some better place to store his liquor. There was a paneled door in the library and a narrow staircase that led down to a wine vault in the cellar. Archie had had the stairway built to save himself steps if the servants were out or asleep.

Mrs. Dunn paused to smile at us as we crossed toward the piano. Abbie plays very well and had agreed to keep things going in that way. "Have you any idea how many there'll be?" she asked.

"Everybody on the island with the exception of Willie Pole and the 'granters,'" Abbie replied as she sat down at the piano.

She started to play "Thanks for the Memory."

After a few opening bars she began to sing in her attractive husky alto. I scowled at her, making her realize how inappropriate her choice was. She changed to "The First Time I Saw You," and looked up to see that I was still scowling. With an apologetic shrug, she changed to swing music and was playing when the others started trooping across the porch. I've lived through the development of jazz music from the cake-walk up to modern swing and the only difference I see in any of it is more and worse discords. I guess I like melodies rather than noise.

The room is approximately forty by twenty and can accommodate a great number of people. They scattered into small expectant groups as they wandered in. Baldwin came down first and I must say he was an expansive and gracious host as he tried to get things under way.

Dave, Pete and Jerry were standing in front of one of the windows on the porch. As I looked up Dave and Pete began making weird signs at me. Finally I understood what they were doing. They wanted Abbie and myself out on the porch. I nodded that I had understood and a few moments later Abbie and I went out to join them.

Pete was rollickingly high, Dave was keenly enjoying it all, and Jerry was glumly serious. "Look, girls," Pete said, "we're the Three Musketeers! All for one and one for all. That right?" he demanded of Dave, who had a protecting arm about Pete to control his sudden lurches.

"That's right," Dave agreed.

"The note," Jerry asked tensely. "Did you give it to her?"

We explained what had happened.

"Jerry's gotta see Mary alone and we don't think Baldwin will let him do it so we're going to make it possible, see?" Pete demanded. At our nod he went on. "That's why we're making you one of the Three Musketeers; there were four of 'em anyhow. Right?" he appealed to Dave.

"Counting D'Artagnan," Dave agreed.

"He knows everything," Pete told us appreciatively. "You gotta flirt with Baldwin or something to keep him busy. Understand?"

"I'll lure him to his doom," Abbie promised.

"Good old Abbie!" Pete leaned forward and planted a wet kiss on Abbie's cheek. Then he turned and limped inside, his eyes roving about the room searching for Del. Abbie and I followed. Dave and Jerry remained on the porch.

Pete's entrance livened things up a bit. Then Mary came down. She wore a dark-russet velvet that very nearly matched the soft sheen of her hair. Her eyes were moist as if she had been recently crying. She was slim and lovely as she passed from group to group greeting them graciously.

When Jerry finally walked in with his head up, he looked too much like a man determined to meet his doom bravely. There was a moment of charged silence until he said rather too casually, "Hello, Mary."

She advanced several steps and took his hand, saying, "I'm so glad you're back safe."

"Thanks," he said and would have turned away if Baldwin had not stepped beside them and said with an effort at banter, "But you haven't kissed the bride."

Jerry and Mary exchanged one fleeting baffled look. As her startled eyes looked up at him, he bent down and planted a perfunctory kiss on her quivering lips. A casual observer would never have believed in the utter hopelessness of that kiss. The whole thing seemed so matter-of-fact and yet so charged with possibilities. The moment passed, robbed of everything but its unrecorded drama.

Mary returned to her other guests and Baldwin, as if he knew what Jerry had planned was never more than three feet from her elbow at any time, playing up to her, assuming the role of an anxious and gracious host.

The party grew dull right after that. The big moment had come and gone and nothing had happened. Dave sidled up to us and whispered to Abbie, "If you're going to get Baldwin out of the way, you'd better do it before the party dies on our hands."

Abbie took Dave's arm and said, "I'm going to pretend I'm a little drunk. I'll present you to Mary and Baldwin. I'll take care of him. You talk to Mary and get her to Jerry."

Abbie and Dave moved away. When the introductions were over I heard Abbie say to Baldwin, "Dave, here, says I'm a poor business woman because I didn't get any alimony out of my divorce. What do you think?"

"I'd say it depended on the circumstances," he replied rather pompously, his eyes on Mary. "Perhaps you didn't deserve any."

"Listen, brother, don't fool yourself," she grinned up at him. "A woman deserves what she can get. That a woman pays and pays may be old stuff to you, but it's true." She hiccoughed "I just didn't happen to want slimy money, that was all." She turned, deftly lifted a cocktail from a passing tray, saluted Baldwin impudently and said, "Here's to your divorce!"

Baldwin flushed and would have left her standing there had not Pete rolled up to seize him by the arm. "Don't pay any attention to her," he advised. "Good old Abbie! She's drunk again." He grinned thickly and winked at me in understanding.

Baldwin jerked his arm away from Pete, but Abbie seized him from the other side. "Don't go away," she begged. "I want to talk to you about some business. I need advice. Now that I'm beginning to make some money I want to know what to do with it."

"Some other time," he suggested, but that didn't deter Abbie.

"Right now," she insisted, clinging to his arm.

He was caught. He couldn't tear himself away without seeming ridiculous. Pete ambled off. Dave came back alone and said, "This is a charming house you have here, Mr. Baldwin. Fine home, lovely wife. You're a lucky fellow."

I think by then Baldwin realized that the whole thing had been staged. He broke away from us as soon as he reasonably could and headed for the porch, where I had seen Mary and Jerry through one of the windows. His progress on the porch was blocked by Pete, who was holding Del in his arms.

Every one, sensing what was happening, had moved as close to the porch and windows as decency allowed and since Baldwin made no effort to control his voice they all heard his tirade. He called Pete a fortune-hunting deckhand who wasn't worth enough sea-water to drown him.

To which Pete replied, "That's your opinion."

"And I know what I'm talking about. You're no good—a waster. But let me tell you here and now, you'll never marry my niece for her money—not as long as I live."

Pete moved forward threateningly. "Maybe you won't live very long!" he cried as he made a vicious swing which Baldwin ducked.

"Leave my home!" Baldwin shouted.

That sent little Del into a magnificent rage; it would have been worse if Mary had not come back alone to make peace. Baldwin flashed his eyes about the porch, but Jerry was nowhere in sight. He turned and stalked into the house, definitely the loser in that round, thanks to Del, whose sweet eyes still snapped with their unexpected fire. Mary tried to smooth over the impossible situation that had arisen. Pete's grumbling as he declared what he would do to Baldwin was a sotto voce accompaniment to the rumbling thunder from the north as it boomed across the Sound from the Connecticut hills.

"I'm a little tired of all this," Abbie said. "How about you, Ethel?"

Before I could answer Stella Ketcham in passing said, "Abbie darling, you are a marvel with men. I do wish you'd tell me how you do it."

"It's a gift," Abbie replied

"Oh, is that what it is? I thought it was something you studied after your divorce." She slinked across the room.

"Why is she so bitchy to you?" Dave demanded.

"Women are like that when they understand each other," I answered. "Stella knows that Abbie can see through her, so Stella thinks Abbie is the same breed."

"I'm going home before the storm breaks," Abbie announced as another roll of thunder passed over us.

"Mind, if I come with you?" he asked.

"For once in your life, I'll be glad to have you," she replied honestly and started to locate Mary to say goodnight.

Pete prepared to leave too, but Del clung to his arm.

Mary was standing at the door leading into the library as we approached. Just beyond her near the fireplace I could see Jerry and Mary's father, Judge Verity, sitting close together, their backs to us. I heard the Judge's voice clearly and distinctly saying, "I was worried myself for a few days when you were reported missing. If you hadn't turned up, young man, it might have been a little difficult for me to explain the discrepancy on the books. I'll never do a thing like that again without something to show why it was being done."

I saw Mary's hand give a convulsive jerk on her handkerchief as Jerry scoffed, "No one would have doubted your word."

Mary turned to us and tried to smile, but it was a wasted effort. Her eyes were hollow pits, the color in her face had drained away.

After we had said goodnight, I heard her say to Mrs. Dunn, "I'm going to my room. Will you send Mr. Baldwin up at once?"

I looked back as we went through the door and saw her mounting the stairs.

Dave took a deep breath. "Well, everything but murder happened," he said as he took Abbie's arm.

I was interested in the white billows of lightning which flashed like star shells in the sky. From far off the thunder rolled and rumbled. Below us the cove lay darkly gleaming under the mooring lights of the many boats. Beyond the sandspit a steam yacht seemed to be moving toward the channel. Many yachts put into our cove when they fear a bad storm on the Sound.

"We're going to have company," Abbie said, pointing down at the yacht.

"That's the kind of boat I ought to have," Dave said with a reminiscent grin. "No booms to bang you."

"And no particular thrill," Abbie added.

As he took my arm going down the long steps to the car Dave said, "You know, I have a hunch we ought to stay."

"Why?" I asked, interested.

"I've followed hunches all of my life—many of them have worked."

"It's such a perfect set-up for a murder. Frustrated young love, tense situation, approaching storm and all. It's part of the pattern."

"It will look different in the morning," Abbie cut in.

"You hope," he said and took over the wheel.

"You know," he went on, "I'm the seventh son of a seventh son and my hunches never fail."

"Then go back," Abbie suggested.

With a laugh he guided us down the hill. As we swung into the shore road where we had our encounter with Stella earlier in the day, we had a full view of the yacht. She was feeling her way toward the mouth of the channel, her searchlight sweeping across the dark water.

When we reached the shed Abbie took the glasses and looked at the yacht. "It's the *Starfish*, all right, just as I thought," she announced.

"And who owns the *Starfish*" I asked

"Claude Graham, a friend of Baldwin's."

As we stood on the little balcony outside the loft door I heard a bell strike seven times, clear and distinct, coming across the water in an interlude of rumbling thunder.

"Eleven thirty, and all's well, Dave said thoughtfully. He didn't believe it. Neither did I. I shivered apprehensively.

CHAPTER THREE

DAVE AND I HAD A highball while Abbie improvised a bunk for him on the broad window-seat at the end of the living-room. After that we all smoked a cigarette. Then Abbie remembered Dave's clothes and went out to the back porch to bring them in. They were still damp, so she draped them hopefully over the backs of chairs near the hot-water boiler.

"I've been a lot of bother," he said, glancing at Abbie. "I've made a lot of extra work for her."

"One doesn't mind doing things for people one likes," I reminded him.

"I hope you're right." He raised his glass in salute and drank to his hope. Abbie joined us, yawning, which set us all off, so we decided to retire.

I was in bed when Dave turned out the light in the living-room. I heard him swear softly as he bumped into a piece of furniture. "Abbie," he called over the partition, "I don't think the Harbor is a good place for you."

"Why not?" She pitched her voice to carry over the rumbling thunder.

"Too relaxing." I could almost hear him yawn.

"Humph!" I grunted as I thought of the tenseness which had pervaded the island all day and listened to the threat of the storm which growled and rumbled as it marshaled its forces for an attack.

The pending storm, however, did not keep any of us awake. We were roused very soon, though, by a terrific clap of thunder which pulled me straight up in bed. There was a moment's ominous silence. After it had rumbled away, before the wind and rain hit the roof with the force of a hurricane Abbie bounced out of bed and scrambled into a robe and slippers. She scuffled out to see that windows and doors were properly closed. I followed, helping as best as I could, as the rain lashed and pounded at the walls with thudding onslaughts. Dave sleepily offered to help, but Abbie refused because we were practically done. It's just like a man to wait until the job is nearly finished.

The shed seemed to lift and rock with each impact of the wind. The rain sloshed against the windows viciously. In back of us the trees whipped and swayed, bending and tossing. We paused before the front window, which was protected by the overhang of the porch. Below us the big willow swung and threshed like a tortured octopus. In the cove, anchor lights jerked and swung as the boats bobbed under the fury of the gale. Beyond the spit, a heavy sea, whipped in from the Sound, pounded against the bar, rolling up and crashing in clouds of spray etched by lightning-flashes.

"Lucky the tide's on the ebb," Abbie said thankfully, "or the bar would go."

I knew she was referring to the cloudburst we had had on Labor Day in 1926. We nearly lost the bar that time.

We both recoiled from the window as a sizzling, snapping white flash slithered before us glinting on every bright object in the room.

"Afraid?" Dave asked, sitting up.

"No," Abbie replied.

"But I saw you jump, both of you."

"We don't like to shake hands with thunderbolts," I replied.

At that moment I saw Abbie lean forward and peer down at the shoreline below us. In the next flash I saw a dog bounding along the edge of the water. It was the Dalmatian that belonged to Art Tobias, the island's amateur radio operator. That dog never roamed about the island alone. Where he was Art Tobias would be nearby. I listened, half expecting to hear steps on the stairs or the noise or Art seeking shelter in the shed below. There was no sound but the wind and the rain and the constant cannonading of thunder.

"What time is it?" Dave asked

"Want to catch a train or something? Abbie quizzed.

The radium dial of an alarm-clock said twelve-fifteen. I gave Dave the information.

"Pete in yet?" he asked.

"No," Abbie answered.

"Well, if you're not afraid and there is nothing more I can do for you, I'll go back to sleep." He grinned impishly, knowing he had done nothing. At Abbie's disdainful sniff, he slid down under his blanket.

I continued to watch the boats lashing and straining at their, moorings, but trying to peer through the driving sheets of rain soon became monotonous We were completely shut in by a falling wall of water. I imagine the Deluge must have been something like that, a heavy wet curtain pouring from an angry sky.

It seemed to me when I tried to recall it later that I heard Pete come in very cautiously, but I couldn't be sure. Abbie says I must have been dreaming because Pete had never been known to be quiet in his whole life. She may have said that however, to cover him. If your conscience is bothering you, if you think you have something to hide, you are apt to be careful. At any rate, he was apparently sound asleep when I wakened the second time. I wanted some bicarbonate of soda. I will eat clam chowder and it always acts the same way. I didn't want to disturb Abbie. I took my flash and slipped into the kitchen. I thought I knew exactly where I could find the small box, but I was mistaken. Then, too, I thought of the mistakes people make in the dark, so I lit a candle which stood on a glass shelf across the kitchen window.

I don't know which is the worse, the distress or the cure. I had just swallowed the last of the dose when I heard the unmistakable sound of someone coming up the steps. It did startle me. I don't know what I expected, but for some reason I thought of what Dave had said about the pattern for murder. There was something relentless about the sound of those footfalls punctuating the boom of diminishing thunder and the even steadiness of the downpour.

For a single moment the face of Weeks, the Club steward, was reflected in the window. What on earth! I opened the door for him to slip in.

His face was worn and drawn from anxiety and lack of sleep. "I saw your light. I thought you ought to know that Baldwin has been murdered," he said all in one breath.

I was not surprised. Dave had conditioned me to expect Henry Baldwin's death.

"I found him a little while ago," he explained. That statement did surprise me.

"You found him?" I asked.

"Yes, in his room at the Club. I've been up to the house to tell them. I saw your light and thought I'd tell you. You'll probably want to take charge."

The man was tired and bewildered, he was not thinking clearly. "We'll call the police," I suggested.

"We can't. The lines are all down. We're cut off from the mainland. The bridge has been washed out and has taken everything with it. There's a new channel twice as wide as it was before which has cut across the neck. We're completely isolated and will be for some time unless the wind dies down. There's an awful lot of rough water surrounding us, Miss Thomas."

"Couldn't we send a boat ashore?" I asked.

"Not with things as they are. We've got to take care of this thing alone for a little while. Will you come down, Miss Thomas? It's sort of lonesome down there."

I knew exactly what he meant. "I'll get Abbie and be right down," I promised.

He slipped out of the door, pulling it shut behind him. A pool of water where he had stood was the only proof that his visit and his news were not part of a nightmare.

Abbie wakened easily. I sat on the edge of her bed and explained the situation. She began to dress quickly. We had just finished dressing when a gentle but persistent tapping sounded on the kitchen door. It was the regular repetition of the knocks which attracted my attention. The house creaked and grumbled under the heavy strain of the wind. Rafters groaned and cracked, but that gentle repeated knocking was as relentless as the wind itself. Abbie had heard it too. We went to the kitchen together, not knowing what to expect.

As we opened the door Clara, Mary's maid, squeezed through. Her dark face shone under the polish of rainwater. Her large eyes were round and frightened as she said, "I waited until Weeks left. I didn't want him to see me. It's a terrible thing, Miss Abbie, and you gotta help Miss Mary."

"Shhh!" I cautioned and looked back into the living-room through the kitchen door. I couldn't see a thing as we three stood listening for a moment. I thought of the witches of Endor as I heard that snoring duet carried on by Pete and Dave. Pete was what I would call a basso profundo. Dave's snorts were pitched in a higher key and ended in a shrill note about every fifth beat, slightly out of harmony but quite effective.

Abbie and I had the same idea. She handed me a slicker and an oilskin hat. She, too, wanted to get some facts before Dave could pounce on the story and tear it to shreds. What was it he had said yesterday about a perfect set up for a crime with a chance for the real criminal to go free because of the Baldwin Mary Jerry situation? But would Dave believe that in the cold light of murder in the morning? Being a newspaper man he would probably tell his story first because of its sensational aspect and then look for facts later.

"Come outside," Abbie whispered.

"It's raining, honey. You'll get your death," Clara warned, forgetting that we were fully dressed "It's so damp and cold," she complained as a shiver shook her body.

We went to the shed below. The little brook that normally trickled down the hill from the spring below the Taylor house was a mad swollen torrent that growled down the wide gash it had made in the side of the hill.

"Good heavens!" I cried in amazement

"Yessum, things is bad, Miss Thomas. Sure is! The brook has cut up the road some. You can't go up no more in a car."

We groped our way into the dark, dank interior of the shed, where the ribs of a new boat which Pete had framed loomed like the skeleton of some prehisitoric monster.

"Now, Clara," Abbie said, "start at the beginning and tell us why you are here."

"I thought you ladies ought to know," she began. "Miss Mary, she don't know I'm here. Nobody knows. She's sort of shocked and stunned-like. It's so terrible to see her. I come because you know all about murders and things like this. You'll be able to help her, won't you?" she begged.

"Of course we'll help her, Clara. Tell us what you want."

The poor girl was cold, upset and incoherent. We had to drag the story out of her, stopping, interrupting, going back, picking up bits and replacing them before we had a clear picture.

"Tell us what Baldwin was doing at the Club," I demanded.

"Didn't you know?" she exclaimed. Then remembering, she went on, "That's right. You went home early. A lot of things happened after you left. Miss Mary had another row with Mr. Baldwin."

"Another?" I prompted as Abbie and I exchanged glances, knowing nothing about the first one.

"Yes, ma'am. You know when you gave me that note, the one from Mr. Jerry, that was the first one."

"You shouldn't have read that note, Clara," I said severely.

"Lord, Miss Thomas, I didn't read it. I didn't have to. I'd a knowed who it was from with my eyes shut," she defended. "Well, anyhow, I tried to give it to her on the sly, like you told me, but that old thing, he caught me. He was a powerful man for seeing things, Miss Thomas. Seems like he knew what you was gonna do afore you did it. I gave Miss Mary the note as if it was nothing at all. She read it and tossed it careless-like onto her dressing-table where she was sitting fixin' her hair. She musta seen him in the mirror because the next minute he came in without saying a word, walked hisself right over to the dressing-table and took up that note before Miss Mary could reach it. He read it out word for word right there in front of me." She paused for a deep breath.

"He folded the note and put it into his wallet and said, mean-like, 'Very interestin'. Now perhaps the Board will understand why Carter has always opposed me.'

"'You wouldn't show them that note!' Miss Mary cried.

"'Certainly,' he say and then after a minute he went on. 'I forgot to tell you that the Board postponed their meetin' when they heard the *Albatross* was safe.'

"That took the gimp right out of her, Miss Abbie.

"She sort of crumpled for a minute and I thought she was going to faint, but she didn't. She turned on him after a minute full of fire and sort of spit at him like a hell-cat. 'I could kill you for that!' she cried. Yessum, that's what she said. I ain't never seen Miss Mary so mad. She ain't like that, Miss Thomas. She's good."

I nodded in agreement.

"And then he say, aggravatin'-like, 'Not in front of your maid, or would you like to discuss crooks too?'"

"What did he mean, Clara?" I asked quickly.

"Lord, I dunno what he meant. They wasn't no crooks that I knew of. He say a lot of things that don't mean nothin'."

"You are sure he kept the note?" I asked, thinking of that as damaging evidence.

"Yes, ma'am. That's why I come down here to you right away. I want you should get that note, either you or

Miss Abbie. It's gonna look powerful bad for Miss Mary and Mr. Jerry does they find the note."

"The police will find it," I said—regretfully, I must admit. Then like a flash I remembered what Dave had said about murders. He had accused me of being partial and my first thought was of protecting Jerry and Mary.

"They ain't gonna be no police for a while. That's another reason why I came. Don't you all know what has been happenin' round here this night?"

"Yes, we know. Weeks told us."

"Last night remind me of a hurricane down in Charleston when I was a little girl. It sure was bad," she reminisced.

"Tell me about Mr. Baldwin," I prompted.

"I tole you, Miss Thomas. He's shot dead."

"Yes, we know that. But what was he doing at the Club and who shot him?"

"Lord, Miss Thomas! Don't you know? I thought you always knew who killed people," she added in surprise.

I laughed at her credulity. "Not always, Clara. Let's get back to Baldwin."

"But, Miss Thomas," she objected, "hadn't you better hurry and get the note so as nobody will think they done it?"

"That's why I want you to tell us things, so people won't think they did it or if they do we can prove that they did not," I argued. "The more we know the more we can help Miss Mary."

"I ain't a-gonna tell nothin' when the police come," she, vowed stoutly. "I've seen 'em askin' questions in the movies and I ain't gonna have them twistin' words around in my mouth."

"But we're not the police, Clara. We're friends and we want to help Miss Mary if we can. Why did Baldwin go to the Club?"

"I don't know exactly. He went off in a huff. His face was a sight to see, all red and mad. He stomped across the room to the door just as Mr. Venter come in from fixin' the porch furniture. Mr. Baldwin turned to him and said loud enough for everybody to hear, 'I'm goin' to the Club for the night. Take care of my interests and let me know in the mornin' after Mrs. Baldwin has left. I'll come home then. There's goin' to be a divorce.' With that he slammed the door and pretty nearly busted the glass, he banged it so hard. He was powerful mad."

"Did that break up the party?" Abbie asked.

"In a way, yes, but they didn't leave, not then. They stood around not knowin' exactly what to do, wonderin' about what had happened. Miss Ketcham was the first to go and Mr. Taylor said he'd ride down along with her. One or two of the others straggled off. They'd have all been gone if the storm hadn't broke just when it did. I guess they all wisht they'd gone because that wind just licked around the house tearin' at the vines, bendin' the trees over and all. They talked a while restless-like. About then the Judge come along all dressed in a sou'wester and would have gone out only Mr. Jerry stopped him and said, 'You stay here. That's my job.' The Judge didn't want to give in, but Mr. Jerry made him. That's when Mr. Jerry left right in the worst of the storm.

"When the others realized the storm wasn't gonna let up none they started for home. After they had all gone, we settled down for the night and nothin' more happened until Mr. Weeks come up and told us about the murder."

"Why are you so worried about Miss Mary?" I asked suddenly, trying to startle Clara.

She refused to look at me and said, "On account of the scandal."

"What did you neglect to tell us, Clara?" Abbie demanded. "Don't you know that no one will think that Miss Mary killed him? Everybody will suspect Mr. Jerry."

"Yessum, I know that and when you help Mr. Jerry you help Miss Mary," she replied with irrefutable logic.

"Go home, Clara. We're going back to bed," I said and started for the door.

She caught hold of my arm. "You got to help her, Miss Ethel! You can't go back to bed! We need you!"

"There's nothing we can do when you insist upon hiding things from us," Abbie cut in. "We can't work in the dark, Clara. We must know what we're doing."

"I've told you everything!" she answered, but I knew from the sound of her voice that she was lying.

"Very well. Tell Miss Mary that we'll be up to see her later in the morning."

"Wait a minute, Miss Ethel! You're the only one that can help us, but you got to promise you won't tell the police when they come."

"I'll temporize," I said.

"No, ma'am," she said shrewdly. "I don't know what that big word means, but I can tell from the way you say it that it ain't no promise."

"Very well then, I promise."

There was a long pause before she whispered, "Miss Mary was out in the storm. That's why I'm so worried about her."

"And you think she went down to the Club?" Clara refused to answer.

"We're wasting our time," I said. "If she was out, she probably has the note."

"No, ma'am, she didn't get it. I looked through her things," Clara replied quickly.

"She probably destroyed it."

"No, ma'am, I know she didn't get the note. She's too worried, too upset. It's that note that's on her mind. We got to get it for her."

CHAPTER FOUR

"BE AS QUIET AS YOU can," Abbie cautioned as we left the shed and faced the relentless rain. "We don't want Dave messing into this yet. He's a newspaper reporter," she explained to Clara.

"No, ma am," she agreed heartily, "we sure don't. He'll probably find out about Mr. Pete and Miss Del too."

Abbie stopped right there in the rain to ask, "What about Mr. Pete?"

"Didn t you know about the ruckus? Mr. Baldwin told Mr. Pete he couldn't marry Miss Del but she didn't put no store by that. For such a sweet looking little trick she sure is dynamite when she gets herself worked up and explodes. Yes, ma'am! She and Mr. Baldwin done had it. Things is awful mixed up, up there, Miss Abbie."

I chuckled. That was a lovely understatement if ever I heard one. "Wait under the stairs," Abbie instructed and went quietly but quickly aloft while Clara and I waited like drowned rats.

She was back a moment later tucking a pair of cheap, red-rubber gloves into her pocket. She led the way with her flash. "Ain't you gonna drive?" Clara asked as we walked past the parked cars.

"No. They probably wouldn't start anyhow."

"You sure you'll get the note?" Clara asked anxiously.

"I'm going to try. Does any one know that you came down here?" I demanded.

"No, ma'am."

"Then keep it a secret between us. I don't want to be accused of blocking justice."

"No, ma'am, it don't sound good," she agreed.

"Then say nothing."

"Yessum, Miss Ethel, but ain't you comin' up to the house with the note?"

"Don't worry about that."

"I won't worry, honey, 'cause I know if anybody kin help Miss Mary it's you and Miss Abbie. When you do come, I'll have some nice hot coffee for you," she promised.

We parted at the little rise where a path went straight up the hill making a shortcut across the tortuous twistings of the road.

As we sloshed through puddles and runnels of water, I had plenty of time for thinking. As Clara had said, things were "awful mixed up." Jerry had a quick temper. There was no question about that, and it was quite conceivable to think of his doing a quick, brash, hot-headed act of passion; but this was obviously a planned crime. Planned so that suspicion would fall on Jerry. Why had Mary quarreled with Baldwin the second time? Was it their quarrel which had made him leave the house? Where had the Judge been going when he was stopped by Jerry, who had said it was his job? Why had Mary been out in the storm?

"It's a mess," I said to Abbie as we reached the comparative shelter of the Club porch.

"That is an understatement," she replied grimly.

We went past the kitchen windows. Our soft shoes made no sound on the wet porch. When we reached the door into the lounge, Abbie paused for a moment to gaze out at the dark hull of the *Starfish*, which loomed over the smaller sailing craft straining and tugging at their moorings.

Weeks was peering out into the windswept darkness. He opened the door for us. A lone candle burned dimly on the shelf over the fireplace where dull-red embers glowed. I noticed the clock in the flickering light of the candle. It was twenty-five minutes past three.

"Are we really cut off from the mainland?" Abbie asked.

"Completely. It was a terrible night. I thought the whole island was going to be washed away. I didn't sleep a wink."

"Then that ought to simplify things about the murder," I said matter-of-factly with no implication intended.

"But I don't know who did it," he protested quickly.

"That's too bad," I replied. "Any ideas?"

He gave us one long queer look and shook his head deliberately. I knew what he was thinking, he didn't have to say a thing.

"We'd better look at the body," I suggested briskly to Abbie. After all, Abbie and I are supposed to be authorities and it was necessary to play up to the idea.

Weeks lit a second candle and led the way down the hall to one of the four bedrooms which the Club boasted.

Even in the dim flicker of the fluttering candle it was an attractive room. The soft shadowy glow seemed to go with the maple furniture, the dainty white curtains and the lemony chintz draperies. Baldwin, too, might have been asleep except for the dark blob of color on his undershirt. He was stretched diagonally across the bed in a careless pose as if he had lain down for a minute and had fallen asleep.

The posture told me a great deal He had been standing beside the bed facing the door leading out onto the rear porch of the Club. The chair between the bed and the desk had been shoved back. I rather fancied I could see the person with the gun moving that chair out of the way with his free hand. There was no evidence of a struggle. There had been a shot. Baldwin had fallen back on the bed and the scene was ended.

I circled the floor with our small flash. Abbie stood beside Weeks, allowing me full charge. On the imitation hooked-rug there was a dark wet stain. A telltale pool of water left by the murderer's rain-sodden clothes, just as Weeks dripping clothes had left a pool in the kitchen of the shed not a half-hour before.

I could see Baldwin, terrified facing that gun, backing, trying to escape inevitable death, until his retreat had been halted by the edge of the bed. He had been trapped.

I switched the flash over the room. "Turn on the light." I said, forgetting for the moment that we had no power.

"Sorry, the current's off." Weeks reminded me.

"Can you get me something stronger than this flash? Isn't there a gasoline lamp in the place or a powerful flashlight?" I asked because we wanted to be rid of Weeks for a few minutes if it was possible.

"I have a larger torch. I must have left it in the lounge. I'll get it." He hurried away.

He was barely out of the door when Abbie started to pull on her rubber gloves. The next instant she was going through Baldwin's coat, which was draped over the back of a chair.

As I watched her, I had a definite feeling that other hands had searched through that wallet looking for the note. She replaced the wallet and went through the remaining pockets. There was no note. She pulled off the gloves and crammed them into her pocket. She stepped toward me, her eyes telling the story of defeat. Something crunched under her feet. She bent forward and removed a tiny object from the floor. I couldn't see what it was and didn't ask because Weeks was returning. A white beam of light flashing in the hall warned of his approach.

Now we had a better opportunity to study the room. Weeks stood in the door, his tired eyes widely interested in everything that we did. I moved closer to the body and said to Abbie, "Shot at close range."

"How can you tell that?" Weeks asked.

"There are powder marks on the undershirt," I explained as I ran my hand under the pillow and felt about carefully. There was no reason why the note or anything else should be there, but since a pillow as a hiding-place is as old as man I had no intention of omitting it in our search. There was nothing there.

"When did you discover the body?" Abbie asked.

"About twenty minutes of three. I had been very busy from the time the storm broke until about two-thirty when the wind lessened a bit."

"How do you explain this wind?" Abbie asked.

"It's a Northeaster that was carried in by the storm," he explained with the wisdom of men who follow the ways of wind and water.

"Then we may be in for a two or three day blow," she said a little forlornly.

"Never mind the wind. We can do nothing about it," I interrupted. "Tell us about finding the body. You said something about two-thirty," I reminded him.

"That's right. I made a pot of coffee and thought he might like some. It had turned cold and I didn't believe any one could sleep through the storm. He was afraid of electric storms, anyhow, and I'll admit I was feeling a bit lonesome myself just about then and I didn't dare go to bed. I came down here and tapped on the door. There was no answer. I knocked louder. There was a lull in the beat of the rain at that moment and I thought I heard something move in here. I listened, thinking he was coming toward the door. There was a loud rumble of thunder followed by complete silence as it died away. I tried the knob. The door was locked. I knocked again louder, but he did not answer. Then I knew something was wrong. I went through the next room and out onto the porch. That door," he pointed to the one opening onto the porch, "was unlocked. That struck me as being queer. If I were in here and was going to lock any door, I'd have locked that one."

"Quite right," I agreed. "Did you see any one?"

"No, ma'am."

"When did Baldwin arrive last night?" Abbie asked.

"I don't know exactly. I was interested in the arrival of the *Starfish* and I was busy taking care of things, fixing windows, closing doors and odd jobs like that. The barometer had fallen and I was afraid we were in for it.

As I worked I saw the *Starfish* steaming up toward the channel. I kept my eye on her as I worked. I knew if they wanted me for anything, they'd either signal or come ashore after they had moored. They didn't need me because I heard a boat come into the float. Four or five people came up the pier and went along the front porch toward the parking lot. Soon after that I heard a car drive off. I supposed they had gone up to Baldwin's for the party. It was a minute or two later when I heard the boat going back to the *Starfish*. I turned the floodlight on for a moment, and while I can't be sure, I thought I saw some one swimming beside the *Starfish*'s boat. I turned off the floodlight and was still watching the *Starfish* when Mr. Baldwin startled me by asking for a room. I was surprised and asked him if he had seen the people from the *Starfish*."

"What did he say?"

"He just nodded and mumbled something about landlubbers who were afraid to stay on the boat and had gone ashore. It was a funny thing for him to say because he was a landlubber himself."

"I knew very little about him," Abbie replied uncertainly.

I think she hoped Weeks would go on. He did.

"I've often wondered why he wanted to come to Hidden Harbor, Weeks continued. "He never got in a boat, didn't own one himself, and though he bought a nice catboat for Miss Del and Sidney, he never used it. He rarely ever swam either. I guess he just liked being with the people down here. He seemed, to set a great store by his seagoing clothes," he said with a rueful look at the inert body.

'Yes, I noticed that," I said absently, thinking about the people who had arrived on the *Starfish*. "How did those people get away from here?" I asked.

"Must have used Mr. Baldwin's car unless some one drove over for them. Willie would know that if they ain't up to Baldwin's," he added.

"And what time did all that happen?"

"Just about midnight. I remember the clock striking eight bells as we talked."

I smiled at the unconscious nautical touch.

"Then Baldwin must have talked to Graham for a few minutes last night," I suggested.

"No, ma'am. I don't think Graham came ashore. It wasn't Graham in the boat. It was one of the deckhands. Graham is a big man."

"But you aren't sure," I insisted.

"Yes, I am. I was in here talking to Baldwin when things began to pop outside. Before I dashed away he told me to call him at six because he wanted to have breakfast with Graham before he sailed."

"Have you notified Mr. Graham?"

"No, I haven't told anybody but Mary and you folks. I thought she ought to know," he said with a true countryman's feeling about death no matter how sudden or unexpected.

"That was thoughtful of you, Weeks. I'm sure Mary appreciated your kindness."

"I don't think it was much of a kindness but I thought she ought to know. I tried to get the police before I went up there, but it was useless. The lines were gone even then. It's a good thing you people know what to do."

"We'll get word through as soon as we've finished here," Abbie said.

"Abbie, you can't send a boat out of the harbor against the sea that's pouring through the channel!" he objected. "She'd founder sure. We may not have a channel if this keeps up much longer."

"We'll have to wait for daylight before we can do anything about boats," she said as she played the flash across the floor, disclosing small bits of mud here and there on the rug between the bed and the door.

I went to the door and was greeted by a damp blast as I opened it. There were small pieces of mud on the sill. I rather expected to see some muddy footprints on the porch floor as Abbie came with her torch. The sweeping rain, however, had eliminated any clues that might have been there. Disappointed, I turned back into the room to inspect Baldwin's shoes. They were not even damp.

Except for the body, the mud on the sill, the wet spot on the rug and the possibility of fingerprints, there seemed to be no clues. The storm had erased many things that might have helped us. I went over the room again, inspecting each thing carefully.

"When did you last see Baldwin alive?" I asked Weeks, who had been following my every move with cat like curiosity.

"When the storm broke. I didn't see him after that."

"Then he might have been killed a few minutes after that," I suggested to Abbie.

"It's probable," she agreed. "Did you see any one while you were busy?" I asked Weeks hopefully. His eyes flickered as he hesitated.

"Come on," I urged. "You may as well tell me, because you'll have to tell the police when they arrive."

"I don't see how you're going to get hold of the police, not for several hours, anyhow," he argued, trying to avoid an answer.

"Listen, Weeks," Abbie said. "We don't want to incriminate any one in this any more than you do, but we have a murder on our hands and I rather think the murderer is still on the island with us. If you saw any one or anything during the night, you should tell us."

"Well, I guess you like Jerry as much as I do and I don't believe you're anxious to believe he did this any more than I am," he replied thoughtfully.

"What about Jerry?"

"He was down here. I saw him out on the float. I guess he was worried about his boats, which is natural enough."

"Did he see you?"

"No, I was in the lounge. After I had finished all the work I could do, I lit the fire in here and stretched out on the couch. I sort of kept an eye and an ear open for anything that might go wrong. I looked up once and saw him standing down there as the lightning flashed."

"What time was that?"

"Must have been about two o'clock."

"Why didn't you speak to him?"

"I had a feeling he might want to be alone. I guess after Mary, he loves the sea the best," he explained with nice feeling.

"Did you see Art Tobias?" Abbie asked.

"No, but I did see his dog and I remembered thinking at the time that Art must be somewhere around because you know you never see the dog unless Art is close by."

"That was just about midnight, wasn't it?" she asked.

"It was when I was busy trying to keep ahead of the storm, right after it broke."

"Art may have been delivering a message," Abbie suggested.

"There was nobody down here to get a message," he reminded her.

"There was Baldwin," I said.

"I don't think that Art Tobias—" he cried, alarmed. "Now, Miss Thomas!"

"I'm simply trying to get at the core of this puzzle," I answered calmly. "You saw Jerry down here and you don't want us to think he did it. We can't just pin this onto some one we don't like and call it a day, you know. It isn't that simple."

"Art Tobias never had anything to do with it!" he defended stoutly.

"I didn't say that he did," I agreed. "Doesn't he get an occasional message for Baldwin over his radio?"

"That's right, he does," Weeks admitted. "He might have had a message for him."

"And if he was down here delivering a message he might have seen some one, the murderer perhaps," I suggested.

"Then you're thinking of him as a witness," he said relieved.

"Exactly," I answered as I recalled the telephone message Baldwin had received just before we left the house last night. It might have been from Art Tobias. There was a way of finding out, but I didn't want to worry Weeks. "We'll go up to see Art," I suggested to Abbie.

She turned to leave the room. "Better keep this room locked up until the police arrive," she advised. "Don't let any one in here."

"When will you be back?" he asked anxiously.

"I don't know. Much will depend on what Art has to tell us."

"You think he had something to do with it," he accused.

"No such thing," she replied. "We will get Art to send a radio call ashore for police help."

"By George!" he said as he locked the door behind us. "I'd forgotten all about that!"

As we left the Club, I was thinking about Art Tobias. "What about Art as a suspect?" I asked Abbie.

"As far as I know, except for an occasional message he received for Baldwin the men had nothing in common," she replied.

We trudged on in silence, the wind and the rain at our backs.

Art Tobias lived alone in a little house over on the north ridge in what we called the "grant" section. When the land was given to the old families most of them wisely chose the north ridge where they have the double advantage of a Sound and cove view. The granters live on the island the year round. They are good friends and fine neighbors. They mind their own business, and while they probably do not think much of us as a class they keep their own counsel. They are thoroughly dependable people and take excellent care of our possessions when we are away from the island. They are a bit touchy about the difference in the social scale, but through the years we have managed very well to maintain a comfortable balance. This new situation would have to be handled delicately. We could make no accusations against Art until we had proof.

I looked across the cove and rather fancied I could see his aerial mast dimly outlined against the sky. That was pure imagination. It was much too dark to see anything. We were moving along the road by instinct and Abbie's unfailing sense of location.

"What about Art?" I repeated.

"I'm trying to be reasonable," she said. "I'm so darned anxious to keep the crime away from Jerry and Mary that I'd suspect my own brother."

"There is Pete to consider," I said.

"I know that, too."

"Art Tobias may have had a very good reason for being out," I suggested.

"I've been thinking about that. He has a reputation as a heart-breaker. He's a handsome devil. He may have had a date with one of the girls who work at the Club. Why didn't I think of that before?" she explained.

We had reached the fork in the road but she trudged straight ahead.

"Aren't we going to see Art?" I asked.

"If we see Art, we'll have to have to ask him to radio to the police. That can wait for a little while. There are other things I'd like to know before that happens. It's bad, Ethel, very bad for our friends." She stopped and reached into her pocket. "Look," she said and thrust her hand toward me.

In the ray of her small flash, I saw one of those silly little trinkets that have come into vogue again for charm bracelets. It was a tiny spinning-wheel, broken and bent.

"Well?" I asked.

"I stepped on this in Baldwin's room. I gave it to Mary just before I left for the West. I guess we know where the note is."

CHAPTER FIVE

"THOUGHT YOU WERE never coming! Did you get it?" Clara whispered as she opened the door for us.

Abbie placed a warning finger over her lips as we stepped inside and shed our wet slickers. Clara 's manner had changed. She was now possessed of a hushed funereal attitude as she took our things and then preceded us toward the huge fireplace where an inviting fire was blazing. Mary, Del and Sidney, quite unaware of our arrival, sat on the large divan staring into the fire like three blinded owls. Clara, on tiptoe, with her presence of death attitude, announced in a hushed voice, "It's Miss Thomas and Miss Abbie, honey."

Mary sprang to her feet and rushed into my arms "You know!" she sobbed.

"Weeks told us," Abbie explained

"Then you've been down there, seen him?" Del asked.

Abbie nodded while I tried to soothe Mary, who kept saying over and over, "What are we going to do?"

During our little scene Sidney had bounced to his feet and said to Clara, "Some coffee for the ladies, Clara."

She gave him an odd look, since she was at that very moment pouring two cups of steaming hot coffee. Coffee has never tasted so good. As I alternated between sipping and inhaling the gratifying aroma, I had an opportunity to study Mary. She sat poised on the edge of a chair facing me and in her troubled eyes I saw a thousand questions. Behind the questions I saw stark terror as her eyes watched every move I made.

"It was good of you to come," Del said. "We were wondering what we should do."

"Any trouble getting up the road?" Sidney asked, offering us cigarettes.

"We walked," Abbie replied as she passed her cup for more coffee and accepted the light which Sidney stood ready to provide.

We talked about the storm, the damage, the condition of the road and our isolation before anything further was mentioned about our real reason for being there. I wonder why it is that people who have one definite thing on their minds seldom go directly to the point? Why is it that most of us indulge in circumlocution? Is it a form of preparation? Do we marshal our forces secretly as we talk of other things?

It was Abbie who brought the conversation home to the subject uppermost in all our minds by saying, "While we are isolated in one sense, there is always Art Tobias' radio, and if that fails us because the power is cut off, there is the outfit on the *Starfish*."

"We do have to call the police, don't we?" Del asked hopelessly.

"Daylight will be time enough," Abbie said as if she didn't think it too important.

"I wish we'd be cut off forever," Del cried, and went over to the hearth to kick an ember back into the coals.

"Now, Del! Don't be like that," Sidney protested, taking a position beside her. He put an arm about her waist.

They looked like troubled children standing there in their pajamas covered by woolen bathrobes.

"It's all right for you to talk, you've—"

I saw him nudge her. She stopped abruptly and looked me squarely in the eyes; asking, "Who did it?"

"I've no idea, child," I replied.

I heard Mary sigh with relief.

"Are there no clues at all?" Sidney asked.

I shook my head as I handed my cup to the hovering Clara.

"But you will find clues, won't you?" Mary asked anxiously.

"Perhaps! In the daylight!" Abbie replied. "But whether or not the clues will lead to the suspects I don't know."

"Suspects?" They all asked the question at once, showing how definitely their minds had been playing with the thought of one suspect and one only.

"Yes," Abbie answered.

"Tell us," Del said—somewhat relieved, I think.

"Well, there's Weeks. He was there all the time. Then there is the *Starfish*, which came in just about the time your uncle arrived at the Club. There is the murderer, the person who was there when Weeks tried to call Baldwin sometime before three o'clock."

I saw Mary's hand go to her throat and when she realized I was watching her she fumbled with her handkerchief.

"All those people?" Del asked.

"All those and Art Tobias," Abbie replied.

"Art Tobias?" Sidney asked, surprised.

"Suspect or witness," Abbie explained. "Weeks saw his dog just after the storm broke, and where the dog is, Art is or vice versa."

"But that's ridiculous!" Del protested. "Why should Art Tobias want to kill Uncle Henry?"

"Why should any one?" I countered.

There was an abrupt silence as they exchanged glances like conspirators. I felt a rank outsider, standing just beyond the intimacy of those glances.

"But Art Tobias," Del finally managed to say as if she were forced to continue the discussion.

"I didn't say Tobias did it, Del," Abbie said patiently. "He was near the scene of the crime."

"Sand-spooning with one of the waitresses probably," Del suggested.

Mary stood up. "It's all too horrible and ghastly, this speculating and wondering."

"Then let us face the facts and see what we can make of the situation," I said crisply. "We know what we think and we'd rather believe something else. We know what most of the people on the island will think when they hear the news."

"Are you trying to tell us that we must be prepared to see Jerry locked up?" Mary asked angrily.

"Not necessarily, but you know and I know—"

"Why don't you accuse him openly?" Del cried hotly. "It's a shame that we have to deal with innuendos!"

"Of course it is," I agreed, "but life is like that at times. Jerry is going to be accused of this murder and unless we can do something to prove him innocent, he may be convicted. That is a fact which must be recognized right now."

"Ethel! You don't believe that!" Mary cried desperately.

"What I believe has nothing to do with it. We are facing possibilities. Everything that has happened here at the island and in this house for the past twenty-four hours should be raked with a fine-tooth comb. If there is another answer to the riddle, we must find it."

"Oh, dear!" Del cried.

"Don't, Del," Sidney said gently.

"What will you find if your mind is already made up?" Mary asked bitterly.

"Straws, we hope," I answered.

"What happened after we left last night?" Abbie asked.

"Don't tell them!" Del cried to Mary.

"Now, Del, you only make things look worse than they are," Sidney argued gently.

"But I don't want them suspecting Pete!" she cried and then clapped her hand over her mouth, horrified at what she had said.

"You will suspect all of us, won't you, Miss Thomas?" Sidney asked.

"I'm afraid so," I replied thoughtfully.

"That's why I say tell them nothing!" Del cried defiantly.

"We can't do that, Del. It wouldn't be fair to Jerry and Mary. We must tell all we know. It's the only way," he said sensibly.

"You've got nothing at stake. You're the only person in the house who didn't quarrel with him sometime yesterday!" she cried desperately.

"That's not true," he replied quietly. "He fired me yesterday."

"Oh, that!" she scoffed. "He fired you at least once a week."

"But this was different," Sidney insisted as he lit a cigarette. "He told me to get out. He no longer wanted me here on the island. He did say I could work in the town office if I couldn't find anything else to do."

"I'm sorry, Sidney. I didn't know," Del said contritely. "I'm sorry I made you tell about it."

"It would have been discovered, such things usually are," he said hopelessly as he tossed his cigarette into the glowing coals. "I think we ought to answer questions now."

"Very well," Mary said. "What do you want to know?"

I leaned forward to deposit my coffee cup. "What was going on in the library between Jerry and your father about the time we were leaving?" I asked.

"I don't know. I didn't talk to either of them," Mary answered, but I knew she was not telling the truth.

I shrugged. "There is no point in our trying to help you and Jerry if you won't help yourselves. You heard something when you stood at that door, something that made you go to your room and send for Baldwin. What was it?"

"He had tricked me," she said bitterly.

"And Jerry and your father, did they know it too?"

"I don't know. They might have suspected."

I glanced at Abbie to see how she felt. I didn't want to force Mary to tell her story in front of Del and Sidney.

A slight shake of her head indicated, "Wait."

"Now, Del," I said. "What about you and Pete?"

"Uncle Henry and I had a row. He said I couldn't marry Pete and I said I would."

"And where does Pete enter into it?" Abbie asked.

"You know how Uncle Henry insulted him?" We nodded. "That made me mad. I told Uncle Henry a few things and then . . . and then . . ." She bit her lips, her little face contracted, her eyes squeezed together to keep back the tears. "I won't tell you!" she declared. "I won't! I don't care what happens!" She turned and fled up the stairs.

"Go with her, Clara," Mary ordered. "Put her to bed."

Sidney stood at the foot of the stairs looking up. "Mrs. Dunn will take care of her," he said, as he turned back toward us.

"Why is she so upset?" Abbie demanded.

"Uncle Henry threatened her."

"About what?"

"I don't know. He always had something to hold over a person's head. It was the way he worked," he said bitterly.

I thought of the note and knew exactly what he meant.

"This is getting us nowhere," Abbie said.

"What can we do?" Mary asked.

"Nothing for the moment, I guess," Abbie answered. "You're all wrought up. I think you'd better go to bed. When you're more composed, when you've had a chance to think clearly, you'll be better able to answer questions intelligently."

"I don't like to leave Sidney alone," Mary said, considerately.

"I'll be all right," he assured her. "I'm really awfully sleepy." His uncontrolled yawn was proof. He rubbed his hand over the dark sheen of his hair. "Goodnight," he said and turned toward the library, which had an entrance to his room.

"Did Baldwin know the *Starfish* would be in last night?" I asked, stopping him.

As he paused in the door, he rubbed his hand up and down over his robe. "I'm not sure, but I think he did. He talked to Tobias on the telephone at least twice last night."

"Don't you know?" I asked. "After all, you were his secretary."

"That's why he fired me. He took particular pains to keep his conversations with Tobias a secret."

"What secrets could he have with Tobias?" Mary; asked.

"I don't know. The first row we ever had was over one of Tobias' messages. That was when we first moved down here. Then last week I saw one."

"What did it say?"

"Something about guests."

"Then you did have guests?"

"No, the *Starfish* came into the harbor but no one came up here. When I mentioned it to him he was very angry and told me to mind my own business. Art called him last night before he went down to the dinner. I took part of the message. That was what made him fire me."

"Did Baldwin expect guests last night?" Abbie asked.

"I'm sorry, I don't know."

"We'll check with Tobias," I suggested. "It is puzzling."

As I turned to follow Mary and Abbie up the stairs, Mary said, "Poor boy! He's been so sweet to Del and me. I think he feels very bad about this. In his way Henry was good to both of them."

On the upper landing several candles were aglow on an old mahogany chest of drawers. From the door of Del's room I heard Clara say, "Just relax, honey, and I'll rub your neck the way I do for Miss Mary. You'll be asleep before you know it".

"Yes,ma'am." She followed the remark with a low musical chuckle, warm and friendly.

Mrs. Dunn was rather startling, appearing suddenly as she did, in a long sweeping negligee. She seemed darker than ever in the shadowed light of the candle she carried. She cupped the flame with her hand, which spread the light against her face. Her eyes seemed sunk in deep shadows. I felt rather than saw that she had been crying. "Are you all right, Mrs. Baldwin?" she asked solicitously.

"Yes, thank you. You might look in on Del. She's rather upset. Clara is with her now." She was majestic and rather tragic as she moved away from us.

"Try and get some sleep yourself," Mary suggested. "Miss Thomas and Miss Abernathy say there is nothing we can do for several hours."

"I couldn't sleep," Mrs. Dunn replied and I believed her.

With the door closed behind us, Mary asked deliberately, "What do you want me to tell you?"

"You'd better begin at the beginning," Abbie said with that direct bluntness of hers. "Why did you marry Baldwin?"

Her story seemed incredible for the year 1937. When I was a young girl and "East Lynne" and "St. Elmo" were popular novels, the story would have seemed real enough, but in this day and age of complete emancipation from all things smacking of the Victorian era it was almost unbelievable and yet it was exactly what any decent girl might have done at the age of twenty-one.

Baldwin, who had been trying to take a hand in the Club management ever since his arrival in the community, had finally managed to get himself elected to the Board in spite of Jerry's opposition. After Jerry had left on the unfortunate trip of the *Albatross*, Baldwin looked over the Club books, which was the right and privilege of a Board member. It just happened that the strong-box which the Judge and Jerry cared for between them was in the Club safe. After a careful inspection of the books, Baldwin called on Mary one evening and told her that he had discovered a discrepancy of approximately fifty thousand dollars, that cash and negotiable securities equaling that amount were missing.

The statement in itself would not have worried her, but she knew her father was very short of cash at the time and had had several unfortunate investments which he had informed her made them practically penniless.

Baldwin had been very polite about it but he had inferred that her father was a thief and would have to be exposed as such as soon as the Board of Directors met and the loss was discovered.

She couldn't bear the idea of her father facing disgrace after his long career on the bench as one of the outstanding judges of Long Island. The *Albatross* had been reported missing for over a week. Life without Jerry didn't seem worth living.

When Baldwin asked her to marry him and promised to return the money as a wedding present it seemed a simple and easy thing to do, since Jerry was undoubtedly gone.

"Sounds like an old-fashioned melodrama," I interrupted.

"But it was very real to me at the time," she said quickly. "I pictured Father's disgrace; the horrible things that would be printed in the papers. It would have killed him, Ethel. I didn't care what happened to me, anyhow. I didn't even feel that my promise to marry Baldwin was a sacrifice. It was just an easy way to save Father."

"Did he keep his part of the bargain?" Abbie asked.

"Yes, or rather I think he intended to do so. He showed me the fifty thousand dollars in cash and said he would put it in the Club safe before the Directors' meeting."

"You poor child," I said tenderly. "I know how you must have felt. What happened tonight? Why did you tell him you would get a divorce?"

She repeated the conversation which I had overheard between Jerry and the Judge as we said goodnight. "When I heard Father say, 'Why, if you hadn't come back or been reported when you were I might have had some difficulty explaining to the Board about the absence of those bonds and securities,' I felt nothing but relief for a moment. I had saved Father. When it dawned on me that Jerry knew all about it, I was completely stunned. There had been no emergency, no theft; Father had been carrying out Jerry's instructions."

"That must have been a shock," Abbie sympathized.

"Shock! I was furious. I talked to Henry immediately after that. He told me that he had acted in good faith, that he really had believed Father guilty of stealing the funds. He also admitted that when he returned the money he found new issues of bonds and securities to replace the ones he had thought were stolen. He knew that before we were married, but he didn't tell me.

"When I realized he had tricked me, had not played fair, I lost my temper. I called him a liar, a cheat and everything else I could think of at the time. I wasn't very ladylike."

"And no wonder," I agreed.

"I suppose he told you that he loved you and wanted to take care of you and all that rot," Abbie suggested.

"That's exactly what he did say, but it only increased my rage. I wasn't fair or decent to him. He wasn't all bad," she said with some regret.

"But bad enough," I said cynically.

"Was it then that you asked for a divorce?" Abbie asked.

"I didn't ask for a divorce. I told him I would get one and tell everybody how he had tricked me."

"And what was his reaction?" Abbie asked with a glance in my direction which clearly conveyed to me that she had some plan in mind.

"He laughed at me, told me to go ahead." She flushed anew with an old resentment as she recounted the scene. "He said he would produce Jerry's note, in court, use it as evidence to kill my chances of getting a divorce."

"And you told Jerry about your quarrel?" Abbie suggested.

"No," she denied quickly.

"But he must have known about it."

A guarded light flashed in Mary's eyes. "But he couldn't have known," she defended. "I didn't see Jerry again last night."

"Then who told him about it?" Abbie demanded.

"It may have been Father," she said thoughtfully.

"Then you finally told your father?"

"No, Father came to my room just as Henry and I finished our quarrel. He overheard the end of it. After his talk with Jerry he had somehow sensed what had happened. He had come up to ask me why I married Baldwin. He had never asked me before."

"Then there was a scene between Baldwin and your father?"

"Oh, no!" she denied quickly. "Father was furious, burning with an inner rage, but he was quite controlled as he said to Henry, 'I'll see you downstairs in a moment.'"

Abbie looked across at me and said, "Then, that is why the Judge was going out."

Mary was startled and gazed from one to the other of us really frightened. "Abbie," she cried, "you don't think that Father . . ."

"No. Your father didn't go out. Jerry stopped him and said, 'This is my job.'"

Mary turned to me desperately. "Ethel, you don't think Jerry did it, do you?"

"We're not thinking, Mary, we're trying to get at facts. Until we have a perfect picture of what happened we can't reach a decision."

Abbie nodded approval.

"But all your questions, your attitude is one of suspicion and doubt all directed toward Jerry," she accused.

"That," I pointed out to her, "is your own attitude. We have made no accusations."

She bit her lips hard at that until I saw the color drain away from them.

"How about the rest of the household?" Abbie stepped into the gap. "Tell us about Sidney, Del and Mrs. Dunn,"

"I know so little about them," Mary answered. "I've only been here for a week. You know as much about Del as I do. She's a sweet child most of the time, gay, full of fun and has been the one bright spot in the household."

"How did she get on with Baldwin?"

"Fine until we had news that the *Albatross* was safe. They argued incessantly after that. Del is determined to marry Pete and Henry was just as determined that she should not. You know what happened tonight on the porch"

"Why was Del so upset a little while ago?"

"I don't know."

"And Sidney?" Abbie asked.

"He and Henry seemed to get along beautifully. In fact, I rather think Sidney sided with Henry on the question of Pete. I have felt that Sidney is in love with Del himself, but you can't tell, he is so quiet and rarely ever expresses an, opinion. His self-effacement may be the result of his long association with a man as forceful as Henry."

"Just what was Baldwin's business?" I asked.

"He's an importer, that's all I know. Sidney could tell you all about that."

"And Mrs. Dunn, what of her?"

"A thoroughly efficient and capable housekeeper who has been with Henry for years and years. She is very devoted to Del, brought her up. She's a little like Sidney, self-effacing and quiet, never saying very much but always actively occupied with her duties. She has been very kind to me, has made life quite bearable these last few days, as if she understood how I was feeling."

"And is there nothing except Del's tantrum last night that might suggest a motive?" Abbie asked hopelessly.

Mary's eyes flashed fear again. "You want to think Jerry did it!" she accused.

"And what are you thinking?" Abbie asked deliberately.

"I know he is innocent," she replied defiantly.

"Did you see him last night when you were down there?" Abbie asked bluntly as she opened her hand and displayed the crushed trinket from Mary's charm bracelet.

Mary actually recoiled when she saw it. "So you know!" she said.

"I only know that you were down there," Abbie replied gently.

"All right, I was," she admitted bravely.

"And you saw Jerry down there. Did he see you?"

"No."

"Why didn't you speak to him?"

"I didn't see him," she denied deliberately.

"But Weeks did," Abbie said. "Why don't you tell the truth?" she asked relentlessly. "Ever since you saw him down there you've been wondering what actually happened. You went to Baldwin's room to get that note. You found him dead and the note gone. Then you saw Jerry. There was only one conclusion for you to make."

"No! no! no!" she cried as if the forceful repetition of the words would erase the idea from our minds.

"But you have been wondering," Abbie insisted. Her eyes were baffled, trapped, full of fear as she tried to avoid our glances.

"Forget we're investigating a murder and remember we are your friends," Abbie reminded her.

"Friends!" she said bitterly.

Abbie shrugged. "I didn't want to believe that Jerry did it. I had hoped to find that it was some one else. It's not your fault or mine that all the indications—"

"Indications!" she cried. "What indications? There is proof! What more do you want?" She pointed to Abbie's hand, which still held the trinket. "I killed Henry! What's the use of pretending? I hated him for the thing he had done to me, hated him not because I married him but because when he knew Jerry was alive he hurried me into the marriage."

"Do you realize what you are saying, Mary?" Abbie demanded.

"Do you think I have thought of anything else for hours?" she answered.

CHAPTER SIX

CLARA WAS WAITING for us in the living-room. "Better have some more coffee," she suggested, handing us each a cup which she had evidently poured when she heard us on the stairs. I sat on the couch in front of the fire and leaned back. I was tired. I felt something cold and damp on the back of my head. I turned round and felt the upholstery. There was a damp spot where my head had rested. I looked up at the ceiling suspecting a leak, but nothing showed.

"What's the matter, Miss Thomas?" Clara asked solicitously.

"Nothing, nothing at all."

I knew she was dying to ask if we had found the note. Before she could muster enough courage to ask questions, I said, "Clara, I want you to do something for me. I want you to check the wardrobes of every person in this house. If you find any wet clothes, let us know at once."

"Yessum," she promised, wide-eyed.

A dismal wet dawn was about to break as we left the house.

"Why did you ask Clara to hunt for wet clothes?" Abbie asked.

"Because one never knows."

"No, one doesn't. I hardly expected Mary to confess to the murder."

"No more did I."

"But you know perfectly well that Mary didn't kill Baldwin. She thinks Jerry did it."

"Obviously."

"It's going to be an awful mess, Ethel."

"Unless, of course, Mary or Jerry did kill him," I replied.

"You sound like Dave. I want to think the real murderer was an opportunist and I am inclined to think that he was, that he counted on suspicion falling on Jerry immediately."

"Now who's sounding like Dave?" I asked with a chuckle.

"Dave is no fool!" she defended. "I can't, because I don't want to, believe that either Jerry or Mary did this thing, but if we seem to believe that one or the other of them did, we may lull the real murderer into a sense of security. If we can do that, we'll have a better chance for observation."

"I hope you're right."

"I've got to be right, Ethel. From now on we must pretend to believe Jerry or Mary guilty. It is our only hope."

I agreed. There was a great deal of logic in her reasoning. "Of course Jerry has the note," I said.

"I think so. Baldwin must have been dead when Mary arrived at the Club or she would not have believed Jerry guilty."

"Rather heroic her attitude," I suggested.

"May be helpful," Abbie replied thoughtfully as we sloshed down the wet, mud-streaked road.

It was shortly after five when we approached the fork near the store. There was a dim flicker of light behind the wet windows. Abbie led the way to the porch and peered through the glass. Martin was bustling about energetically, getting things ready for the day's business. The door was open. We stepped in over the damp circle where the wind had whipped the rain over the sill.

"Hello!" Martin called in surprise. "What are you two doing here, or are you smarter than I think you are?" He stopped his dusting. "You know, I've been wondering who'd be the first customer this morning. I sorta expected Mrs. Baylis, because she worries so about those children of hers. This food supply won't last too long," he said with a calculating glance at the well-stocked shelves.

"Then you know we're cut off from the mainland?" Abbie asked.

"Yes, Willie stopped by to tell me that the bridge washed out along about two-thirty this morning taking everything with it. You know, Abbie, I never figured that bridge was built right. It was too low. Why, the water always came up over it every time we had a high, fall tide. The next bridge they build had better be mounded up, if they build another one," he added doubtfully.

He chattered on, positively loquacious for him. His tongue must have been loosened by what he considered our common problem. After all, we were a group of people cut off from supplies and communication from the mainland.

"Will you lock the front door for a few minutes?" Abbie asked.

"Sure, but why?" His, eyes twinkled at me rather suggestively.

"I want to ask you a few questions and I'd rather not be interrupted by Nora Baylis should she come," Abbie explained.

"She'll think it mighty queer if she finds us locked up in here at this hour of the morning," he cackled.

"Don't do it if you're worried about your reputation, Martin," I challenged.

"Shucks!" he replied, as he shuffled forward to bolt the door. "I ain't supposed to be open till six anyhow. That'll give you plenty of time to ask questions."

"Henry Baldwin was murdered last night and you've got to give us the information we want, since we can't get through to the police."

"No! You don't tell me! Who done it?"

I chuckled inwardly at the calm way in which he accepted the news. Just like him to remain unruffled.

"We don't know."

"So somebody killed him, eh? Well, this is the first murder we've ever had on the island." He bit off a sizable chew of tobacco and looked at us for a moment. "It's hard to believe, ain't it?

"Come back here," he suggested and led the way to the storage-room behind the store proper. There was a comforting smell of ham and bacon, spices and other foodstuffs. I took a stool, Abbie sat on a box and Martin teetered on the edge of a barrel. "Got any ideas?" he asked.

"Some that we don't want," Abbie replied. "We are trying to keep away from the thought that everybody on the island is going to have."

"You mean the people that ain't got no sense," he replied juicily. I don't believe I could ever live with, or love a man, who chewed tobacco.

"Exactly," Abbie agreed.

"Well, what can I do to help Jerry? I'll do what I can," he promised.

"Who was on the switchboard last night?" Abbie asked.

In addition to operating the community store, Martin runs the local telephone exchange and the summer post office

"I was. Suzie went ashore to the movies."

The granters always speak of a trip to the mainland as going ashore even though they now do it by automobile.

"Then you can tell me who called Baldwin last night sometime before twelve."

"It was Art Tobias," he replied immediately.

"Oh," I said.

"What's the matter? He leaned forward "Say, you ain't aimin'—"

No," I interrupted him quickly. "I was just trying to get something straight in my mind. The *Starfish* came in about eleven thirty last night. Do you happen to know if Art had a radio message from her at any time yesterday?"

"I wouldn't know about that, but I reckon he did, because he called Baldwin down at the Club last night and sometime later he came by here and left a letter for Baldwin. Art's very particular about that radio of his," he hurried to explain before I could interrupt him. "If he gets a message for you it don't make no difference to him that he has telephoned you. He always puts a copy of the message in the mail. He likes folks to have a copy of the message same as the Western Union does."

"Did Baldwin get the copy?"

Martin looked more like a turtle than ever as he shuffled into the store to look in Baldwin's box. "Nope, he didn't get it. Still in there," he said on his return. "Why are you so interested in the messages?" he asked after he shot a long dark arc of juice into a box of sawdust.

"We're interested in everything Baldwin did last night. What time was he here?"

"It was about ten o'clock, I guess. It was soon after Art called him down at the Club, anyhow. I didn't notice the time. He was in a hurry. Just dashed in and asked me for the package he left in the safe. I was busy so I handed it to him and off he went. Seemed to be in an awful rush."

"And you are sure that was after Art talked to him at the Club?" I insisted.

"Yup."

"Do you know what was in that package, Martin?" I asked.

He shook his head and again squirted a long brown stream toward the sawdust.

"What did it feel like?" Abbie asked.

"Darn me, Abbie, if you ain't the beatenest woman I ever did see!" He grinned sheepishly. "You know things folks does without even seein' 'em do it. How'd you know I felt it?"

"You did, didn't you?"

"Sure, I did." He turned to me. "I'd hate to be married to a woman like her. She'd be powerful hard on a man." He stopped abruptly, confused by the implication of what he had said. Everybody knew that Tim Abernathy had

run out on Abbie. The last thing in the world Martin
would do, however, would be to hurt any one's feelings.

Abbie understood his confusion. "It's all right,
Martin," she said. "I know you weren't being personal. I
wasn't thinking about being a detective when I was living
with my husband. It's rather too bad, too, in a way," she
added.

"That's right, you wasn't," he agreed self-consciously.

"Now how about the package?" I reminded him.

"A man don't have a chance with the two of you after
him," he teased. "That package could have been a lot of
papers or it could have been money. I couldn't figure it
out. It wasn't jewelry, of that I'm sure, because that's
what I thought it would be."

"Why?"

"He give it to me just about the time him and Mary
got married. I don't know if it was before or after, to tell
you the truth, but it was just about then."

"I wish you had had X-ray fingers," I said
thoughtfully.

It was his turn to ask, "Why?"

"Because we'd like to know what was in that
package."

"The best I can do is to tell you what it looked like, if
that will help." At my nod he continued, "It was a long
manila envelope—a big one—the kind that have sides
that bulge. There was nothing on it but his name."

"Thanks."

"You reckon that package had something to do with
his death?"

"I hope so. If it doesn't, it's going to be hard on Jerry,
you know," Abbie said and moved away into the store.

"If you think of anything, Martin, get in touch with
us," I suggested as I followed her.

"I sure will, Miss Thomas. Say, how are you fixed for
food? Don't you want to take some extra eggs and things?
It may be three or four days before we can get any
supplies across the bay."

"Fix up a bundle and send it over. We have a guest, so send enough," Abbie answered.

Abbie moved toward the door but I remained at the counter. Martin sort of hung between us. He looked at me expectantly. "What, if anything, have you heard about Stella Ketcham and Baldwin?" I asked.

"You're asking because you think it may have something to do with the murder, ain't you?" he demanded.

"For no other reason," I replied emphatically.

"Well, there has been talk. There are some of the women folks who think Stella had her mind all made up to marry him." He looked at me quizzically. "How'd you know anything about them? You ain't been around lately."

"Call it intuition," I suggested.

"I've heard it said that Stella was mighty disappointed when he married Mary. I'd have done the same thing myself in his place if it was a question of one or the other," he added.

I moved toward Abbie. "Don't say anything about the murder, Martin. We want all the time we can get before people start swarming down to the Club."

"You ain't gonna have more than an hour's grace, once it gets light. Soon's they can see, the men will be coming down to look after their boats. The first thing you know the whole island will be down there trying to see the corpse."

I moved over to the post-office section of the store and asked, as if I had just that moment thought of it, "How about letting me see that letter Art Tobias left for Baldwin?"

He considered for a moment as he scratched the fuzz behind his right ear. He shook his head. "I couldn't do that, Miss Ethel. It's in the mail under the protection of the United States Government."

That stumped me. I wanted to know something about those radio messages and I had to get that envelope out of

the protection of the United States Government, as he so
aptly put it. "I'm going up to see Mary. Is there any mail
for the Baldwins?" I asked innocently.

"By gum!" He slapped his side and cackled
delightedly. "You're a smart one! With you and Abbie on
the job the murderer had better watch out. Now, I can see
no reason for not giving you the mail in the Baldwin box.
Folks does that all the time when they know each other
as well as you folks do." He shuffled behind the partition
and came back with two envelopes. "There's two of 'em,"
he said.

"One for the eight-o'clock call and one for the later
one," Abbie reminded him.

"That's right, but I was trying to remember when it
was put into the box." He considered a moment. "I know.
Suzie got something out of the box last night after she
came home. I heard her canceling something. This is
probably what it was."

"And what time was that?" Abbie asked.

"Pretty close to midnight."

Abbie smiled at me with satisfaction. We had fixed
Art's reason for being down near the Club.

"A lot can happen in a short time, can't it?" Martin
asked philosophically as he ambled toward the door.

"Sometimes too much, sometimes too little, I replied.
"That's our problem right now, too little time.'

"Well, if you got things to do while the murder is still
a secret, you'd better get going," he advised as he drew
the bolt. "Daylight, what there is of it, is practically here."

He was right. The eastern sky was a dull dark-gray,
thick and heavy, with no sign of a break anywhere. The
rain, however, was less violent although the wind still
blew sharply. I saw the gleam of a pair of headlights
coming from the base of the hill, "Looks like a customer, I
said, "probably Nora. Sorry we kept you so long!' I
crammed the envelopes into my pocket. He knew
perfectly well that I intended to read them, but I could

see no reason for doing it under his eyes since he felt as he did about the post-office.

He was peering over my shoulder. "Yup, you're right. It's Nora Baylis. I hope she misses the hedge this time," he said hopefully.

But Nora didn't miss the hedge.

"Damnation!" he cried "That woman ain't got no sense of distance!"

"'It's something constitutional," Abbie suggested, as the front wheels of Nora's car whacked the porch Steps

Disgusted, Martin turned into the store Nora began talking as she backed out of the roadster.

"Wasn't the storm terrible! When I woke up this morning and saw the bridge gone, I told Bill that unless I was smart some one would get down here ahead of me. I do think in an emergency like this, children should have the first consideration, don't you?" There was some kind of an accusation in her voice.

"What emergency?" I asked.

"Why, the storm, being cut off the way we are and all. I never heard or saw anything like it in all my life! I was terrified. I had my head under a pillow most of the night."

"Then you couldn't have seen or heard a great deal of it," I said as I moved away.

"Well!" I heard her gasp at Martin as she side-turned into the store. "Well! What's the matter with her this morning?"

"What's the next step, Abbie?" I asked as we trundled down the road in a hippity-hop, puddle-jumping marathon.

"How about a conference as we go?" she suggested.

"Confer away! There's one thing certain, if Baldwin had an envelope full of money it might reasonably be the motive for the murder."

"Just what I was thinking," she replied. "The money somehow seems to be connected with the 'phone calls from Art Tobias."

"And Art Tobias seems to be connected with the arrival of the *Starfish*," I suggested.

"And Art was down here. If he knew about the money and also knew that Baldwin would be at the Club, it makes a nice case against Art," she mused.

"All of which has nothing to do with Mary's reason for confessing that she killed Baldwin. I think we'd better see Jerry and find out, if we can, why Mary believes him to be the murderer."

"We may learn things we'd just as soon not know," she objected.

"If he killed Baldwin, there's nothing we can do about it," I reminded her.

CHAPTER SEVEN

JERRY'S COTTAGE IS on the shore road, as it is called, about halfway between the fork and the boat shed. It snuggles in a grove of trees peering out at the cove from as pretty a setting as one would wish.

"Phoebe is up," I said as I spied a light in the kitchen.

We went up the walk and tapped on the glass pane of the kitchen door.

Phoebe Raynor, startled for a moment, looked up from the stove. Then she came across the room to let us in. She was a comfortable soul, rather tall, and built as a woman ought to be with the proper amount of padding over her bones. Her gray hair was pulled into a tight little knot on the back of her head. She beamed a welcome.

The doughnuts she was making made the kitchen smell warm and nice. A kettle of hot fat bubbled over the fire, a plate of crisp brown cakes sat on the back of the range, their fragrance mingling with the sharp smell of wet pine. Phoebe was an old-fashioned housekeeper who, winter or summer, cooked over a wood fire.

"Sit down," she invited, pushing an adorable old rocker toward me. "Here, Abbie, take this stool."

"Give me one of those doughnuts before I faint," Abbie cried.

"Wait until I get the powdered sugar," she chuckled as she bustled over to the corner cupboard.

They were delicious doughnuts. After the second one I asked, "Jerry up yet?"

"Oh, dear no! He'll probably sleep late today. He was up till all hours last night worrying about the boats."

"We've got to see him, Phoebe," Abbie said quietly.

"But, Abbie!" she protested. "It isn't six o'clock yet!"

"I know. I've been up most of the night myself. So has Miss Thomas. Something has happened, Phoebe, something bad." She paused purposely for effect.

"You mean about the electricity, telephone and things?" Phoebe asked.

"No. Something worse than that. Mr. Baldwin was murdered last night. We've got to see Jerry about it."

Phoebe gazed at us, all the friendliness gone from her usually calm face. "Now, listen here, Abbie, if you think, because you've turned into one of those detective women like Miss Thomas, that you can come around here and accuse Jerry of . . ." She stopped and looked at us helplessly, realizing, I think, that her sudden outburst would do Jerry no good. With an immediate change of tone she said, half-pleading, "He didn't do it, Abbie. You know that, don't you?"

"Of course, Phoebe, but it's going to look bad for him until we can prove him innocent. You just said yourself that he was out until all hours."

"Very well, I'll call him." She left the room weighted with an air of doom.

"If Jerry had been her own son she couldn't love him more, nor could she have done more to spoil him," Abbie said warmly.

Phoebe was back in a minute. "He says to come up," she said. She went toward the stove to lift another batch of rich-brown doughtnuts from the hot fat.

Jerry's room was large, low-ceilinged and comfortable, snuggling as it did under the roof over the kitchen ell. Through the dormer windows one had a view of the cove on one side and the woods on the other. A newly lighted fire crackled cheerfully.

He stood on the hearth facing us, looking very slim in a dark-blue robe wrapped tightly over maroon pajamas. What little sleep he had had seemed to have refreshed him.

"I thought you'd better come up here," he said. "Phoebe told me why you had come. There's no need for her to know things that may worry her." He rubbed the golden stubble on his chin speculatively. "When did it happen?" he asked calmly, as if he realized there must be a careful marshaling of all facts.

"Sometime between twelve and two-thirty," Abbie replied.

"And every one on the island is going to think I did it," he said thoughtfully.

"Unfortunately, yes," she answered. "You were seen at the Club."

"I expected that. Was it Weeks?"

Abbie nodded.

"And what do you think?" He included us both in the question.

"Nothing yet, Jerry. We believe Baldwin was killed soon after twelve, but that is only a guess on our part. You might have followed him down from the house and in a fight or an argument have killed him."

"You're basing that conclusion on my quick temper?"

Abbie nodded.

"But do you believe I killed him?" he insisted.

"Frankly, Jerry, I don't know. What time did you get to the clubhouse?" she asked.

"I don't know exactly, Abbie. It must have been after two."

"Then you have an alibi to cover the time between twelve and two," she said relieved.

"I'm afraid not," he said after a moment's calculation.

"Can't you prove what you did with your time after you left the house?" she insisted.

"Unfortunately, no."

"That's too bad."

"Yes, isn't it?" he agreed.

There was something defeated and yet maddening about the way he said it.

"When did you leave the house up there?"

"A little after twelve, in the teeth of the storm."

"Then where were you, between twelve and two?"

"It's no use, Abbie. I have no alibi."

"You mean you have an alibi but you won't use it," she accused.

He shrugged, leaving us to draw our own conclusions. He turned to tinker with the fire, thus breaking the tension that hung between us. I stood up and moved about the room to wear off my annoyance at his stubbornness.

"Serves us right," I said as I stopped before a rear window and looked down at the rain-soaked yard the wind-swept lawn and Phoebe's old-fashioned garden bent even with the earth.

"What do you mean?" he asked.

Without bothering to face him, I replied, "We have no connection with the case. We should have minded our own business and allowed things to take their natural course. I'll learn some day, if I live long, enough," I added.

"Don't feel that way," he begged. He may have been looking at Abbie; I don't know because I didn't turn round. "You're the only people who can help me. I need you. I know how bad it's going to be for me the minute the police arrive. I just have no alibi. I wish I did."

"It's all right, Jerry," Abbie said. "We know you have an alibi but you don't intend to use it. That's all right, too, if you want to be a fool. You're the one who'll burn, as they say in the classics." There was a moment's pause and then she demanded hotly, "Don't you realize the murderer counted on suspicion falling on you? Are you going to help him or her?"

"Why do you say her?" he demanded quickly.

"Because any one could have done it, man or woman," she retorted.

"I'm sorry, Abbie," he said relieved, "but it's one of those things." I could feel him withdrawing into a shell.

Abbie began on a new 'tack. "Suppose you tell us what happened up at the house after we left," she suggested. "Just when did you go?"

"We were home before twelve. When the *Starfish* came through the channel."

"Then you left before I had my set-to with Baldwin?"

"Yes."

"Why did you quarrel with Baldwin?" I asked.

"It wasn't a quarrel, really. He wouldn't fight. I learned Mary's reason for marrying him."

"About the Judge, you mean?" Abbie asked.

At that moment I became interested in Jerry's empty garage. The door was open, the floor was soaked and dotted with wet leaves blown there by the gale. As he answered Abbie's question, I said, "Then you know that he told Mary her father was a crook?"

"No, I wasn't sure of that. I was merely suspicious after I had talked to the Judge and had learned that Baldwin had gone over the books in my absence. I could think of no other reason for Mary's marrying him. I left the Judge determined to have it out with Baldwin. I met him at the foot of the stairs ready to fight. He excused himself, saying that Mary was waiting to talk to him in her room. I was seeing red at the time and would have forced the issue except for the intervention of Mrs. Dunn. She made me realize that I was putting Mary in a more difficult position."

"And what was the Judge's reaction?"

"Naturally he was furious. He finally followed Baldwin upstairs."

"And did you talk to Baldwin again last night?"

"Yes, when he came down followed by the Judge. He took us into the library and admitted, of his own accord, that he had honestly thought the Judge had taken Club funds. He said he told Mary about it and she had begged him to save the Judge from disgrace. At that point the Judge called him a liar."

"But he didn't put any money in the strong-box, did he?" I asked.

"No. He said he intended to do it until he found the missing funds had been replaced. I believed him, Abbie."

"That was sweet of you," she said scornfully.

"But, Abbie! He had the fifty thousand dollars in his pocket last night. He showed it to us."

"And was the money in a long manila envelope?" I asked.

"Yes, yes, it was. How did you know?"

"That doesn't matter. Go on!" I prompted.

"There's nothing more to tell. Baldwin told his story, admitted he had been wrong, assumed the blame. You know how disarming that can be."

"I do. What happened to the money?"

"He put it back in his pocket and left us. He took a raincoat from the closet under the stairs and marched across the room. He made a dramatic exit, saying there was going to be a divorce."

"Did Mary tell you the conditions of the divorce?"

"Did the Judge know?"

"He knew more than I did. He had gone upstairs. Even after Baldwin had left, the Judge wanted to follow him."

"Did Mary tell you anything about her talk with Baldwin?"

"No, I didn't see her."

"Now tell us something about that money."

"I've already told you."

"You saw him put it back in his pocket?"

"Yes."

"And you saw him from that moment until he left the house?"

"Yes."

"Did any one else at the house see the money?"

"I don't think so. We three were alone in the library. Why is the money so important?"

"It might make an extra motive."

"I could kiss you for that," he beamed and put an arm about Abbie to give her a nice comradely squeeze.

I turned back to look at the empty garage once more and asked, "Where is your car?"

He actually blushed under his dark tan. His eyes blinked as he replied too quickly, "It got wet and stalled. I had to leave it on the road." To change the conversation he asked, "Have you any ideas about the money?"

"The murderer took the money, we are sure of that now," Abbie replied. "It's important because it clears Mary."

"What do you mean 'clears Mary'?" he demanded.

"She has confessed. She was at the Club," Abbie said quietly.

"What!" he cried. "That's crazy, ridiculous! Mary wouldn't hurt a fly!"

"She had provocation enough!"

He marched toward Abbie as if he would strike her. He towered over her belligerently. "You know God-damned well she didn't do it!" he shouted.

"I know what she says," Abbie retorted; "and shouting won't change things."

That sobered him. "I'm sorry, Abbie, but you didn't expect me to take it calmly, did you?"

"We must face the facts," she replied.

"Even when they are absurd?" he demanded.

"They're not as absurd as you think."

"Why should she kill him when she was going to get a divorce?"

"Because Baldwin was going to use your note at the trial to stop the divorce. I don't know how she happened to kill him; she didn't go into details."

"She couldn't go into details because she didn't kill him."

"Why are you so sure of that?"

"Because I killed him. She must have realized I did it and was trying to save me by taking the blame herself. It is just the sort of thing she would do, the poor kid!"

"And now because you think she really did it you are lying to save her," I suggested sarcastically.

"I'm not lying," he flung the words back at me with venom. He crossed the room to a very damp pair of trousers draped over the back of a chair and fished the note out of one of the pockets. It was crumpled and damp but unmistakably the note we had carried to the house the night before. "If she went there for the note, why didn't she get it?" he demanded as he waved it at us.

"I'd burn that if I were you," Abbie suggested.

"Oh, no! It may be very useful. If Mary persists in her assumption of guilt, this note will squash her story."

"Don't be a fool, Jerry!"

"What's so foolish about that? If you know Mary was at the Club last night, others may also discover it. If she is going to confess to a crime I know she did not commit, I can play at that game myself. They'll never prove anything against her. I was there first, the note proves that."

"And you'll both die, you'll be tried together and convicted. You won't help her by a confession."

"She's doing it to save me, I tell you," he insisted. "You've got to believe me."

"We know that only one of you can be guilty," I said thoughtfully.

"And I'm the one," he declared.

"Then suppose you turn over the fifty thousand dollars and we'll close the case right now," I said. "There's no point in going on with this comedy." I had him there and he knew it. He made me think of an animal caught in a trap as he looked, from Abbie to me. "Love is a wonderful thing," I scoffed, "but it can be so damned foolish at times. Will you stop the heroics and get down to cases? Either produce the money or stop the nonsense."

"But, Ethel, I can't let her take the blame because she thinks . . ."

"She hasn't told any one but us and we don't half believe her."

"You don't really believe her?" he begged.

"We could change our minds very easily. The fifty thousand dollars would convince us"

"I haven't got it. It wasn't there. I never even thought of it when I took the note."

"Then he was dead when you arrived?"

"Yes."

"How long had he been dead?" Abbie asked.

"I don't know much about such things, but I'd say the best part of an hour. He seemed quite cold."

"I'm glad you had sense enough to touch him," I said.

"I wanted to be sure he was dead. I thought I might help him," he replied.

"Then we are definitely sure that he was probably killed between twelve and one, that you entered the room before Mary and that neither of you killed him," Abbie summed up thoughtfully.

"But we can't prove that Jerry didn't kill him, not, unless he changes his mind and gives us an alibi," I reminded her.

"And that I won't do," he vowed.

"Then we'll probably see you in jail," Abbie said with disgust. She went to the window across from me and looked out over the cove. She bent forward and peered anxiously. I was curious to know what had attracted her attention. I stood beside her but could see nothing of particular interest in the cove or on the shore below us.

"Where is the *Albatross*?" she asked.

"What?" he exclaimed with more feeling and interest than he had displayed in the murder except, for the mention of Mary's confession.

He leaped to the window and gazed out over our heads.

"She's gone," Abbie said.

"How in hell could she go anywhere?" he demanded.

"Then, where is she?" I asked.

"Probably on the bottom," he replied, puzzled, "but I don't see how it happened."

"Well, Jerry, you have things to do, so have we," Abbie said. "We'll see you later."

He clutched at her arm. "What are you going to do about Mary?"

"All we can hope to do is to find the murderer. You keep quiet," she ordered.

"I'll never let a charge stick against her," he vowed.

"Now, you listen to me, you snipe," she said scornfully. "You keep quiet! The one chance we have to clear you both is to let the murderer think he is safe because either you or Mary is suspected. If you do one thing to spoil our chances of getting the real murderer, we'll wash our hands of the whole affair, won't we, Ethel?"

I nodded solemnly.

"Then you really don't think she did it?" he asked hopefully, considerably subdued by Abbie's attitude.

"That is something we must prove. Come along, Ethel."

"Why not stay for breakfast?" he suggested. "We can talk about plans."

"We have two hungry men to feed at the shack," she replied, "and we are not going to seem to be too friendly toward you or Mary."

CHAPTER EIGHT

ABBIE INDULGED IN the satisfaction of several emphatic "damns" as we walked down the kitchen path from Jerry's cottage.

The open garage door leered at us, and the wind, caught in the hollows of the eaves, sang mockingly.

"Why must he be so pig-headed about his alibi?" she demanded as if it were my fault. "What does he feel he must hide from us?"

"Well, we are sure of one thing anyhow. Neither Mary nor Jerry is the murderer."

"But they are both fools in love. They'll lie themselves into the electric chair unless we do something to save them, and they're not going to be much help; they are afraid for each other," she added.

"Of course," I replied as I thought of the effect of sudden death, an invisible shuttle weaving mysteriously, leaving a sinister bit of fear-laden weft across their warped lives.

"We haven't begun to scratch the surface of the problem yet," she complained. "There are so many things unexplained, so many loose threads, so many hints of things that are not as they should be."

I crammed my hands deep into my slicker pockets, to encounter the two letters that Martin had given me. Letters that might hold the answer to the riddle. I paused in the road. She halted beside me. Should I open them or take them up to the house and have Mary open them for me? We were on the rise of ground back of the shed. Ahead, looming against the gray backdrop of the sodden sky, I saw Art Tobias' aerial mast. Below in the cove lay the *Starfish*. Between the two there was an invisible connection, but had it anything to do with the murder? Art would know. I moved forward.

As Abbie matched her pace to mine she said, "I'm bothered about the *Albatross.*"

"The storm was too much for it," I replied. "After weathering an Atlantic gale it sinks in a sheltered harbor? That's fishy, Ethel."

"And if it is, I can't see the connection between a sunken boat and the murder."

"Neither can I, but I'm sure it's there."

"It interests me but for a different reason," I said.

"Which is?"

"I am wondering which Jerry will attend to first, his car or his boat."

We were almost past the shed, heading in the direction of Art Tobias' house. Just as we had a clear view ahead beyond the curve, I had two sudden reactions. From behind us a voice called, "Hey! Where are you going?" It was Dave standing on the back porch waving his long arms. Ahead of us, parked in the road in front of the Ketcham house, was Jerry's old roadster. So that was the alibi he wouldn't use!

Abbie, too, had seen his car. "I fear the worst," she said.

"Even so, he doesn't have to pose as a Saint Anthony to us," I retorted.

"He wasn't thinking of us. He didn't want Mary to know that, broken-hearted as he was, he could find comfort with Stella," she said bitterly.

"Didn't you know that most men are not monogamous?" I jeered.

"I guess there's a lot I don't know about men," she replied.

"Hey! Come in out of the wet!" Dave bellowed. "Breakfast's ready!"

We turned back to the shed. Art could wait. There were other things to consider. Jerry spending part of the night with Stella when he . . . I gave it up. There was no point in my trying to rationalize it. Men are a queer lot, more animal than women, or are they? I had always suspected Stella's slinkiness as having a purpose— evidently I had been right. Well, it was her business and Jerry's. No wonder he wanted to keep it a secret—and yet—

Dave's honest gray eyes and amused grin were the only normal things we had seen for several hours. It was a real homecoming to see him standing there in baggy trousers and rumpled turtle-neck sweater waiting for us to climb the stairs. Abbie smiled at him as if she, too, appreciated the qualities he represented.

"I thought the goblins had got you," he said as he helped us off with our things

"They did," I replied as I cast an eye on the breakfast table. "He's forgotten napkins," I said to Abbie in bantering criticism.

"And there's a wet spot where the cream bottle has been sweating on the table," she replied in the same mood, as she went to a cupboard for a pitcher.

"I get so tired of housework," Dave complained, going on with the game. "I work so hard and what do I get for my labors, nothing but fault-finding."

"Stop your nonsense," Abbie replied. "Have you seen a jar of marmalade?"

"There's enough groceries here to last a week," he said, indicating a large carton filled with good wholesome staples "The boy from the store woke us up when he brought them in."

"That's too bad. I didn't think Martin would get them over here so soon—but we'll probably need them," she ended.

"I can't stay that long, Abbie, so don't urge me," he teased.

"You're going to stay for a while unless you want to swim across the bay," she said tersely.

Pete came limping out of the bath all slick and shiny after his shower. "What's that you say, Abbie? Has the storm done much damage?"

"Enough," I answered as I took my turn at the bath. They tell me that rain is good for the skin. It may be, but I wanted to wipe it off, dry the edges of my hair and feel a comforting dab of powder.

"Don't be in there all day," Dave called "The minute I start an omelet you go into the bathroom." He had evidently heard a complaining housewife sometime in the course of his career. Perhaps it had been a wife of his own. That was a new thought. Well, it was something that he and Abbie would have to work out between them.

I hurried. I know how men hate to wait for their food. I've seen more men made grumpy because they are forced to wait for their meals than for any other reason.

I was out in two minutes. The table, a hand-made pine trestle, stood in front of a row of seats built into the rear corner of the kitchen. I slid onto the seat against the back wall because I wanted to have a view of the road from the rear window. Dave was very active for the next few minutes. His omelet, which he served from the pan, was light, and fluffy, the bacon crisp and brown, the coffee smelled delicious and the toast was only half-burned.

"Cozy, I calls it," he said as he sat at the end on my right. Pete was at the far end and Abbie sat opposite me.

When Pete's appetite had been satisfied and he was on his second cup of coffee he said, "You didn't tell me about the damage."

We told them of the ravages of the storm and finished with the news of Baldwin's murder.

"And you let me sleep!" Dave accused Abbie.

"Know who did it?" Pete asked practically.

"It serves you right, Davie, for trusting a woman," Dave grumbled. "You should always follow your hunches. What did I tell you yesterday?" he demanded of Abbie. "Didn't I tell you that Ethel Thomas on the spot, Abbie

Abernathy doing a flop in the harbor, and her whisper to the home-coming hero, equaled a story?"

"Then why didn't you stay on the job last night?" Abbie retorted. "We might know something now if you had."

"You talked me out of it, Abbie. It's your fault. I should have known better. It's like getting a hunch on a horse. You've made up your mind and are all set to bet and then like a dumbbell you let some one talk you out of your hunch. It happens every time. When I play my hunches, I'm always right."

"It would seem to me that you played this one," she replied. "You wanted a story, you insisted upon staying down here, Baldwin's been murdered and you can't get away; so you've lost nothing."

"I've lost the hours you've been roaming around on this island picking up bits of information here and there, and," he added after a wink at me, "probably destroying evidence that would point to your friends."

"I'll tell you all I know," she replied, "and it won't take long."

"You underestimate yourself," he chided.

"Cut the kidding," she said crisply. "Last night you talked about a pattern for murder and all that rot. In your saner moments you said the Jerry Baldwin-Mary setup would be an ideal situation for a murder. Well, it happened. Do you still think it possible that some one murdered Baldwin knowing that the blame would fall on Jerry?"

"To tell you the truth," he said, "I did it."

"That makes—" I started, but a kick on the shin from Abbie silenced me at once.

"That makes what?" he demanded of me.

"Never mind fooling," Abbie cut in. "Answer my question."

"I still think a smart man who wanted to be rid of Baldwin would have utilized the setup. The only trouble with the idea is the fact that it throws a swell story overboard."

"I'm not interested in a story for your paper. Are you going to follow your hunch and forget your paper for the time being, or are you going to write a lot of junk first and dig for the real story later? Is it to be hunch or story?"

"And what happens if I say story?" His eyes laughed at her.

"You hunt alone."

"So that's my reward for cooking your breakfast. Suppose I say hunch?"

"Then we'll tell you what we know up to now."

"Hunch it is, old girl. Go to it."

"Don't call me old girl."

I knew exactly how she felt. I hate people who call me mother or grandma. They may mean well enough but there is a sting to it somewhere.

I interrupted the recounting of the story once to get up from the table and run outside. As I had expected, I saw Jerry coming up the road. I thought he was on the way to rescue his car. I could have saved myself the trip out into the drizzle, because he produced a bag of Phoebe's doughnuts from under his coat.

"Come in," I invited.

"No. I feel like walking around a bit," he said.

"If you can't get your car started, come back. Pete or Dave will push you over the rise. You can coast down from this knoll," I suggested.

If detection was my life-work instead of an avocation which came by accident, I'd probably have been unaffected by his confusion when he realized I knew who and what his alibi was. The human factor always gets in my way and I'm still woman enough to get a personal satisfaction out of a situation. I really think he was ashamed. At any rate he refused to look at me as he said, "Thanks."

"You may not need an alibi. We won't mention it unless we must," I promised. Having satisfied that feminine streak in me I began to feel sorry for him.

"What difference does it make?" he asked defensively.

"None really, except that Mary might not understand."

"And why not?" he flared. "You women are all alike! I'd been at sea for six weeks going through hell. I came home to find my girl married to a blighter, my life wrecked and just because—" He paused and demanded angrily, "What did you expect me to do—enter a monastery?"

It was so typically my idea of a man's reaction that I laughed. If the situation had been reversed; if it had been Mary who had returned to find him married, I doubt very much that she would have found relief or comfort in the arms of another man. No normal woman would. She would have spent a sleepless night on a lonely bed crying her heart out for the man she had lost. Oh, well! Men and women have followed the same pattern for so many years that it's useless to think about it.

"I'm glad you think it's funny," he growled and turned on his heel. I let him go. He was in no mood for an ethical discussion; neither was I, for that matter.

"It was Adonis with doughnuts," I explained as I transferred them to a plate.

"Mind if I dunk?" Dave asked as he poured another cup of coffee.

"Dunk away. I rather enjoy it myself," Abbie said.

"Why didn't Adonis come in?" Dave queried.

Pete looked at me anxiously for a moment before he asked, "Think I ought to go out and walk around with him?"

"I'm sure he'd rather be alone just now. You can see him later. We want to talk to you."

"You're positive Jerry didn't do it?" Dave asked after his third doughnut.

"Reasonably sure."

"Okay. Go on with your story."

They were an attentive and interested audience. There were few interruptions. "These are the things that bother us," Abbie said as she began to sum up. "Jerry was on the loose for an hour or so during the night and he refuses to tell us where he was or what he did."

"He's a fool to keep quiet," Pete sputtered.

"He has his reasons," Abbie retorted. Then she went on, "Mary was out in that wild storm. She saw Jerry at the float. The Judge was angry enough to horsewhip Baldwin. We can't ignore the Judge. Del had a row with her uncle, a bad one. Baldwin fired Sidney last night. And you, Pete, you were probably smoldering with that slow anger of yours. You came stealing into the house sometime during the night and did it very quietly, stealthily for you. Was it your conscience, or consideration for our guests?"

He bridled but he made no reply.

"Baldwin had fifty thousand dollars. It is gone. He was shot but there is no revolver in the room. Where is the gun? What has the *Starfish* to do with it and why did the *Albatross* sink?"

"What?" Pete gasped and jumped up from the table and limped through to the other room to make sure.

"It's a pretty little riddle," Dave mused. "Very pretty!"

"Now what have you to say for yourself, Pete?" Abbie demanded as he came back, unbelief in his eyes.

He braced both hands against the edge of the table as if in that way he would steady himself. "I might as well tell you now. I didn't want you to hear me last night when I came in because I knew Baldwin was dead."

"You did, Pete?" There was a deep accusation in Abbie s voice.

"Nice going, Pete," Dave said with admiration "Your confession is going to save us a lot of trouble, isn't it, Abbie?"

"It's no confession. I didn't kill him!" Pete denied loudly.

"Oh, heck! Why not?" Dave complained. "That's the way with these cases. Just when you think you're all set, bango they blow up."

"It's nothing to kid about. I don't like being mixed up in it," Pete grumbled as he ran his finger around the edge of his collar, which suddenly seemed uncomfortably tight.

"They don't hang you in New York, Pete. They get you on the pants." Dave reminded him.

Pete was self-conscious and smiled rather sourly.

"Why did you go there?" I demanded.

"Because I didn't like him, that's why!' he exploded. "I was sore. I knew about the note. I saw a good chance to get even with him for calling me a fortune-hunting deckhand. And," he added what was probably his real reason, "I was a little tight."

"Did you have a fuss with him after that session on the porch?" I asked.

"Well, he wasn't satisfied with that row; neither was Del, for that matter. I was mad and instead of leaving as I should have done, I was itching to take a sock at him, but Del wouldn't let me do it. She followed him into the house. They had a private battle of their own."

"What about?"

"She wouldn't tell me the details. All I know is that she was awfully upset, crying as if her heart would break when she came back a half-hour later. She just sobbed and cried, asking me all sorts of darned fool questions," he explained with the bewilderment a man feels in the face of a woman's unexplained tears.

"What sorts of questions?" I asked.

"If I'd love her no matter what happened; If I'd believe in her no matter what I heard. If I'd go on loving her in spite of anything Baldwin might tell me."

"Just blind promises for future use?" I remarked.

"Yeah, that's right," he agreed.

"So it was because of Del you went down to the Club?"

"No, that was only part of the reason. Clara told us about the note, that Baldwin had taken it and had it in his pocket. On the way home I got to thinking about Baldwin and decided I owed him one. I thought it would be a nice trick to go to the Club, beat hell out of him and take the note for Jerry. I'd been stewing all evening and was just ripe for action, so down I went."

"What time was that?" I asked, hoping to fix a definite time through Pete.

"I don't know exactly. Del and I had been sitting in front of the fire for a long time. It must have been one-thirty or later when I left Del. I went directly to the Club. Baldwin was stretched across the bed, deader than a smelt, grinning up at me in the light on the match I held. I came home right away."

"But the note. Didn't you look for it or did you have some other reason for going?" Abbie demanded.

"Sure. I looked for it. Hell's bells! With him dead like that I wanted to protect Jerry. It wasn't there," he stated flatly.

"Did you see any one at all?" Dave asked.

"Nope! Not a soul. I don't suppose I would have seen any one anyhow. I was what you might call chastened or something. At any rate, I didn't feel very comfortable about it, wondering who had killed him."

"Naturally," I agreed.

"Why did you ask me if I'd seen any one, Dave?" Pete asked curiously.

"I'd like to know who was in the room when Weeks tried the door."

"It wasn't me," Pete denied stoutly. "I'd have been scared to death."

"What difference does it make?" I demanded, anxious to get Dave's line of reasoning.

"The murderer might have returned for something he or she had forgotten."

"Before we finish with this case, I'm afraid we're going to find that the American Legion trooped through that room," I said.

"You sound annoyed," Dave chuckled.

"I am. Weeks was there, he didn't kill him. Mary was there, we don't want to believe she killed him. Jerry was there and was willing to accept the blame to shield Mary. Pete was there. An unknown person was in the room when Weeks tried the door."

"And," Abbie added, "the murderer was there sometime."

"Marvelous," Dave teased.

I glowered at him and continued. "There are some questions I'd like answered. For example: Who was the man with whom Baldwin had been having an argument just after his meeting with Stella? Why was he down there on the sandspit with Stella, anyhow, when he had seemed determined to keep Jerry away from Mary?"

Dave made me think of an elephant as he sat there listening carefully to every word, his head nodding up and down in approval. I went on.

"Why did Baldwin want to get rid of his nephew, Sidney? Why did he suddenly decide that he didn't want Sidney out here? Why the secrecy? Was there any connection between the call Baldwin received at the Club and the money which he took from the store safe? Why did Baldwin suggest that the party be transferred up to his house instead of letting it die a natural death at the Club? Did that have any connection with the expected arrival of the *Starfish*? Was there some reason why he didn't want people at the Club when the *Starfish* arrived? Was he killed because of the fifty thousand dollars or is that just one of those things that happened and may cause us a lot of confusion because we won't let ourselves see beyond it? If on the other hand he was murdered for the money, how many people knew about it?"

"A nice point. A very nice point, and fifty thousand bucks, cash in hand, is a lot of money." Dave tapped the table with his fingers "Let's see. Jerry and the Judge knew about the money. Also your friend Martin had a pretty good idea, and if we knew what was in those letters which your Puritan conscience and a good law-abiding respect for Uncle Sam has kept you from opening, we might be able to include Art Tobias in the list

I slipped from the table and produced the envelopes. I ran a knife under their flaps and pried them open. The dampness had loosened the glue.

"When it comes to tricks and ways and means of covering up, Pete, woman is a master," Dave said with a lot more admiration than criticism in his voice.

The first message read:

HAVE FOUR GUESTS EXPECT
ACCOMMODATIONS.
GRAHAM.

The second read:

ARRIVE ABOUT MIDNIGHT.
GRAHAM.

"Nothing there to tell us about money," Pete said with relief. He was afraid we would suspect Art and he didn't want that to happen. They were good friends, spending many a long evening together in the spring and fall when the harbor was quiet and deserted of summer people.

"It might be a code message," Dave suggested.

"Art wouldn't have to know the code," Pete protested.

"That's right," Dave agreed. "We'd better talk to this chap"' he suggested. "How about it, girls? We've got to send for the police, anyhow,. and I might get a line or two through to my paper."

"Your paper can wait," Abbie replied. "These dishes will have to be done. Breakfast dishes are such a mess if allowed to stand too long."

"I'll clean up," Pete volunteered "You fellows go ahead."

"You're not to mention anything you've heard here," Abbie warned as we prepared to leave.

"Mum's the word," he promised.

CHAPTER NINE

DAVE CUPPED HIS hand under my elbow as we moved up the slippery rise in back of the shed. The wind, less strong now, came in fitful gusts, blowing the thin rain into our faces.

"There are a lot of angles to this, things we don't even suspect at the moment," he said gravely.

I flashed him a quick suspicious look. His face was sobered by thought. All the banter had gone out of his clear gray eyes.

"Do you mean something you suspect which we have missed?" Abbie demanded.

"I wouldn't be at all surprised," he replied as an impish gleam returned to his eyes.

"Then tell us," I suggested.

"Not now. There's no point in cluttering your mind with an idea until we have seen and talked to Art Tobias. I may be all wrong."

"In other words, we'll just have to be patient until you've made the decision in your pompous masculine way," she accused.

It was a good sign, Abbie taking exception to things he said in that way. Dave was fresh, pert and even sassy at times, but I had not seen him pompous, praise be.

He made a pucker of his face which somewhat resembled a snoot as he grinned at her. "Do you want that lovely head of yours fogged with ideas that may be beside the point?"

"Rubbish! Don't do or say anything to Art that may tend to get his back up. Remember he's a granter and touchy like the rest of them," she cautioned.

"I'll be a master of diplomacy if you permit me to talk. We'll all handle the situation with the utmost delicacy," he promised.

I had stopped with one ear cocked against the wind.

"What's the matter?" he asked.

"Quiet!"

They both paused and strained their ears against the sound of the wind in the trees and the booming of the surf below.

"Isn't that a dog howling?" I asked.

"I believe it is. Why?"

"People in these parts are superstitious about such things," Abbie replied.

"Now, don't tell me that they think a wild bird in the house brings sure death," he chided.

"They do," she answered thoughtfully.

"And strange knockings are portents," I added.

"A broken glass dish in the cupboard is a warning and if a picture or a mirror falls, there is bound to be a major catastrophe."

"And a howling dog means a death," Abbie supplemented.

"Then we're heading for death," he scoffed, "because that is a dog howling most mournfully."

We went on up the road toward the top of the ridge. As we turned off at the path leading up the rise to Art's house, the dog's cry was more distinct, a cross between a yelp and a forlorn howl. It gave me the shivers, it was so plaintive and helpless too. Somewhere not far from us a dog was in distress, doing his best to attract human attention.

"We ought to find that dog. Art can wait," I suggested, suffering agonies with the dog. They are so pathetic when they try to convey their feelings.

"I believe it's Art's dog," Abbie said anxiously as we neared the top of the hill. She increased her pace.

I found it difficult to keep up with her. Dave very gallantly stayed at my side.

"It's Art's dog," Abbie I called from the top of the path.

"So what?" he called back between puffs. The hill and the extra help he had been giving me had taken toll of his wind.

"You ought to lead a better life, you're puffing like a grampus," she flung back over her shoulder as she started ahead.

The dog had either heard us or had picked up our scent, because the howling stopped to give way to loud barks which would challenge our attention. "It certainly is his dog," I said as we reached the crest and followed Abbie.

"Then our friend Art seems to have skipped and left his dog behind."

"How could he get away?" I asked contemptuously. "He had no plane and there is no other way off the island, today."

"He might have left before the bridge went out," he argued wisely.

"He didn't. His car is in the garage." I pointed at the swinging door which must have been banging in the wind for some time. "And what is more, he never leaves his dog behind him."

"There's an exception to every rule to prove the case. He has left him behind this time," he said grimly, more so than I felt the situation warranted. And yet I found myself hastening on unaccountably afraid of what we would find.

We moved across the grass toward the low one-story house which was bound to the earth by battered masses of petunias and the honeysuckle vine which shaded the narrow porch. We followed Abbie to the rear of the house because the sharp staccato barks came from there.

The dog was in the outer or summer kitchen, as the natives call the small utility room, usually a lean-to just off the main kitchen, which serves as a shed for wood, coal, the kerosene can and other odds and ends. The door was not locked. Abbie lifted the latch and the Dalmatian, unimaginatively called Spotty, rushed out emitting glad yelps. He pawed at her dress and licked her hand.

"Look!" she cried. "He's been hurt!" She pointed to a long ugly gash on Spotty's head just behind his right ear.

"Something fell on him or he's had a hard wallop," Dave cried and dashed through the shed past the rusty old iron stove into the main kitchen.

With the dog jumping and leaping about us, we followed Dave through to the living-room.

The room was a shambles. Furniture was knocked about. A center table had been upset. Chairs were scattered in disorder.

Spotty ran to the corner, alternating between whimpering over and licking at the silent face of his master, who sprawled so grotesquely on the floor. Art lay there, a dark blob on the top of his pajamas.

His dressing-gown was open, the tasseled cord snaked away from the body. For one awful moment as I thought of what had happened, I thought of Jerry.

Perhaps he had not been with Stella, after all. Perhaps this was the alibi he did not have, could not use. Perhaps his car did stall, after all, on the rise near Stella's house. Innocent or guilty, it was one more thing which would throw further suspicion on him.

Abbie glanced at me as if she read my thoughts. Dave seemed to know what we were thinking as he cast a speculative glance in our direction, then moved forward and knelt close to the body.

While he knelt there, I studied the room. The windows were blurred by the rain. There was a steady drip, drip, drip from a leak in the roof. A rug had been dragged along the floor through the puddle made by the leak. The radio outfit had been smashed to bits and on the floor just off the hearth a fire-iron lay where it had been dropped. On the center rug there was a round wet stain similar to the one I had seen in Baldwin's room. It was a tell-tale mark left by the murderer. I looked across at Abbie, who stood motionless watching Dave. The water was dripping from her coat to the floor, leaving a large round ring. If she stood there long enough, she would leave just such a mark as the murderer had left.

Dave stood up and turned to us. "I think he's been dead for a long time."

"Shot?" Abbie asked.

He nodded. We hunted for the gun, but it was not there. One lone candle burned on an old cherry chest which I would have given my eye-teeth to own. The flame flickered in a pool of melted grease. As I watched it the wick fell over, the flame died.

We went into the bedroom. Wet clothes were draped over chairs and on wooden pegs along the wall. The bedclothes were rumpled and tossed about on the old pineapple four-poster. It was a gorgeous piece of furniture. I bent down to see if it was still roped. It wasn't; the spring rested on slats. As I straightened up I could hear an alarm-clock ticking hollowly from its perch on an old hickory chair which stood at the head of the bed. "He'd been in bed for some time," I said.

"And just how do you know that?" Dave asked.

"By the depression in the mattress and the condition of the under sheet in that particular spot. Also you might take a look at the dent in the pillow. It's deep and the feathers are either old or they have not had time to spring back into shape."

"Then he must have been killed in the last couple of hours," Dave suggested.

"I'm afraid so. It was after the bridge went out taking the power line with it."

"We don't have to check with Willie. According to Martin, it was about two-thirty."

"We'll check with Willie nevertheless," I said.

"Why?"

"Because the current is often interrupted during a storm."

"Check," he said.

"Then he was killed sometime between two-thirty and five, just when, we will never know, but it was still dark or he would not have lighted the candle," Abbie said.

"Check again," Dave said with a new admiration for her really keen powers of observation and deduction.

Abbie continued her reasoning. "Art evidently knew his visitor, suspected nothing when he was roused from his sleep, probably by the barking of the dog."

"Right," I agreed.

"Then why is the room in such a mess?" Dave demanded.

"Aren't you forgetting the dog?" Abbie reminded him.

"Check again, but why not shoot the dog too?"

"Perhaps he tried," I said and hunted for bullet-holes about the room. I found two.

After we had all inspected the bullet marks, which were obviously new, Dave said, "I don't believe the murderer got away without some torn and ripped clothing if not a bite or two."

"That's a job you can have," Abbie said, "hunting for torn clothing."

"All this brings up a pretty question," Dave said. "If the murderer knew or thought he had been seen by Art, why did he wait two or three hours before coming up here to do this job?"

If we had only followed through on that line of reasoning, we would have saved ourselves a great deal of work and considerable danger. It was not until later when we went back to that thought that things really began to happen and the dark way opened for us. It was Dave who veered away from the subject for reasons of his own which he didn't divulge at the time.

"Of course," he went on, "the murderer may not have thought about Art or the dog until later and when he did he knew that a two-fold danger waited for him here." We followed him back to the living-room. "Our murderer was afraid of that radio outfit," he said.

"And the dog," I reminded him. I glanced at Spotty, who was crouched beside his master looking at Art with mournful eyes.

"But he didn't kill the dog," Dave objected.

"That was his mistake. He must have thought the dog was dead. Now, I wonder why he dragged Spotty out into the shed and closed the door. Those marks were made by the dog's body as it passed over the mud stains left by the murderer."

"Tobias may have made them himself," Dave objected.

"But he didn't. Art left his wet and mud-caked shoes in the shed when he came in. Funny you didn't see them, they were just inside the door," Abbie taunted.

"Check to you," he said with an admiring grin.

"This damp spot on the floor marks the place where the murderer stood while he talked to Art before he fired the shot."

"That's reasonable," he agreed.

"But it gives us nothing except a picture of the killing," I said hopelessly.

"And the fact that the murderer was some one well known to Art, along with his reason for being here." He pointed to the smashed radio apparatus.

"Those two facts don't seem to fit together, Dave," I objected.

"Why not?" he demanded.

"If we assume that Jerry had nothing to do with this and the murderer was hoping that Jerry would be suspected, why did he do anything which would delay sending for help?"

"It was no good without current, anyhow," he said after a general inspection of the outfit.

"Then why was it destroyed? It doesn't make sense. There's always a chance that power will be restored immediately after a storm. If the murderer came here after the bridge was washed out, he must have known there would be no current."

"It's possible that the murderer did not know about the wash-out down at the bridge."

"I don't believe the murderer wanted us to send for the police, and that seems stupid, because the more time we have to work on the case the better Jerry's chances will be," Abbie reasoned.

"Perhaps the murderer doesn't think much of your ability as a sleuth," he said without trying to be facetious.

"There's always that," she admitted, "but don't forget Ethel is here too."

"We may be entirely wrong," I said. "The murderer may not have considered Jerry in it at all. We may be blinding ourselves by a preconceived idea of the murderer's reason."

"Don't kid yourself," Dave interrupted. "This thing has been too carefully planned. If Jerry didn't do it, the murderer intended him to be blamed."

"I wonder if Art's death could have been prevented?" Abbie mused thoughtfully.

"I don't see how. Now, don't go blaming yourself, Abbie. You girls have done a lot in a short time. The whole police force could not have done more," he reassured her with a warm friendly pat on the back.

"Don't be too nice to me, Dave. After all, I'm a woman," she warned.

"I couldn't be too nice to you, Abbie."

She sighed. "If I ever propose to you, you can't say you didn't put your neck out and ask for it."

"I'll live for the day," he grinned. "You know the old jingle, 'First's the worst, second's the same, but last's the best of all the game.'"

"Yeah, I know, but twice bitten, three times shy," she misquoted.

"Listen, love-birds," I interrupted impatiently, "we have a murder that we're trying to solve. Dave, suppose you bottle your ardor for the moment and take a look at Art's records over there. They may help us."

"Thanks, Ethel," Abbie said. "The man unnerves me."

We found a log-book into which Art had carefully recorded all his incoming and outgoing messages. I had no idea so many people on the island had used Art's wireless as a means of communication. There were messages to all parts of the country, greetings to friends, messages of arrivals and departures, all the things one usually sends in haste.

Among them we found a number of entries for the *Starfish*. They began about the time Baldwin came to the island and covered the entire period since that date. They occurred intermittently about twelve to fourteen days apart and always mentioned the arrival of guests.

Baldwin's replies to such messages were brief and to the point. "Ready." "Not now." "Wait." "Tomorrow." "At once." These were typical of Baldwin's answers, but his reply of the preceding evening had stated: "Six overdue expect ten."

As we finished looking at Art's entries Dave said, "Funny thing, this guest business. Do you suppose Baldwin charged for putting them up?"

I was pondering that. Abbie shrugged. He continued, "I wonder why people didn't stay on the boat when they got here? She probably has accommodations for eight or ten extra."

"You know how yacht parties are," Abbie said, a little disappointed, I think, because there was no mention of money in any of the messages.

"Sorry, but I don't. Yacht parties have been a little out of my line. The Coney Island steamer and Sunday-school picnics up the Hudson cover my boating experiences." He closed the book and asked, "How many rooms are there available at the Club?"

"Four. They were put in originally for overflow. They are rarely ever used."

"Baldwin may have entertained Graham's guests there, however, since they never went to the house," I suggested.

"Why did those people rush to the mainland last night in the teeth of that storm? Why didn't they stay at the Club or at Baldwin's house?" Dave insisted, following his train of thought.

"They may have been scared stiff by the approaching storm," Abbie offered.

"A lot of people have come here on the *Starfish*," he said thoughtfully. "I wonder if they always rushed 'ashore,' as you call it. I'd be interested to know if any of them ever stayed at the Club or were taken to Baldwin's house."

"We can easily check on that," Abbie promised.

"It will be interesting to know. I'm going to take this book with me—any objections?" he asked.

"Just what is on your mind, Dave?" I asked.

"It's on the fantastic side at the moment," he evaded. At my scowl of annoyance he begged, "Let me hang onto it and think about it a little longer, will you?"

"Which means you don't want to tell us," Abbie said.

"Not now. Where do we go from here?"

"The *Starfish*. They have probably heard about the murder. I hope they have had sense enough to send a message if they have."

"They might prefer silence," he suggested mysteriously.

"They undoubtedly would if the idea which has been growing in my mind means anything," Abbie replied.

"Want to tell us?"

"Sure. I'm not nearly as secretive as you are." She covered Art's body with a sheet.

"He won't budge until Art's body is removed," Dave advised, wise in the ways of dogs, as Spotty refused to leave.

"What about that gash on his head?" Abbie asked.

"It looks healthy. When we move the body we can have a doctor look at it. No need to worry him now."

"I wonder if he realizes he failed last night?" I asked as I closed the door on master and faithful friend.

CHAPTER TEN

AS WE WALKED ACROSS. the spongy grass toward the path, Dave reminded Abbie that she had not explained her idea.

"I'm leaving Jerry out of this," she began.

"It's all right with me, but will the police be as generous in their thoughts?" he asked bluntly.

"We still have an hour or two before the police arrive, time enough, if we're smart, to investigate Graham."

"That's going to take some doing," he said thoughtfully.

"Not with you around to help us," she jabbed back at him.

"Your servant, as always," he replied. "Proceed."

"Graham was probably swimming last night at the time his guests left the yacht." She began telling Dave what Weeks had said about seeing some one in the water near the *Starfish*.

"Go on," he urged, interested.

"There was nothing to prevent his swimming ashore after things settled down at the Club."

"What about the gun? Did he carry it in his teeth?" he asked.

"It could have been carried in a waterproof bag tied to his neck or tucked into his trunks," she replied.

"Very interesting. Go on."

"He wore a pair of those close-fitting rubber swimming-shoes. He came out of the water at the end of the Club porch, slipped round to Baldwin's room and murdered him."

"I don't believe it, Abbie; too fantastic," he objected. "And what is more, how did Graham know that Baldwin was spending the night at the Club?"

"We don't know that Graham didn't come ashore with the boat and we don't know what Baldwin might have told the man who did if it wasn't Graham."

"I'll admit that, but—"

"Wait a minute, Dave. There's a lot in what Abbie says. In Baldwin's room at the Club there was a water mark on the rug, a round wet spot. There was a similar one back there on Art's rug. I noticed Abbie as she stood watching you work over Art's body. The drip, from her raincoat made a much larger circle, than the one on the floor. If she is right, and I'm inclined to think that she is, the two wet spots were made by a person who wore no clothes."

"That would be a swell headline, wouldn't it? 'Naked Murderer Found,'" he quoted thoughtfully. He shook his head. "I'm afraid not, Ethel. You don't mind my calling you Ethel, do you?" He smiled at my consent. "It presupposes Graham knew about Jerry."

"Of course he did. He's been coming here for a year or more."

"Do you know Graham?" he asked Abbie

"No. But that's because I didnt hobnob with Baldwin."

"And neither did Jerry," he argued.

Dave stopped under the shelter of a large tree and opened Art's log book. We waited while he checked something for his own satisfaction. "Baldwin lived here the year round, didn't he?" he asked as he closed the book.

"No, I wouldn't say that. He often came down for weekends and in between for a day or two, but the house hasn't been officially open as an all-year residence."

His next question was an abrupt change of subject and seemed to have nothing to do with the case. "Ever go to Bermuda in a small boat?" he asked.

"I sailed down once as crew in a race. Why?" Abbie replied.

"How long did it take?"

"Quite a while; we had to beat our way down. We came back in about a week, however, with a fair wind."

"But you wouldn't have to worry about wind in a boat like the *Starfish*."

"Certainly not. What are you driving at?"

"It would make a swell honeymoon trip, wouldn't it? You know, you've made me very boat-conscious these last twenty-four hours. The open sea, a boat and you, with seagulls soaring overhead," he pretended to day-dream; but I was not fooled for a moment.

"Stow it, Dave, and be serious. We're trying to solve two murders to save a young man we believe to be innocent."

"And while I don't want to spoil anything that might border on romance," I interrupted, "I'd like to call your attention to what is going on in the cove, since we are supposed to be interested in the *Starfish* and Mr. Graham at the moment. Look down there!" I pointed dramatically, toward the cove.

The *Starfish* was definitely under weigh. She had left her mooring and was heading slowly toward the channel. There was a deckhand forward in her bow as she nosed her way into the opening of the inlet.

"Maybe we're both right," he said.

"Right about what?" Abbie asked as she began to hurry.

"Ideas. Graham is on the run. He may or may not know about the murder, but he is anxious to get away from Hidden Harbor, which is an interesting move."

"I hope she gets stuck!" Abbie cried. "If she goes, she takes with her our only chance of communicating with the mainland until the sea calms down more than it is now."

She was absolutely right. The Sound was a mass of whitecaps which rolled and rumbled into the bay churning that usually calm strip of water into a mad sea.

"He may have thought of that, too," Dave said annoyingly.

I was beginning to get a little tired of his cryptic remarks. "Graham can't run away from the police," I reminded him, "even though he gets out of the cove, which I doubt."

"He seems to be doing all right so far."

The *Starfish* had entered the channel and was proceeding slowly toward the boiling water at the end of the sandspit. The sea pounded and boomed on the bar. Great long rollers raced through the channel, buffeting the *Starfish* as she nosed ahead.

"Do you think he'll clear the bar, Abbie?" I asked anxiously.

"I don't know, Ethel. With the sea running, the channel may have filled up or it may be twice as deep as it was yesterday. You can't tell about sand and water in a storm."

We stopped to watch the boat's halting progress as she nosed into the rolling waves. She took them neatly, head on, rising and falling with their onslaughts, casting sheets of foamy spray as they cracked and split against her sharp prow.

"She's struck sand!" Abbie cried as the *Starfish* came to a hesitant stop and the waves pounded and broke over her bow, washing her decks. "He's backed her off! He's going to try another spot!" Abbie was excited. "She's struck again!"

Once more the *Starfish* was engulfed in bow-breaking waters.

"Oh, the fool!" Abbie cried in contempt. "He's going to try to force her over! He's backing up again—watch him!" She clutched at Dave's arm. "He's going to wait for a good high wave and then he'll give her all she's got and try to ride across. The man is mad to try it, but he has nerve," she admitted in admiration.

"Looks like risky business," Dave said.

"Of course it's risky. He must feel there is a great deal at stake to try it," I cried, excited myself.

The *Starfish* took one violent plunge forward and then shivered to a dead stop. I could see the churn from her propellers as they whirled. The waves broke over her, hiding her almost completely from view at times. She had struck too hard. Graham couldn't back her off. He had gambled and lost.

"She's going to be there for a while," Abbie stated with satisfaction, and started down the hill as fast as she dared over the slippery ground.

"Won't the waves push her off?" Dave asked.

"On the contrary, they'll probably dig a hole for her to rest in while they pile the sand behind her. The fool! To block the inlet like that!" she cried indignantly.

We made the rise at the back of the shed very quickly. At Abbie's suggestion we climbed into her car, which fortunately started at once. The parking lot was dotted with cars. Most of the community seemed to be down there or arriving behind us to watch the *Starfish*. Probably all the old islanders were remembering the bad wreck we had had in the inlet once before when a big power-boat had been caught on the bar. Two people had been drowned that time. It had been rather dreadful to stand on the shore and see the, boat pounded, to pieces and yet be unable to do anything about it.

When we left the car we joined the others who were racing down the sandspit, where the shore ahead was lined with spectators watching the *Starfish*. We joined a group including Jerry, Bill Baylis and Sidney Venter. Over the roar of the waters I heard Bill shout to Jerry, "She'll break up sure!"

"Not with the tide coming in," Jerry answered.

"But we didn't have much of a fall last night," Bill shouted back "The wind kept most of the water in the cove. We ought to get a line out to her."

"Can't reach her from here, and I'll be damned if I'll try to swim out to her," Jerry declared.

"We've got to do something!" Bill called back. "If we let her stay there too long, she'll block the channel."

I smiled at that. Good old seagoing Bill! His chief concern was the channel and not the people on board the *Starfish*.

"We'll go back to the Club and set off some rockets," Jerry said. "They may see them from the shore or there may be a cutter or some boat on the Sound. If that fails we can try to pull her off with small boats." He turned and started for the Club on a run.

We divided our interest between the Club and the yacht for the next few minutes The distress flag was whipping from the mast, making a mute appeal for help. In a few moments rockets went soaring into the sky.

Dave looked dubiously at the thick gray sky overhead. "I don't believe any one will see the rockets—it's too murky," he said hopelessly.

Jerry came dashing back. He was soaking wet, his curly hair was plastered tightly to his skull. He was panting for breath after running through the sand.

"Maybe they'll have sense enough to send out an S.O.S.," I suggested hopefully.

"Can't," he replied crisply. "Graham claims that some one went aboard last night, cut down his aerial and smashed his radio outfit."

We exchanged glances at that. I'm sure we were all wondering if Graham had done it on purpose.

"Why did he venture out?" I asked.

"Because he was as sore as a boil. He came ashore, fighting mad, but he didn't tarry very long when he heard the news. He was disgusted when he learned that two women were trying to solve the case. He went to his ship. She got under weigh at once."

"Was he going for help?" I asked.

"Nobody knows," Jerry replied. "Say, where have you people been?"

"We went up to see Art. We thought we would radio for the police from there."

"His set is no good without current" he replied scornfully.

"It's no good anyhow," I replied.

Abbie and Dave were watching Jerry as he said, "It has always worked before."

"But you don't understand, Jerry," I said with an assumed patience. "Art's set has been smashed too."

"He must be pretty broken up about that," he said with feeling and-concern.

"He's dead, Jerry. Murdered!"

"Good God! You don't mean it! When? How?"

I told him what we had found. I was convinced by his reaction to the news first, and his interest and questions afterward, that he had nothing to do with Art's death.

"Where is it going to end?" he asked helplessly. I shrugged.

He bent forward and spoke close to my ear. "Don't tell a soul on the island what you know about last night. The maniac seems determined to kill any one who might possibly have seen him."

Jerry's statement was startling enough in itself. I knew he was thinking of the possible danger to Mary, but when Dave too, who had overheard, bent closer and said, "He's right, my lady, the murderer may think you know too much," my blood actually ran cold for a moment. I don't believe I'm afraid of anything that walks the earth; at least I never have been and I've been in some pretty tight spots. I've faced a madwoman who with a knife in her hand was determined to kill me. I've looked down the dark muzzles of revolvers expecting them to bark sudden death to end my career. I was carried by a murderer one night, when he thought I was the body of his victim, not knowing where he was taking me or what he intended to do with me. It's an exaggeration to say that I was not afraid; we all are when it comes to that fraction of a second between life and death when we are awed by the mystery of what lies just beyond oblivion. What I meant to say was that I have never anticipated fear in the form of dread. Jerry's frantic fear for Mary and Dave's warning made me shiver because we were facing an unknown force, an unseen power that struck in the dark relentlessly, finally.

A shout from the crowd standing at the water's edge attracted our attention. I rather expected to see a rescue boat coming up outside the bar. I peered through the gray mist, but there was nothing in sight. The group, necks craned forward, were watching the churning water between the *Starfish* and the shore. Jerry sprinted away. We followed.

At the water's edge we saw what was interesting them; A body propelled by powerful strokes surged through that turbulent sea. There were moments when it seemed that the man could not win. He appeared to be on a rolling treadmill of waves that would hold him until he became exhausted. There was another shout as he gained perceptibly.

"That man certainly can swim!" Jerry cried with admiration.

CHAPTER ELEVEN

IN A FEW MINUTES the man emerged from knee-deep water. He was tall and powerfully built. His great, hair-matted chest rose and fell under the stress of his heavy breathing. He was a magnificent creature, with his broad shoulders, tapered waist and lean thighs encased in dark blue swimming trunks. With powerful hands he wiped the water from his eyes and pressed his turbulent hair back from his forehead As he came up the sand breathing heavily he glowered at us, his dark eyes full of contempt for the men who stood on the beach. "And you call yourselves seamen!" he challenged.

"I'm beginning to respect your idea," Dave said to Abbie. "That man could have swum across the cove without any difficulty. Is he Graham?'

Abbie nodded.

"Well?" Graham was demanding of the men who faced him at the water's edge.

"Seamanship doesn't mean making a fool of one's self," Jerry took up the challenge. "You should have known you couldn't clear the bar after a storm like last night's."

They reminded me of fighting cocks as they stood there measuring each other. Jerry was fair and lithe, Graham dark and heavy. While Jerry was not as built as Graham, he suggested a cleaner, more enduring strength. Jerry won the battle of concentrated stares. It was Graham who gave in and asked, "Well, are you going to stand there and watch my boat pound to pieces?"

"We've sent up rockets which may bring help," Jerry replied.

"Rockets!" Graham spat with contempt.

"There's one other thing we can do if the men are willing. We can try to pull you off," Jerry suggested.

"With what?" Graham demanded.

"All the boats that have motors, large and small."

"Let's try it," Bill Baylis said eagerly.

"Willing, Graham?" Jerry asked.

"I'll try anything," he replied in desperation.

The men gathered about Jerry. I heard his voice shouting instructions. "We'll get every boat with a motor. Line the small boats with outboard motors in tandems. Let larger boats pull directly. Be sure you have plenty of rope long enough, so we won't get in each other's way, and be careful you don't upset in the sea at her stern. Let's go!"

They were like small boys as they raced down the beach eager for an adventure in their boats.

Within fifteen minutes they had ten lines attached to the stern of the *Starfish*. The air was a perfect din of throbbing, barking engines. Small boats with outboard motors, run-abouts, power dories, speedboats and small cruisers strained and pulled at the *Starfish* while her own propellers churned and boiled in the water. It seemed a hopeless task as the sea raced and broke over her bow. I expected to see the *Starfish* ripped apart by the terrific pull on her stern.

The *Starfish* listed to starboard. I held my breath, expecting anything to happen.

"They'll never do it," Dave said gloomily.

The next minute there was a shout from the men and boys in the boats and a cheer from the watchers on shore. The *Starfish* began to move slowly. On the next huge roller she settled on an even keel again and floated, back toward the calmer waters of the cove.

I was elated myself by the rescue as we turned to follow the crowd moving back toward the Club.

"Well, she's clear," Graham said with satisfaction.

"And you're lucky," Peter remarked. "Why did you try to run out?"

"Because my friend Baldwin was bumped off during the night and what were you people doing about it? Nothing!" He spat the words out. "You were standing around wide-eyed and scared, twiddling your thumbs and doing nothing to bring aid to discover the murderer."

"We've been working on the case," Peter retorted deliberately—a sure indication that his dander was rising.

"What do a couple of women know about a crime like this!" Graham sneered.

Dave gave me a sly poke in the ribs and grinned at Abbie, his face a tantalizing mass of wrinkles.

We had reached the Club porch then. I stepped forward, accepting Graham's challenge. The others pressed close behind me, full of curiosity, relishing the situation. They were with me at that moment, Harbor people backing one of their own against a stranger. In one way Abbie and I were on trial in their eyes and I had no intention of letting them or ourselves down in front of that hairy mountain of smug contempt. "I happen to be one of the women you mentioned just now, Mr. Graham."

His dark eyes were full of questions. "All right, who's the murderer?" he demanded. I liked the way he carried the battle to my territory.

"We don't know—yet," I replied, trying to emphasize and point up that "yet." He sneered. "But the field is narrowing down," I added.

"Sure it is. That's an old alibi when people know nothing," he scoffed.

There was a titter behind me. Stella's low mocking laugh cut across the nervous mirth.

"Is that why you tried to run away?" Abbie asked pointedly.

"And who are you?" he asked as his eyes went over Abbie inch by inch.

"I'm the other woman. Why not answer my question? Were you afraid? Have you something to hide?" Abbie asked as she glared back at him.

At my elbow I heard Dave's subdued voice give a warning, "No, no!" But Dave's advice was too late. I knew that, the moment Abbie had flung the taunt in her desire to save my face. Graham's mind worked with the quick precision of a steel trap. I fancied I could hear the interrelating parts click as a shadowy veil of protection and calculation lowered over his eyes and his whole body stiffened for a moment.

"Are you accusing me?" he demanded hotly.

"Miss Thomas told you we did not know the murderer," she replied with the poison-sweet repetition that only a woman can manage.

"Then what are you driving at?" he growled.

"We were just trying to point out to you that since we are all marooned here on the island your sudden and unexplained departure seemed shall we say, suspicious."

"You can say anything you like," he retorted. "It won't prove anything."

"But it still leaves the stigma of suspicion and puts you in the position of explaining your unwarranted action."

"I'll explain nothing to you!" he snorted and turned away.

"Let me talk to him," Dave whispered. "He may be one of those men who hate women—like me," he added as he stepped forward toward Graham.

"Any chance of repairing that radio of yours, Mr. Graham?"

"The boy has been working on it," Graham replied.

"Was it badly messed up?"

"The set's all right but all the outside wires have been cut and destroyed."

"Too bad," Dave commiserated, "for you and for us. Tobias' set has been wrecked too."

I watched hoping to see some telltale flash in Graham's eyes at the mention of Tobias, but there wasn't even a flicker a he looked over the group and asked, "Where is Tobias? He could help my man."

"He has been murdered, too," Dave announced loud enough for the entire group to hear.

Graham's truly amazed, What? was accompanied by a gasp of unbelief all about us.

"He knew too much," came promptly from Graham on the heels of his amazement.

"About what?" Dave asked quickly.

"The murder, of course," Graham retorted

I stepped to Dave's side and said, "Mr. Graham, let's bury the hatchet, you and I. We're both interested in the same thing. You have lost a friend, we here on the island have lost two of our members. Since we are cut off from help we ought to do all we can to make the work easier for the police when they do arrive. Some of us are in danger even now—you, myself, and—"

"Why me?" he interrupted.

"Because you were close at hand at the time of the murder, which took place shortly after your arrival last night." He listened to me as I talked, but his attention was fixed on Abbie. His awareness of her as a woman burned in his bold glance. I felt as though he were disrobing her there in front of us all.

He laughed audaciously with a challenge in his eyes as he continued to look at her and asked, "Are you suggesting that I—"

"I wouldn't be as crude as that," I said with a challenge of my own. His eyes jerked to me. He knew what I meant. "You took a swim last night after your boat arrived. You might have seen something that would lead us to the criminal." I could see Dave's disapproval of my tactics even as I noticed the sudden flicker of Graham's eyes. I had succeeded in surprising him.

He hesitated for a second. I saw something other than lust and disapproval dawn in those amazing strong eyes of his. A new respect flashed there. At last he accepted me as an equal or an adversary, I didn't know which. "I don't see how that follows," he evaded.

"You saw your friends off, didn't you?" I ventured.

"In a way. I was in the water when they put ashore, but I didn't swim in. It was just a dash of bravado on my part. They were afraid of the approaching storm and were so anxious to get away from the water that I took a swim to shame them."

"I'm sorry you admitted that publicly," I said and meant it.

"I'll take care of myself," he assured me. "I may even put myself in your hands," he said to Abbie with suggestive assurance.

I heard Dave mutter, "Swine!" under his breath.

"Be on your guard; we have other things to do!"

"Art Tobias was down here," I cautioned solemnly, "last night at the time of the murder—he's dead now."

"Thanks for the tip."

"Glad to be of service."

"Of course," he said thoughtfully, "I'm not a detective and don't know much about such things, but have you been looking in the right place for the murderer?" His eyes followed Jerry's progress up the pier from the float.

"We've checked all obvious suspects," I replied coldly.

"Who had a motive?" Graham demanded.

"We're not sure, but we think it was a robbery," I suggested.

Once more I scored. This time it was the quick clenching of his fist that gave him away as his eyes gazed steadily into mine for a moment. "What was stolen?" he asked.

"Fifty thousand dollars," I answered flatly.

Again that ripple of surprise ran through the group pressing close behind us.

"Fifty thousand dollars!" he exclaimed. "Why should he have fifty thousand dollars on him?"

"We don't know. That's one of the points we had hoped you might be able to clear for us, since you were such a good friend of his," I added suggestively.

"It doesn't make sense," he protested. "Baldwin was too cautious a man to have that much money on his person."

"But he did," I insisted. "At least two people saw it."

"Then you'd better concentrate on those people. One or the other of them ought to be your murderer," he replied with sound logic throwing the money situation right back into my lap. He took a step forward. "Look here, I want to get back to the boat. Why don't you come aboard later? We can have a talk. I'll help you all I can but I am worried about the boat. I want to check to make sure that no damage has been done." With the agility of a young boy he leaped over the porch rail to the soft sand below and strode toward the water.

"You've warned him! He's prepared now!" Dave grumbled.

"Which was part of my idea Keep your eye on Graham and the boat. I'll tell you why later."

The crowd pressed in on us asking foolish questions about the double murder.

Sidney plucked at my elbow to ask if there was anything new to tell Mary. "She's awfully upset and worried," he said.

"Tell her to sit tight. We'll be up when we can make it," I promised as we moved out of the inquisitive circle where we could talk without being over heard.

"That money, Miss Thomas, are you sure about that?" Sidney asked.

"Positive."

"But he didn't keep money at the house .You must be mistaken," he insisted.

"He had it, nevertheless. Did you handle any money matters for him recently?"

"Nothing but petty cash and household expense accounts."

I took the two messages from Art Tobias and handed them to Sidney, explaining that I expected to take them to the house.

He slit the edges of the envelopes and handed them to me to read.

"Know what they mean?" I asked as I handed them back.

"No; they don't make sense; they never did."

"Any ideas about them?"

"No. The *Starfish* usually came in at night. Uncle Henry always watched for her. The moment he saw her putting in, he would rush down to the Club for an hour or so and come back alone. He never brought Graham or any one from the yacht to the house. There were times when the *Starfish* didn't stay in the cove more than an hour or, two. When she lay here overnight, Uncle Henry usually had breakfast aboard and went in to the city right after that."

"How long does it take to drive from here to the mainland?" Dave asked.

"Not more than fifteen or twenty minutes to the center of town, depending on how fast you drive."

Dave digested that thoughtfully then asked, "What about trains to New York?"

"You're stuck here," Abbie reminded him.

"I wasn't thinking about leaving; I was just curious about train connections," he replied.

"There's a time-table posted in the lounge," Sidney said. "We usually drive in, so I don't know much about trains."

"Is there any way to check on the fifty thousand dollars?" I asked.

"We could telephone the cashier at Uncle Henry's office," he suggested.

"Unfortunately there's no telephone," Dave reminded him.

"I wish I could help you about the money," Sidney said. "Is there anything else?"

"Just tell Mary to keep a stiff upper lip, that's all."

With an understanding nod he walked down the porch toward the group near the entrance to the lounge.

"Why are you so interested in the distance to town, time-tables and things like that?" I asked.

"Because of Graham, the *Starfish* and those guests of his. You made a slip with him," he accused. "You shouldn't have left yourself wide open the way you did."

"I think I scored a couple of bull's-eyes," I replied.

"You did, but he's a clever marksman too. Don't underestimate that man," he warned.

"Don't worry, I won't. When are you going to tell us what's on your mind?" I demanded.

"When I've figured it out," he replied.

"While you're meditating, will you keep your eye on the *Starfish*? Get Pete to help you. There's no one else I can trust. Unless I'm mistaken, Mr. Graham is going to be very active. In fact, I rather expect him to drop something overboard if he gets a chance, so don't let your attention lag for a moment."

There was a warm appreciative gleam in his eye as he said, "Okay, boss. What do you expect and why?"

"I don't know exactly what to expect, but he was much too eager to get aboard after he heard, about the money. There was no great rush, but he felt a terrific urge. You can see that man's mind at work. I may be wrong, but I think he has something he wants to hide."

"So do I. We'll have to get together on Graham."

"We can depend on you?" Abbie asked.

"More than you seem to realize," he replied.

"Good," she smiled at him.

"In the meantime I think I'll have to have words with Nora Baylis, who is bearing down on us under full sail. See you later," I promised as I tucked my arm under Abbie's and moved forward with her to meet Nora Baylis and a new idea in crime detection.

CHAPTER TWELVE

NORA HOOKED ME into the fold of her plump motherly arm and said, 'We were so afraid you wouldn't get here in time! It's been so trying for you, my dear, and you too, Abbie, but of course you're younger."

I felt like crying "meow" to that dig, but I didn't. I'm just a little touchy about my age because I'm rather proud of myself and my stamina. I let it pass. I had no idea what was coming—one never does when Nora is on the loose, but something told me it would be good whatever it was. I tried to get out of that aim of hers, but I wasn't woman enough to accomplish it. I think for the first time since their marriage I understood Bill. I'll admit I had often wondered why he stuck it out. In that moment, I think I knew. You can't escape from Nora and her kind. They do something to you, rob you of your defenses. I could have given her a vicious poke in the ribs somewhere beneath her bosoms but I didn't. Nora was the eternal epitome of good woman and motherhood. She exuded maternal instincts and I've no doubt in a moment of stress her warm bosom would have been a haven of comfort.

I thought of all those things as she steered me down the porch. I could have liked her if she wasn't so damned ubiquitous. "Where are we off to?" I asked as I tried to slow our pace.

"A meeting," she replied as she swept me toward the door of the lounge.

"But—" I tried to protest because I hate meetings.

"Here we are," she cried as she thrust me through the door, Abbie following. And there we were.

A good half of the members of Hidden Harbor were in the lounge. Weeks, standing behind the desk, looked as if he had swallowed a hot potato. Bill Baylis stood over near the fireplace, his bulk looming over the slight figure of Archie Taylor. They were all there, the Cravens, the Franks, the Cotters, the Huetts, the Deanes, the Smiths, the Robertsons and the Defran boys. Even Willie Pole waited patiently.

"Where's Jerry?" Nora called as she joined Mrs. Deane and Mrs. Smith, who completed the formidable trio. We call them The Three Graces.

Jerry, looking rather sheepish, came in from the bar. Tommy Baylis, the oldest of the Baylis offspring and a young imp, stopped Jerry and cried, "Look, Jerry, I'm playing detective, will you give me your fingerprints?" He thrust an inked pad under Jerry's nose.

"Sure," Jerry replied and obliged the child by imprinting a piece of paper which Tommy held ready. Tommy scampered away with one of the Dean boys.

There was an embarrassed hush as conversation died away at Jerry's approach.

"What's the idea, Jerry?" I asked.

He didn't answer my question directly. He addressed the group. He was fussed, poor lad, and no wonder, but it didn't last more than a minute. "It's a special meeting, an emergency meeting. As you know, any six members of the Club can call a special meeting if in their judgment it seems necessary. At this time six members feel we are faced with an emergency. We have had a bad storm with disastrous results. As President of the Club, it is my duty to preside at such a meeting, but under the circumstances, I prefer to hand the meeting over to our friend, Judge Verity."

"What on earth do you suppose Nora is up to?" Abbie whispered as a light round of applause greeted the Judge when he stood up and faced the group.

"There is always some doubt in my mind as to just what constitutes an emergency," he began, "but since some of our members feel that an emergency exists, I shall be glad to preside instead of our President if the members who called the meeting will tell us what they want and what they propose to do. Mrs. Baylis, will you explain the purpose of this meeting?"

Nora had the perfect club-woman manner. She wasted no time over preliminaries but plunged directly to the heart of the matter. "We have had a murder, two murders, in the past few hours. Since we are solely dependent on our own resources until outside help can arrive, we thought that we should take the matter into our own hands and go about the solution of this crime, or crimes, in a proper and orderly fashion. I say this with no idea of casting aspersions on the ability of two of our members who are versed in such matters. In fact, I think we are all proud to have here with us, and are deeply grateful to, our own Ethel Thomas and Abbie Abernathy."

She waited for the applause to die down.

"There is a fiend in our midst, a force for evil working against us, our homes, our very lives There is work for each and every one of us. We feel that at such a time of stress it is too great a responsibility to rest upon the frail shoulders of our friends, no matter how strong and willing those shoulders may be. We feel there should be a committee formed to help and protect these two brave women."

Nora sat down. While the judge waited patiently for someone else to speak, Abbie and I had a chance to exchange amused glances.

One of the Defran boys stood up. "I don't know anything about solving a crime, and I don't believe any one else in this room does except the capable owners of the frail shoulders which have just been mentioned so poetically. Since most of us wouldn't be able to tell a clue from a sheet-rope, I think the whole idea is a lot of damned nonsense. What can a committee do but get in the way and gum things up?"

Charlie Cotter jumped up and said, "I agree with Bill Defran."

There was some applause. I felt sorry for Dave, sitting out there on the porch missing one of the funniest shows I had ever seen.

The Judge was in something of a spot. "We can't take the matter of murder, lightly," he said, "nor can we shirk a responsibility that is rightfully ours."

"And you can't solve a crime with Robert's Rules of Order, either," Archie Taylor snapped.

"But we can have some semblance of order," Nora cried, bouncing to her feet. "I, for one, think we're all entitled to know what is and has been going on here. Will you tell us, Miss Thomas?"

I stood up and gave them: what I hope was a cold stare. "I most certainly will not tell you a single thing. This is not a tea party nor is it a time for idle chatter. Murder is serious business, although some of you do not seem to realize it. If we knew or had any idea as to the identity of the criminal, I would be the first to let you know."

"'Atta girl, Toots," Bill Defran called across to me as I sat down. I don't know that I've ever been called "Toots" before but I liked it coming from Defran.

Nora jumped to her feet. "Since we are outside the law for the moment, we must be a law unto ourselves. I propose that this meeting become a court of inquiry into the murders of Henry Baldwin and Arthur Tobias.

Mrs Deane seconded the motion

"I think it might be wise to waive discussion," the Judge said "I'll take a vote."

Those in favor of Nora 's motion seemed to win. I don't know why, but the Judge seemed to think it a good idea. He didn't ask for a negative vote. He turned to Nora and asked, "Just what sort of inquiries would you like to make?"

"I'd like to know if Miss Thomas or Miss Abernathy think the murderer is in our midst."

The Judge turned to Abbie, who replied, "He is unless he or, she left the island immediately after the murder."

"Have you done anything to determine whether he left or not?" Nora demanded.

"Since I have no idea as to the identity of the guilty person, I cannot answer your question."

"Did any one leave the island last night?"

"No one left by boat. The only other means was via the bridge. Willie Pole, will you answer a few questions?"

Willie moved forward a few paces to face Abbie. "Did any one leave the island last night after the storm broke?" she asked.

"Only the people who went off in Mr. Baldwin's car."

"Did you know them?"

"No, ma'am; only Mr. Baldwin."

There was a gasp of astonishment at that statement.

"Mr. Baldwin, Willie! Are you sure?" Abbie asked.

He favored her with a glance that was a mixture of contempt and annoyance. "Mr. Baldwin couldn't be dead if he left the island, could he?" After the titter that greeted his answer had died down, he went on, "He rode down with them so's I'd let them out in his car."

"Did he make any explanation?" Abbie asked.

"Same as usual."

"Then that sort of thing has happened before?" she asked.

"Yes. About every time the *Starfish* puts in here some one goes ashore. Sometimes Mr. Baldwin drove 'em in, sometimes he sent his car same as last night."

"How did Mr. Baldwin seem last night?" I think she intended to elaborate the question but Willie didn't give her a chance.

"Mad," he replied immediately.

"What did he say?"

"I couldn't hear too well, because he was talking in the car. You can't hear people talking when they are inside a car."

"But you knew he was angry?"

"Yes, the moment she drove up."

Every one leaned forward at that, waiting anxiously for the next question, the one which had to be asked.

"Who drove up, Willie?"

"Miss Del."

They all settled back disappointed.

"Tell us about it," Abbie urged.

"Well, she drove up right behind Baldwin's car, which was parked at the gate. She come just as Mr. Baldwin stepped out of his own car. He seen her and told her to go back home. They had words. He made her turn round." Willie's mouth settled into a straight line. I knew and Abbie realized he had done all the talking he intended to do for that -day.

"Then we should try to catch the murderer," Mrs. Deane said as Willie stepped back.

"What do you think they have been trying to do?" Jerry asked, more annoyed than I think he should have been.

"If it's too much for them to attempt it alone, they should ask for help," Mrs. Smith cried "I propose we appoint a committee to help them."

"Nerts!" Bill Defran cried and stalked out of the room.

"Is there anything a committee could do?" the Judge asked Abbie.

"The most important thing to do is to get the police here as soon as possible," she replied.

"Can't we take care of this matter ourselves?" Mrs. Deane asked.

"We're not equipped to take fingerprints, search properly for the gun, develop and tabulate bits of evidence, make laboratory tests nor any of the other things that the police do in a case of this kind," Abbie replied.

"What has been done to protect the evidence you mention?" Nora demanded.

"We have closed the death room. Weeks, I believe, has roped off part of the rear porch."

"And at Art Tobias' place?"

"Nothing. His dog is there standing guard."

"Much good the dog was last night!" Mrs. Smith sniffed. She was a notorious dog-hater.

"Then we ought to form the committee—"

Nora did not finish her sentence because the imp of satan she calls son dashed into the room clad only in swimming trunks, his pudgy body soaking wet. "Mama! mama!" he cried. "Look what we found!" In his hand he carried a revolver.

"Tommy!" Nora cried. For a moment I thought she was going to faint "Where did you get it?"

"Out of the *Albatross*."

"Out of what?" Jerry demanded and strode forward.

"We were playing divers and pretending the *Albatross* was a sunken treasure ship. We were diving down and trying to bring things up. I found this."

"Perhaps that's the gun you said the police would have to find," Nora said.

"That's my gun" Jerry stated, and then I saw the funniest look cross his face.

"Give the gun to the Judge," I suggested.

As Tommy stepped across the few feet separating him from the Judge, I noticed the small round and rather compact water stain he had left on the rug where he had been standing.

"Has the gun been fired?" Nora asked.

"All six cartridges," the Judge replied.

"When did you last fire your gun, Jerry?" Nora asked.

"I didn't fire it. It was loaded when I brought it ashore yesterday with my duffle."

His statement was greeted by a complete silence.

"You say you brought it ashore?" I asked. I couldn't permit him to put a noose about his neck that way.

"Yes. I left my things at the head of the pier. The revolver lay on top of the pile. I dropped everything there when we came ashore."

"Didn't you miss it?" I asked.

"No, as a matter of fact I didn't. I left my stuff there when I went up to the shed with Pete for lunch. Young Mike Abbott carried my duffle up to the house for me."

Young Mike, his face a mass of freckles, looked at Jerry with adoring eyes and said, "That's right, I did. I always carry things for Jerry."

"Did you see a revolver, Mike?" I asked.

"No, ma'am; there was no revolver on the duffle bag when I took it."

"Then some one in that crowd yesterday stole your gun," I said as emphatically as I could. I got up and walked out of the lounge and straight into the bar and ordered a Scotch and soda.

"Well!" I heard an echo from the Deane-Smith-Nora corner.

Abbie joined me a few minutes later. She refused a bracer, which rather surprised me. We joined Dave on the porch.

"How was the meeting?" he asked with too much amusement in his eyes to suit me just then.

"Just ducky!" Abbie snapped it out. "The Three Graces have put the committee idea across. We now have assistants and deputies, as many as we want."

"Hold everything, Abbie, and count ten," Dave advised. He turned to me and said, as if she were on some distant planet, "Don't look now but I think Abbie is mad."

"And who wouldn't be?" she stormed. "The hell with their murder! I'm through!"

"I don't blame you," he said. "It's a lot of work, anyhow, and what do you get out of it? Nothing but grief. It's like the newspaper game—you worry, fret, work like a dog, lose sleep and for what?"

"You can't let Jerry down," Pete argued as though he really believed she meant what she said.

"And how is your temper, Ethel? You seem quite calm," Dave commented.

"I've had a bracer."

"Lucky girl."

"I'm not going to let Jerry down!" Abbie barked at Pete. "Think I'm going to quit because a lot of old—keep your eyes on that oatsbray!" she cautioned as I saw Nora bearing down on us.

"You must be tired, Abbie," she said with sweet solicitation, "after all the work you've done and practically no sleep, I understand. Couldn't you take a nap now?"

"We'll have to talk things over first, plan our work. My first duty is to the community. I'll think of myself after my duty is done," Abbie carped

"I knew you'd understand," Nora said, giving me a nasty look. "You will keep us informed of your progress, won't you?"

"When I have something to tell you, I'll let you know. It isn't always wise, however, to talk too much. Not in a case of this kind."

"I don't see why," Nora objected.

I loved the run-around Abbie was giving Nora and listened keenly.

"I understand this game a little better than you do, Nora," Abbie said so sweetly. "Talk is sometimes dangerous. Take a tip from me and tell Bill to keep quiet if he makes any discoveries. The person who knows too much is often the next victim."

"You mean—" she gasped.

"Figure it out for yourself. Why do you suppose Art was killed?"

Nora turned a little green. "My goodness! I never—" The balance of her sentence was lost in the wind as she hurried away.

"I'd say you polished her off," Dave grinned appreciatively.

"You can't keep a good woman down," I reminded him.

"Nor an active man," he answered. "Graham is watching the shore."

T'hen let us watch him from a less conspicuous place," Abbie suggested.

"I'll watch from the windows inside. I think your committee men are approaching," he replied before he sauntered away.

Bill Baylis and Archie Taylor were headed in our direction. They stopped and faced us somewhat sheepishly.

"Archie and I have talked it over," Bill said "We'll do anything you say, since we've been pushed into this. What do we do?"

I felt like a school teacher keeping bad boys after school. Bill looked exactly what he was, an ex-football player grown slightly pudgy above the waistline. His nice brown eyes smiled lamely at me across the crooked bridge of his nose. Archie Taylor was a smaller man than Bill. He was sparsely built, decidedly on the slim side. His hair was graying at the temples and he looked more than his forty odd years. There was a beaten expression about his eyes accentuated by the droop of his mouth. It had been there ever since he lost most of his money.

"What are the chances of getting a boat out of the Harbor? Abbie asked

"It'll be pretty tough going for a while, but the sea may go down in an hour or so. It has stopped raining and the wind has let up considerably," Bill said sagely as he looked up at the sky.

"Couldn't you ferry a boy and a bicycle across the creek in canoes?" Abbie suggested. "If we could get some one across to the road they could ride into town."

"It's worth a try," Bill agreed brightly, glad of a chance to do anything connected with boats. "I'll see if I can get that trailer of Jerry's." He dashed off filled with a new purpose.

"You wanted to talk to me alone, didn't you?" Archie asked, looking after Bill.

Abbie nodded.

"Well, what's on your mind?"

"How long did you stay with Stella last night after you left Baldwin's?" Abbie asked.

From his look I gathered that there had been times when he stayed with Stella, but that last night was not one of them.

"She brought me to the house and dropped me there," he said.

Since he had lost his big house to Baldwin, he had been living in the cottage next to the Club which he had built originally as a combination bath and play house. That was in the days when money was abundant, paper profits were high and we rode gaily toward ultimate disaster with our eyes closed to the clouds looming overhead and our ears shut to the rumblings of thunder about us.

"See anything around here?" she asked.

"Yes, I was interested in the people who came ashore from the *Starfish*. I watched them drive away."

"Did you see Baldwin when he returned?"

"I didn't see Baldwin after the car drove away."

"Did you see anything more last night?"

"I saw Art's dog and later I saw a man over by the patch of scrub oaks at the edge of the parking lot. I just naturally figured it was Art."

"Why?"

"Because of the dog, I suppose. The man stood up just as some lightning flashed. Funny thing, I thought he was naked. I couldn't figure that out at all."

"But you're not sure it was Art?"

"No. I'm not sure," he said regretfully. "I wish I were. It might help, since I had an argument with Baldwin yesterday afternoon."

"Want to tell me about it?"

"No. It had nothing to do with this. It was just a private quarrel about Stella and me."

"Then you saw them together down on the spit?" He nodded.

So Archie was crazy about Stella. Well, he was just the type of man who would be. I declare the longer I live the more bewildered I become over the complexities of human emotions.

"I haven't a leg to stand on, Abbie, if you want to suspect me. I live right next to the Club. I was here at the time and I hated him for taking my place away from me. Oh, what's the use, Abbie?"

"We don't want to suspect any of our friends," she said thoughtfully. "We'd simply like to get to the bottom of the case, if possible, before the police arrive."

"It would be a break for Jerry. Things look bad for him. You know what the women are thinking," he said.

"Too well," she answered.

Their conversation was interrupted by a stir and bustle of activity at the end of the porch.

"Must be Bill and the trailer for the canoes," Archie said dully and turned away.

"The naked man bears out our theory, Ethel," she said when Archie was out of earshot. "And we know Graham was in the water, he admitted it himself."

"But Graham was not here to steal Jerry's gun when the *Albatross* came in," I reminded her.

"We don't know that Jerry's gun was used. We can't know about that until a ballistics expert has worked on it."

"And in the meantime those women are going to put Jerry on the grill and have him fired unless we get something definite. We've reached one of those static periods on a case when nothing seems to happen to point the way. We've evidence enough now to hang Jerry, but we neither of us want to do that."

"Jerry would never have hidden his own gun on *Albatross* and then sunk the boat. He thinks too much of the boat," she argued.

"Let's see what they are doing about sending some one across to the road," I suggested, craving action some kind.

Boys and men were busy loading two canoes onto the trailer under the supervision of Bill Baylis. Those two imps, Tommy Baylis and young Red Deane, came round the end of the clubhouse and stood watching the proceedings. The boys put their heads together for a hurried consultation. The next minute they were on their wheels headed up the road bent on mischief of some kind. I thought nothing of their activities at the time and I don't know what I might have done about it if I had. It was of one of those things that happen when boys get ideas.

The canoes were loaded. Bill turned to Buddy Huett and said, "Ride your bike down to the bridge, Buddy. We'll meet you there."

"Okay," Buddy answered with pride, his eyes aglow with importance as he cast superior glances at the less fortunate boys.

"That ought to bring the police in an hour or two," Abbie said as she gazed after them. "Now, how about a sandwich?"

As we entered the lounge Dave beckoned from the easy-chair where he had been watching.

"Smart girls," he said as we stood beside him.

"Graham's been circling the *Starfish* in a small boat pretending to look over the hull. When he reached the stern he took extra precautions to make sure that he was not being watched. I think he lowered something into the water. I rather think that, whatever it was, it was attached to a line."

"Fine!" I approved.

"But how are we going to get it?"

"We'll get it, but we mustn't be too anxious about it. We'll have to give him an hour or two to lull him into a sense of security."

"What do you expect to find in that bundle he lowered overboard?"

"What's your guess?" I countered as I lit a cigarette.

CHAPTER THIRTEEN

IT WAS AFTER FOUR when we had finished our sandwiches and coffee. The day had slipped away from us. Strange that no effort had been made to reach us from the shore. We were thoughtful and silent, particularly Dave. It suddenly occurred to me that he had been unusually quiet. And as I thought about it I wondered why he had been so willing to concentrate on the *Starfish* when there was story material for him all over the Club. Also he had never told us his idea about Graham and the *Starfish*.

"All right, Dave, better tell Aunt Ethel about it now," I suggested as I lit another cigarette.

"Chain smoking is bad for you, Ethel," he evaded.

"Never mind my health; let's concentrate on you. What's your idea about the *Starfish*?"

He seemed unduly cautious as he glanced about the room to make sure we would not be overheard. "We've got to go at this thing carefully, girls. If my guess is right, we're bucking something big and I don't mean a double murder either."

"Don't be so annoyingly mysterious. You don't have to beat about the bush with us."

"Ever hear of illegal entry into the country?" he asked.

"Certainly; it's one of the major rackets," Abbie replied glibly, and then paused as the significance of his remark struck home. "What fools we've been, Ethel, not to have thought of that ourselves! It's a hot guess, Dave, and a correct one if we can depend on Willie and Sidney. Graham's passengers always went directly ashore the moment they landed."

"It's a perfect setup, isn't it?" Dave asked.

"Couldn't be better. How do you suppose he has been operating?" I asked, intrigued by the possibilities of his suggestion.

"If our hunch is right he has been doing a high-class business, bringing in people with money. We've nothing to go on but Art's log-book and the more or less regular entries. My guess is that he works out of Halifax during the summer and probably Bermuda during the winter months. That's why I asked you about your Bermuda trip."

"And I really thought you had a honeymoon in mind." She feigned disappointment.

"Business before honeymoons," he said quickly. "I don't believe the fifty thousand was stolen at all. Baldwin paid it to Graham."

"Isn't that a lot of money for bringing four people into the country?" Abbie objected.

"Depends on the people," he said thoughtfully. "There's a snag in my reasoning somewhere. I've been trying to find it."

"Wait, Dave," I cried. "I wonder if this is it! We know Baldwin's fifty thousand has disappeared and in our efforts to account for it we are jumping at conclusions. Why should Baldwin pay money to Graham? It should be the reverse. Graham is the man who brings the people here, but it is Baldwin who really disposes of them in a way that has not, up to now, aroused suspicion. Graham has probably been paying Baldwin. If we're on the right track at all, your theory explains a number of things about Baldwin—his reason for being at the Harbor, even his marriage to Mary. As the son-in-law of old Judge Verity he would be above ordinary suspicion. We really have something. Check in that book of Art's. What was Baldwin's reply to Graham last night?"

"'Six overdue expect ten,'" Dave read. "I get it now!" he cried excitedly. "Graham owed Baldwin a lot of money."

"And last night Graham swam ashore, had a row with Baldwin, killed him and took the money," Abbie summed up.

"Wait! Would Graham do that?" Dave argued.

"It was Baldwin who provided Graham with a safe port of entry. He wouldn't want to be rid of Baldwin unless he had other means of getting people into the country."

"But if they had a row, anything could have happened," Abbie insisted. "Graham was in the water last night. There was a damp spot on the rug that could have been made by a man in a bathing-suit. It all fits together."

"And explains the nude man Archie thought he saw," I added.

"If we accept this theory it means we are willing to dismiss Jerry and the Judge as possible takers of the money and probable murderers." Dave was thoughtful.

"Jerry has all the money he wants, and as for the Judge . . ." Abbie mused.

"It's okay with me," Dave, agreed. "It's a nice theory if any of it is true. Stranger things have happened and we are assuming that we've already established the facts. How about it, Ethel?"

"It sounds reasonable," I admitted, but I was thinking many things. If Graham had killed Baldwin, why didn't the *Starfish* leave the Harbor last night?

Abbie seemed to read my thoughts, for she said, "Graham should have left the Harbor last night."

"That's a point, why didn't he?" Dave puzzled.

"Because there was a storm, a really terrible storm. You don't know much about it because you were asleep and snored through it all, making nearly as much noise as the thunder. The *Starfish* didn't dare go out last night. It was much too dangerous. Storms can be like that, you know." Her attitude was patronizing as she looked at Dave.

"I guess my staying down here was a mistake, after all," he said regretfully. "Did I keep you awake or was it really the thunder?"

"Let's stick to our theory about Graham," she advised.

"Love, Abbie, is the greatest theory in the world. There will be murders when we are six feet under. At the moment I don't want to be too distasteful to you. If you advise it, I may have my adenoids taken out or something."

"Save your adenoids," I advised with a laugh. "Love can wait while we get Graham's little package which is at the bottom of the harbor, we hope." I led them outside.

There were at least a half-dozen straight-legged, golden-brown youngsters hanging about the porch in swimming-pants.

"I was looking for Tommy Baylis because he is the nearest thing to a fish that I've seen on land or sea, but he's not in sight," Abbie explained.

She selected Sammy Cotter, Teddy Caine and Mike Abbot and drew them to one side. "How would you boys like to do a little detective work?" she asked.

They were as eager as youngsters could be as she outlined a plan to them. They were to take her out to the *Starfish* and while they were waiting for her, they were to drift to the stern of the yacht and dive in and out of the small boat. They were to be very casual about it but on each dive they were to try to fetch bottom and look for a bundle that was probably tied to a line.

"How will you cut the line?" she asked as that difficulty presented itself.

"I can do it the way pearl divers fight sharks," Mike boasted.

At the last moment I decided to go with her. We left Dave watching us from the float as we put off in the dingey with the three boys.

Graham was waiting for us on the deck and helped us up the ladder. "I wondered if you'd come," he said.

"We have to cover all suspects," I laughed, "and now that they have formed a committee we must be on our toes." We explained the situation at the Club.

"That sort of thing must be annoying to women like you," he said. "How about a drink?"

"Why not?" I agreed, glad of an excuse to get him away from the ship's side.

As he moved forward in his blue coat and white trousers, cap at a rakish angle, I had to admit that he was a handsome devil in a fascinating way. A hard man but an exciting one.

"This is a nice ship you have here, rather more beam than I expected," Abbie said. "Do you find her seaworthy?"

"She does very well. I don't venture very far from shore. My friends aren't very good sailors and there's no fun putting to sea alone."

"I prefer sails," Abbie said flatly. "A yacht's good enough, but I enjoy the thrill of supplying my own power."

"You would," he replied with admiration.

Over the drinks he asked, "Anything new on the murder?"

"We can't make head nor tail of it, Mr. Graham," I replied.

"How about the Carter fellow? He had a motive."

"True," I agreed, "but he's not the murdering type, and besides it's too easy. The missing fifty thousand complicates matters."

"It would," he nodded thoughtfully. After a moment he said, "Can't murder ever be simple? Must it always be so complicated?"

"There are always so many unknown factors," I answered. "Things that rarely ever appear on the surface."

"How about Baldwin's family?" he asked.

"They seem normal enough, as far as we can make out. You knew him fairly well. Can you give us any helpful information?"

"He was an odd man. In all the years I've known him, I've never spent any time in his home. I don't believe I know anything that would lead to murder." He spoke thoughtfully and with a certain amount of hesitancy, real or feigned, I don't know which.

"Just what do you mean?" I asked, willing to take the lead if he was offering one.

"You've met Mrs. Dunn?" At my nod he went on. "There's a peculiar situation there. She wasn't always his housekeeper. How has she taken this?"

"Normally enough, I'd say. As far as we know she did not leave the house last night. I don't believe Mrs. Dunn had anything to do with his death."

"Well, I suppose you know more about women than I do. She might not do anything for herself but she'd be likely to fight for that kid of hers."

That was a surprise and my face must have shown it.

"I'm just telling you this in case you need it. If you don't, you'll keep it under your hats, both of you. Del is Baldwin's child by Mrs. Dunn."

"No!" I exclaimed as I realized why Del had been so upset, crying and exacting promises from Pete the night before.

"It's a fact. You see, there's a Mr. Dunn. Religion kept her from getting a divorce, but it didn't keep her from living with Baldwin. Well, since they couldn't get married he has raised Del as a niece. I don't know that Del knows anything about it herself; probably not."

"The poor child," Abbie sighed. "I hope this story doesn't have to come out."

"I don't believe Mrs. Dunn was too pleased with this marriage of Baldwin's," he grinned nastily.

"Would you be, in her place?" Abbie asked.

"I suppose not."

"Why do you suppose he married Mary Verity?" I asked. "Have you any idea of the reason that might have prompted it?"

"Man's vanity. As we grow older we like younger women," he answered with a challenging glance toward Abbie.

"Humph!" I grunted disdainfully. "How about Baldwin's business?" I asked, preferring to change the subject.

"He was an importer, had an office down on William Street. That's all I know."

"I had hoped you might know the reason for his having such large sums of cash on hand at various times."

His eyes flickered at that, but for the life of me I don't know whether it was my question or Abbie's crossing of her knees that caused it. He answered almost immediately, "Hasn't that nephew of his been able to tell you that?"

"No; Sidney handles the petty cash for the family, nothing else."

He seemed relieved, but I pretended not to notice that. He was deep and smooth and on his guard all the time, but he did say, "I never quite understood the nephew setup."

"Perhaps Sidney is still another child. Baldwin seems to have been a man of wide interests," Abbie suggested.

He laughed heartily and gave her a very intimate look as he approved, "That's a good one!"

From below us on the water I heard a boy's squeaky voice call rather plaintively. "Hey, Miss Abbie! Are you ready? It's getting cold."

"Our ferrymen are bored and cold," Abbie said as she rose and moved across the deck.

"Don't hurry. I'll send you ashore," he urged.

"The boys wouldn't like that," she replied. "How's your radio coming?" I asked as he helped me down the ladder.

"We haven't enough spare material to fix it. Sorry. Is there no word from the shore yet?"

I was too occupied with the business of getting from the ladder to the boat to answer. As I settled in the stern seat I knew by the expressions of their faces that the boys had been successful. They were bursting with pride and ready to bubble over. I scowled for silence because Graham was hanging over the rail watching us with amused eyes.

Sammy took one of the oars and with the blade and braced against the hull, shoved off.

"Hey, you!" Graham growled. "Watch out for my paint!"

The boys tittered at that, they were so full of suppressed excitement. Sammy rowed expertly toward the float while I wondered about Graham. He was a strange man. Why had he told us about Mrs. Dunn and Del? Had he done it purposely to get us off the scent? Had he hoped to escape notice by providing us with another motive? He had a reason, of that I was sure. I had seen the type often—ruthess, two-fisted men, born fighters who never gave up, right or wrong. He puzzled me. Somehow I couldn't see him as the murderer, but then I didn't believe that Jerry had done it either. Neither of them was the type to slink through the dark. Graham would mow a man down who stood in his way, and he would do it with brute force, by a blow from me of those powerful fists. I was confused but I felt sure that the wet and muddy bundle reposing under Mike's thin buttocks would tell the story.

"Are you going to show us what's in it?" Sammy asked as he made the painter fast to a ring in the bat.

"I'd rather keep it a secret for a little while, if you boys will promise to keep quiet," Abbie replied.

"I don't want any one to know about this for at least an hour or two. How about it?"

"Sure, Miss Abbie. We're deputies, aren't we?" At her nod, he went on, "And we can't say anything till you tell us to. That's the way it works, isn't it?"

"I could swear you in as deputies if you like," Abbie suggested with a fine understanding of the boy's mind.

"I think it would be more fun to be secret deputies," Mike explained. "Then you can tell us to do other things and nobody'll know we're working with you."

"Fine," Abbie agreed. "Keep your eyes on the *Starfish* and let me know if any one leaves the boat or tries to get the bundle."

"Okay."

"And don't tell Tommy Baylis," I suggested. "He's playing at being a detective and seems to be trying to make things hard for Jerry."

"We'll fix that," Mike vowed.

I was wondering how we would get the bundle up to the porch without its being seen, but our deputies took care of that. Teddy Caine slid it into a wooden bailing scoup and trotted up the pier as unconcerned as you please. He was waiting for us and said, "It's pretty dirty. We didn't want to wash the mud off it out there on account of—you know. Do you want us to wash it now?"

At a nod from Abbie they scampered away. When they returned from the spigot at the end of the porch, the bundle was not only clean but it was wrapped in a piece of white cloth.

"Mum's the word!" Abbie said as it was handed to her.

Mike would have saluted, but Sammy stopped him by saying, "Nobody's supposed to know. Don't forget if you want us for anything else we'll be ready." As we smiled in agreement, they turned and raced away.

"Where are we going to inspect it?" Dave asked as he followed us into the lounge.

Abbie crossed to Weeks' desk and took a key from the board. She led us down the hall to a room next to the one in which Baldwin's body still lay.

Abbie unrolled the cloth. The bundle was carefully wrapped in oiled silk. Dave produced a penknife and cut the cords. He unrolled that silk with eager hands and surveyed the contents with satisfaction. Under the neat flat piles of thousand-dollar bills there was a good solid strip of lead which had been used as a weight.

Dave whistled. "It must be the fifty thousand dollars!" There was excitement in his voice.

I glanced at him quickly. I have heard that man's cupidity often rises to an uncontrolled impulse at the sight of a great deal of money. Dave's eyes, however, were merely thoughtful. He seemed to be estimating the amount.

A noise on the porch startled us. We all turned toward the window. I thought I saw a head disappear below the window-frame but I wasn't sure. Dave dashed across the room, but unfortunately the door, swollen, from the rain, stuck. He finally resorted to some good round curses, but it wouldn't budge.

"Some one was snooping;" he said as he came back. "What are you going to do with that stuff, now that you have it?"

"We'd better hide it," Abbie said.

"That isn't safe," he objected.

"Then what do you suggest?" I asked.

"I don't know. I'd say we were running a risk while we have it."

"But no one knows we have it," Abbie objected.

"I'm not so sure it's a secret." I told them about the head I thought I saw disappear from the window just a few minutes before.

"How about the safe in the office?" Dave suggested.

Abbie refused that idea, saying, "We might leave it at the store with Martin."

"Why not give it to the committee? They wanted to have a hand in the case. Let them worry about it."

"Not yet, Dave. It will give the show away."

"But we can't run around the rest of the day with all this money on our persons! Night will be coming on; it will be dangerous."

"I have it!" Abbie cried. "There's an old safe in the shed. It's one that Grandfather used. You couldn't budge it with three men and you couldn't get into it with anything short of dynamite. Will you take the package up there and put it in the safe if I give you the combination?" At his nod of agreement she crossed to the desk and wrote the figures on a piece of Club stationery.

"What will you be doing?" he asked as Abbie prepared the bundle.

"We'll be checking on that noise we heard," she said.

We led him down the long hall to the side entrance beyond, the kitchen, through the door where the unknown man had vanished the night before. We stood there and watched him until he was well on his way up the road.

"I have a queer feeling about Dave and that money," Abbie said.

"You like him, don't you?" I asked.

"I could, if I'd let myself. He's sweet. I wouldn't want anything to happen to him."

"Nothing will," I assured her.

Just as we turned back from the door, we saw Archie Taylor leave the end of the porch and start up the shore toward the shed.

When we reached the lounge, there was a group of people on the porch. They were huddled close together and talking excitedly in low voices. Bill Baylis, Nora, Stella, Sidney and a number of other people formed a circle.

As we paused in the door I called, "Any news from shore, Bill?"

"Nope! Buddy hasn't returned yet. We got him over to the road all right. He ought to be back soon Jerry's down there waiting for him. If he has made town some one ought to be out soon, the sea's going down a lot."

"Have you anything new to tell us?" Nora broke from the group to ask.

"Not a thing," Abbie replied.

Nora turned to face Bill with an I-told-you-so glance.

Sidney came over to us and said in a low voice, "Mary's frantic. She's been expecting you all day. She wants to know what has happened."

"Tell her not to worry. We haven't had time to think. Things have been happening so fast."

"Then you've discovered something?" he asked eagerly.

"Many things but nothing definite. How long have you been here, Sidney?"

"I just came a few minutes ago. Why?"

"When you approached the Club did you see any one at the rear of the building?"

"No, I didn't. I was interested in the people on the porch."

"Too bad! You go home and tell Mary to be patient. Tell her everything is under control." We watched him until he rode away on his bicycle. From behind us Weeks was coughing and making sounds like an indignant tomcat.

With one eye on the group still clustered on the porch he whispered, "You didn't tell me Baldwin had been robbed."

I explained that we had not known it at the time.

"It puts me in a bad light," he complained.

"You were bound to be suspected, because you were unfortunate enough to have been here last night, but don't let it worry you."

"But it makes me uncomfortable. They look at me with their suspicious eyes, and just a few minutes ago, after asking me a lot of silly questions, Nora Baylis made Bill go through the safe. I don't like it, I tell you."

"None of us do. Just sit tight for a little while, Weeks; the case is practically solved," I assured him.

"Then watch the committee or they'll spoil things for you," he warned. "They asked me to fix the time of the crime. They're up to something."

"What did you tell them?" I asked.

"Same's I told you. That I didn't see Baldwin after the storm broke but I did talk to him about one-thirty or so."

"What?" I gasped. "Weeks, you didn't tell us that this morning!"

"Didn't I?" he asked quite as surprised as we were.

"No, you didn't. You led us to believe that midnight was the last moment you knew him to be alive."

"Gosh! I'm sorry!"

"Well, it can make no difference now. What did Baldwin want when you talked to him?"

"Nothing. He said he had knocked the phone off the table. He sounded sleepy."

"You didn't see him?"

"And you are sure you talked to him at approximately one-thirty?"

"Yes, or possibly a little later. I came in here for something and heard the buzzer on the board."

That information knocked all our theories and ideas into a cocked hat. If Baldwin was alive at that time either Jerry or Mary might have killed him. My case against Graham was gone. Jerry had said Baldwin was cold when he touched him. He might have been lying to cover himself or Mary, because that was about the time they were in the room.

CHAPTER FOURTEEN

ABBIE AND I SETTLED into a corner to talk over the situation. If Baldwin was alive at one thirty, why had Art Tobias been killed? There could be but one reason. He knew more about the *Starfish* and her real business than his log book indicated. Perhaps Baldwin gave him a cut of the profits. With Baldwin alive at that hour all the aspects of the case changed. It reopened the case against Jerry, and while it did not entirely eliminate Graham it did not make things as difficult for him as I had hoped they would be. Of course, as Abbie pointed out, there was the money. But why had Jerry told us that Baldwin must have been dead for some time?

We were still discussing the various angles when we heard Jerry's voice on the porch. I went to the door and called him.

He came in announcing, "Buddy is back. The bridge at the other end of the Neck was washed out too. That's why nothing came down this morning. Buddy swam the creek up there and contacted the local police. They will come down by boat. They ought to be here in an hour or so."

I took his arm and steered him down the room away from the door.

"What's up?" he asked.

"Plenty. We've just learned that Baldwin was alive at one-thirty. Why did you lie to us this morning?"

"I didn't lie to you. Baldwin had been dead for some time when I was in the room."

"But Weeks talked to him on the telephone about one-thirty or later," I insisted.

"Oh, that!" he said with irritating calmness. "Didn't I tell you about that? Weeks talked to me. I knocked the telephone over as I felt under the pillow for Baldwin's wallet. I was replacing the receiver when I heard Weeks' voice. I mumbled something about having knocked the phone over and hung up."

"And left all your fingerprints on the telephone?" I cried in exasperation.

"I suppose so. There isn't anything we can do about that now, is there?" he asked matter-of-factly.

I'm sure when he asked the rhetorical question, he had no idea of suggesting to me that I eliminate those fingerprints, and yet that was exactly the thing I felt like doing. As he stood there facing us, he seemed determined to take the guilt on his own shoulders. Did he secretly suspect Mary of the murder? Was that why he had kept the note which, if used as evidence, would be sufficient to put him in jail? More than ever it would be necessary to establish an alibi for him.

"You look worried," he said with a casualness that was irritating beyond words.

"I am. I hope I never again get involved in a case with friends of mine," I said fervently.

"Don't feel that way about it, Ethel. We all feel pretty comfortable knowing that you and Abbie are working for us."

"Even though you let us work in the dark," I accused.

His answer to that was a shrug which seemed to say, "Now you're acting like a woman."

"I could slap him," Abbie complained as he disappeared into the bar.

Stella Ketcham sauntered into the room. Her gait would suggest a casual entrance but I rather felt she had seen Jerry going into the bar. Abbie was on her feet and called, "Stella, I'd like to talk to you."

"And I've been wanting to talk to you," she replied as she came toward us.

"That's just fine then," Abbie said.

"My, how things have changed! Fancy a murder giving us mutual interests," she said as she sank into the chair between us.

Abbie leaned forward. "Look, Stella, we don't have to pretend that we like each other, but at a time like this can't we forget our personal feelings?"

"Women and elephants you know," she said with a smile.

"But since neither of us is an elephant and we are, I hope, sensible women, let's act our ages. I'd like to ask you some questions which I hope you will answer."

"And if I don't?"

"I'll have to tell the police when they arrive; they'll ask them," Abbie answered with controlled patience

"Are you accusing me of the murder?" Stella asked

"Don't be so damn silly!" Abbie blurted, her patience completely gone.

Stella's self control was magnificent. I expected an outburst but she surprised me. "You haven't answered my question," she said.

"I think you're capable of murder," Abbie replied straight from the shoulder, "but I don't know of any reason for you to kill Baldwin."

"That's so gratifying," she answered with a little breath catching laugh.

"Will you tell me why, when Baldwin was supposed to be interested in watching his wife yesterday afternoon, he took you walking down on the Point?"

"Because I asked him to do it. I had some business to discuss with him, and," she added, "I hoped Jerry, and Mary would have a chance to be alone."

That, of course, was a lie and she knew that we both knew it. Abbie pretended to believe it, however, as she said, "Stella, all our lives I've been judging you wrongly. That was noble of you."

Stella flushed and said, "Wouldn't we do better if we covered our claws? Believe me or not, that was my reason."

"I do believe you," Abbie insisted. "When you came back from the Point, did Baldwin leave you to talk to some man?"

"That's right," she acknowledged.

"Who was the man?"

"Archie Taylor. He came out of his cottage and walked across to join us. I left them and went home."

"Did you hear any of their conversation?"

"No. I didn't tarry because I knew Archie was in a temper."

"It probably was not important, anyhow." Abbie changed her tactics and said, "You've no idea how relieved I was to hear you say you were interested in Jerry and Mary having a chance to be together. I think we all love them both and while most of us are afraid that he might have, in a moment of rage, killed Baldwin we none of us want to believe that he killed Art Tobias. The committee seems to have been very active. The finding of Jerry's gun on the sunken *Albatross* won't help him any."

"No one is going to believe he killed Tobias," she objected, "because we all know Jerry wouldn't attack a dog."

"That's a good point," Abbie agreed.

Stella leaned forward and asked eagerly, "Couldn't you get the dog to lead you to the murderer?"

"We might, but at the moment Spotty won't leave his master's side. He is standing guard. We can't do anything about him until we get some help and the body is taken away. I'm not thinking about that now. I want you to help Jerry. I don't want him to be accused of either murder."

"How can I help?"

"I'm positive that Baldwin was killed between twelve and one."

"What does that prove?"

"You left Baldwin's house with Taylor soon after Baldwin came down here. Were you at home in your house when the storm broke?"

"Yes. I brought Archie down here and just made my garage as it started to rain. I was drenched running from the garage to the house."

"Which gave you a swell excuse for being in a negligee when Jerry arrived," I thought but I said nothing, as Abbie was doing remarkably well.

"And that was just about twelve or a little after, wasn't it?" Abbie asked.

"Yes."

"What time did Jerry arrive?" Abbie tried to be casual about it but I saw Stella's eyes blink in surprise. Abbie hurried on before she could say anything. "He was with you, wasn't he, Stella? I figured it out when I saw his car stalled on the road in front of your house. For Jerry's sake, think before you answer. He has refused to tell me where he was between twelve and two. If we can prove that he could not have killed Baldwin, there would be no reason for his killing Tobias. If Baldwin was dead before two o'clock, it is not important that Jerry was seen by two people."

"Two?" she asked, surprised.

"Yes, two. In his way Jerry is a fool, but a nice fool. There's a streak of gallantry, in him. At the moment he is caught between two women. He won't tell what he did during those two hours because he wants to protect both you and Mary."

"My reputation and her feelings," she said, not without some bitterness.

"Exactly," Abbie agreed. "He'll protect you both with his life if necessary."

"Then that's where she was," she said bitterly.

"What are you talking about?" I demanded.

"Mary Verity, of course! I saw her sneaking up the path past my house just before dawn this morning."

"Wait a minute, Stella," Abbie cried. "We're talking about the time between twelve and two."

"And I'm talking about the hour just before dawn." She laughed hollowly. "She could have been up to Art's."

"Are you sure it was Mary?"

"I'd know her anywhere," she replied positively.

"She might have been to see her father," I suggested.

"What for, legal advice?" Stella snapped back. "You like Mary and you don't like me. Naturally you'll try to protect her," she scoffed.

"We're only trying to find the murderer," Abbie answered lamely, recognizing the truth in what Stella had just said.

"Then ask her questions. Ask her where she was at that hour of the morning. She had plenty of motive. When she thought Jerry had been lost at sea she married Baldwin for his money because they are broke. Then when she heard Jerry was safe, she wanted to get rid of her husband. She's a deep one; the quiet kind always are. She has taken everything from me that I've ever wanted. I hope she hangs for this!" she finished with hot vehemence.

"Wait, Stella. Baldwin was killed long before five o'clock."

"But Art Tobias wasn't. How do you know that she didn't have some warning that Art Tobias was down near the Club?"

As she spoke there flashed into my mind the memory of Mary's startled and excited surprise when we mentioned Art as a suspect.

"I don't see how she could have known that," Abbie lied.

"But you admit the murderer must have known it," she argued.

"Yes, the murderer definitely knew it," I agreed.

"Well, then! See what little mealy-mouthed Mary has to say for herself," she commanded imperiously.

"I will," I promised.

"Take care of her. I'll give Jerry an alibi. Why not? I'll be glad to do it. He was with me, and how she'll hate knowing it!" She paused to relish the idea.

"You're not doing it just to be vindictive, are you?" Abbie asked.

That was her exact reason. I could see it in the cold calculation of her eyes.

"You want to save Jerry, don't you?" she demanded. At Abbie's acknowledgment she went on, "Then why worry about my motives?"

"Aren't you forgetting something, Stella?" I asked.

"What?" she demanded, her brows pierced by a frown.

"That Jerry loves Mary. That if it's a question of him or Mary, he'll lie to save her."

"Yes, I know it, that's the hell of it," she said hopelessly.

"I know," Abbie said with sympathy. It was probably one of the first genuine moments the two girls had ever had. Abbie had loved Tim Abernathy in that way and he hadn't cared a tinker's damn about her and I honestly think she knew it from the very first but she wanted him none the less. She couldn't have been happy without him and God knows she wasn't happy with him and she hasn't cared much about anything since he left, until yesterday when Dave's understanding grin seemed to penetrate the shell in which she has lived. Stella was looking at Abbie with unbelief in her eyes as Abbie said, "You'll get over it after a while."

"If we're not careful we'll be letting our hair down, Abbie," she said with a twisted smile. "It would be a strange state of affairs after all these years, wouldn't it?"

"Maybe we've never understood each other," Abbie suggested.

"Or have understood each other too well."

"And I'd miss your dirty cracks at my expense," Abbie added.

"And I, your quick retorts. You're the only woman I know who can take it on the chin and still come right back, strong."

"Then we won't change, Stella, but don't be surprised if I begin to show a little respect for you."

"Please don't. It might be catching."

"But you've such a hard shell, you could resist it."

"After all, isn't that a question of vitality?"

"Either that or brass," Abbie replied with a shrug as they became antagonists again, back on their old footing.

"That's better," Stella approved. "Anything else you want to know now that you have torn my reputation to shreds?"

"It was pretty ragged, anyhow," Abbie depreciated.

"Okay, Abbie, you're one up on me. I'm not in a fighting mood but just remember this, if you don't accuse Mary Baldwin of the murder, I will."

"So that Jerry can go gaily to the chair?" I scoffed.

"I'm not going to save him for her," she vowed vehemently.

I believed her. It was exactly the sort of thing she would do. Well, we had a little surprise for her in the form of Graham and his activities and we couldn't ignore the Archie Taylor angle either.

Jerry came back from the bar bringing us each a drink. "I thought you'd need some fortification," he said.

"We need more than that," Abbie remarked pointedly, "but the drink will do very well at the moment."

We were having a very pleasant interlude when there was a commotion on the porch.

"Oh, Oh!" Jerry said, looking toward the door where Nora and her two satellites, purpose written on their plump faces, were advancing.

They barged in with Bill and several males in their wake. They spread out in a circle before us as if it were their intention to block any attempt at escape. There was a glint in Nora's eye that was not to my liking as she opened fire.

"We thought you would play fair, Abbie, and you haven't," she accused, choosing to ignore me.

"In just what way have we cheated you Nora?" Abbie asked coldly.

"What have you done with the money?" she demanded with dramatic emphasis.

That was something of a surprise. Before Abbie could reply I asked quickly, "So you were the Peeping Tom?"

"I refuse to be insulted by you," she retorted, turning a hurt glance in Bill's direction. He, poor devil, was trying in masculine fashion to keep out of it.

"No particular insult intended, Nora. We know some one spied on us, much to our regret. You may not believe it or want to realize it, but a great deal depended on our keeping the finding of that money a secret."

"There's been too much secrecy. What are you trying to hide? Why can't this thing be handled in the open?" she demanded, with a good woman's righteous wrath.

"Because I thought otherwise'" I retorted. "Why don't you attend to your children, a job at which you're quite capable?"

"I am attending to my children. It's a fine state of affairs when we must depend upon a pair of boys to supply us with the information which you have wilfully withheld. We have been depending on your knowledge and experience and yet two boys with an amateur detective set have given us more information and have gone further toward solving the crime than you have."

"That's very interesting, Nora, and who are the boy wonders?"

"Tommy and Red," she announced with pride. "They have told us something that you probably don't even know. We have conclusive proof that Jerry was in the room with Baldwin last night. There!"

I saw Del come to the fringe of the crowd and look over toward us as Bill Baylis objected, "Now, Nora, you've no right to say things like that without more proof than fingerprints collected by a couple of fool kids."

"You may think your own child a fool, Bill," she said with icy injury, "but I know better." She took some sheets of paper from her bag. "These are Jerry's fingerprints which he gave to Tommy and they are the exact duplicates of prints the boys found on the telephone in Baldwin's room."

"Nora Baylis!" I stormed. "Do you mean to say that you allowed your child to go into that room and spoil evidence which will be needed by the police? How dared you do such a thing! I hope they put you in jail for it—they should!"

That held her, but only for a moment. "I had nothing to do with it," she denied. "It was the children's idea and the results seem to justify the means."

Jerry gave me the next shock when he said, "Well, Ethel, I guess the jig is up. What would you like to have done with me, Nora?"

Nora gasped.

"Don't be a fool, Jerry," Bill cut in. "No one with any sense believes you're guilty. Why pay any attention to these fool women, anyhow? Abbie and Ethel know what they're doing. If they haven't locked you up, it's good enough for me."

"Well! Bill Baylis! How dare—"

"Now listen here, Nora," he said firmly. "I've had enough of this. You go home where you belong and take Tommy with you, or apologize to Jerry, one or the other."

Nora didn't know what to do with such open and public revolt. She finally managed to say, "I didn't accuse you of the murder, Jerry."

"But the inference is that I did it, isn't it?" Jerry asked.

"Unless you could explain why your fingerprints are on the telephone," she suggested hopefully with a wary eye turned in Bill's direction. I had a feeling he would pay for his rebellion later.

"I don't care to make any explanations," Jerry said and turned away from her. He selected a magazine from a nearby stand and seating himself began to read.

Nora turned to us. "What are you going to do with the money you found?"

"Nothing at the moment, and I don't propose to have you and Tommy messing into things any further. You've already done irreparable damage. If there is another murder it will be your fault and yours alone. Do I make myself clear, Nora?"

"We'll see!" she cried and turned to her companions.

After some discussion, Mrs. Deane took up the banner and advanced in Nora's place. "Are you going to tell us what has been done with the money?"

"No," I answered firmly.

"She can't," a voice said from the rear of the crowd. "It's gone."

It was Dave with a nasty cut on the top of his head. A cut that needed immediate attention. Even as he spoke he swayed. Abbie jumped forward and supported him lest he fall.

"I'm all right, Abbie. Head feels a little big, that's all. I could do with a shot of whisky or somehing," he said as he eased himself into a chair.

When the wound was sterilized and covered by a piece of gauze taken from the Club first-aid kit, Abbie asked, "What happened?"

"I don't know. I was up there at the safe trying to make the combination work. I guess I was pretty engrossed, because I didn't hear a thing. I felt a wallop and saw a lot of stars and then, blotto! How long have I been gone?"

"Long enough for things to happen," Abbie replied, ignoring the others. "Jerry's given himself up for arrest."

"What the hell for?" he asked with spirit.

"The committee has been learning things. You have them to thank for your crack on the head."

"Abbie," he said thoughtfully, "those damned fool women are going to spoil everything. Can't some thing be done to muzzle 'em? Can't we use poison, drop 'em in the harbor or just tell them to mind their own business?"

Outraged mutterings followed his query, as I replied, "It's useless Dave. Three people can't back a virtuous organized society."

"But we don't have to talk to them do we?

"Not unless you want to," I agreed.

"Then we won't."

I think Nora and her followers would have left us if young Tommy had not dashed in at the moment crying, "Mama, Mamas We know something else!"

"Hush, baby! Nora cried, but her effort to smother the boy's speech was futile.

"We've been up to Art's!" he announced. "The radio is all busted! There are fingerprints all over everything and the dog is dead!"

"What's that?" Dave asked.

"Spotty is dead," Tommy replied. "He's been shot. We found his body."

Dave leaned forward and beckoned to Tommy, who advanced somewhat hesitantly. "Are you the fellow who looked into the window when we were in the room back there?"

Tommy nodded.

"Smart fellow!" Dave approved. "How many people have you told about the money?"

"Just my mother and the people on the porch."

"How did you happen to go up to Art's?" Dave asked.

"Well, you see we figured Jerry killed Mr. Baldwin, and—"

"Now, why should you think that?" Dave asked.

"It's what everybody is saying. You see, I found some of Jerry's fingerprints in there on the telephone and so I thought I might find some up at Art's," he explained breathlessly.

"When did you go up to Art's?"

"Soon after we saw you with the money in that room."

"Didn't you pass me as I was going toward the boat-shed?"

"Yes. We saw you."

"Tell me, Tommy. Did you see any one near the boat-shed?"

"Only Mr. Taylor, who was walking along the shoreline; nobody else," he replied.

"Thanks, Tommy. Say, that's a nasty scratch on your leg. Where did you get that?"

"I tripped over Mr. Venter's bicycle out back of the Club when you tried to chase us."

"You'd better put some iodine on that scratch," Dave suggested kindly.

"Shucks, it'll be all right."

"Tommy, come here to me!" Nora called. She had taken the iodine from the first aid kit and was ready for the boy.

He screeched as she applied it, but I paid no attention to that as I walked over to Jerry and sat on the arm of his chair. 'Well, they can't accuse you of killing the dog. That's one break" I said.

His reply was a definite shock as he said, "Give them time, Ethel. I was up there."

CHAPTER FIFTEEN

THAT STATEMENT OF Jerry's was all I needed to throw me into a fine quiet fury. I was furious at everybody, including myself, for being too sure of the case and the ideas which had been forming—Nora for interfering in things; Jerry for the calm complacent way he was taking it all; Dave for losing the money. As my fit of annoyance died away I had to admit, in all fairness to Nora and her committee and particularly that youngster of hers, that they had turned up some startling facts which could not be ignored.

We had reached an impasse and every one sensed it. Jerry was on a spot and unless something was done and done quickly he would be put under arrest the moment the police arrived.

Bill Baylis was restless. Even Nora and her cohorts seemed at a loss. They had fired their bolt and were waiting for a counter-charge, but there was nothing for us to do at the moment. I turned to Bill, "Will you find Archie Taylor for me?"

He welcomed the opportunity to get away. "Come on," he suggested to the others.

"And what is going to happen to Jerry?" Mrs. Smith asked.

"I'm going to sit right here," he announced, looking up from his magazine.

"Where could he go?" Bill scoffed. "Don't be silly!"

Most of them made a reluctant if somewhat relieved exit from the lounge. Del Baldwin was perched on the arm of the chair occupied by Pete. As the room cleared she rose after giving Pete's head an affectionate pat and came in our direction. I paid no attention to her but continued to question Jerry.

"When did you go up to Art's?" I asked.

"A little while ago. I took some food up to Spotty. I wanted to take a look at that cut on his head."

"Why on earth did you do that?" I complained.

"You've had your meals today, haven't you? You fixed Walsh's head immediately, didn't you?" he demanded of Abbie.

What could we say? Abbie and I simply looked at him pityingly.

"You seem determined to take the rap for these murders," Dave said. "Ever been in the hoose-gow?"

"Not yet."

"You're not going to like it. You're going to miss your boats and your freedom."

"Not with Abbie and Ethel on the job," he replied with confidence. "That is, unless they believe I'm the murderer."

"Don't be a fool, Jerry," Abbie moaned. "You might kill a man but we know you'd never kill a dog. It isn't a question of what we believe. It's the circumstantial evidence that is piling up against you."

"All of which will have to be proved."

"We can prove where you were between twelve and two," Abbie said. "We've had a talk with Stella. She's determined to give you an alibi."

"That was rotten of you," he accused.

"Have it your way," Abbie said with disgust and turned away.

"Look here, Abbie," he said. "You ought to know why I'm taking this passive attitude. Until we find the real murderer I intend to let Weeks' statement stand about Baldwin being alive at one-thirty. Stella can say anything she likes for any reason she likes but it will do no good."

"Here's Mary," Del warned.

I looked up to see Mary, her father and Sidney coming into the lounge. She came directly to Jerry, who stood up to meet her. "Jerry, what are you doing?" she asked fearfully.

"Nothing," he replied and took her hand in his.

"It's been frightful sitting up there all day," she said, "getting nothing but little bits of information. Why do you let Jerry take the blame?" she flared at us.

"We have no choice in the matter," I said quietly. "There's enough evidence to hang him right now."

"But—"

"Quiet," Abbie warned

Dave moved over to the window and closed it so that our voices would not carry out to the porch for the benefit of listeners

"'Haven't you learned anything? Mary asked.

"Too much and too little," I answered. "We know that four people and possibly five were in Baldwin's room."

"Four or five?" Mary gasped.

"Yes Jerry, you, Pete and an unknown person. Unless one of you killed Baldwin, there is the unknown person and in addition to him a possible fifth."

"I tell you Mary was in that room after me!" Jerry said hotly.

Del had clutched at Pete's arm and was gazing up at him with terrified eyes.

"And Pete thinks he was there after both of you."

Abbie remarked. "Some one did kill him, we know that."

"I told you this morning that I killed him!" Mary cried. "Why go on and on?"

"You mustn't say such things!" Jerry cried. "It's dangerous!"

"But I did it, I tell you," she insisted tearfully.

"Why, oh why did you kill him?" Jerry asked mournfully. For a moment I was convinced that he believed her.

"To get the note, of course," she answered quickly.

"What did you do with it?" he demanded sharply.

"I burned it."

Jerry looked at me in triumph.

"Did you kill Art Tobias, too?" I demanded. "Is that what you did when you were out just before dawn?"

Both she and Jerry were startled by that question.

"I had to do that too," she admitted with a shudder.

"Why?"

"Because when Weeks came up this morning he told us that he had seen Art near the Club. I was afraid he had seen me down here."

"Mary!" Jerry cried. "Do you realize what you're saying?"

"Certainly not!" It was the Judge who spoke up. "The girl is beside herself. She is trying to protect both of us. She doesn't know which of us killed him. She is afraid it might have been either of us."

He turned to me, "I can't let this go on any longer, Ethel. I killed him. I had hoped it would pass as an unsolved crime, but I can't let the children suffer."

"Oh, Father! Don't say it!" Mary sobbed.

Jerry bit his lips to hold back the tears that rimmed his eyes. Pete and Del were shocked. Abbie and Dave favored me with quizzical unbelieving glances.

"When she was out this morning at dawn, she came to see me," the Judge explained. "She was afraid of my hot temper. She knew I had learned her reason for marrying Baldwin."

"And what time were you here?" I asked.

"I don't know exactly. I was in the room looking for the note when Weeks knocked on the door. It was locked, so I slipped away quietly."

Abbie's sigh of relief broke the tension

"You are three adorable fools," I said. "Each of you is afraid that the other one is guilty and you are all willing to take the blame; but don't you realize that since none of you have all the facts your stories do not jell? Judge, Baldwin had been dead for several hours when you were in that room. Jerry is the only one who can reasonably take the blame, because he has the note, but until he can produce about one hundred thousand dollars in cash I won't believe him guilty. Mary was here, but she didn't get the note nor the money. Pete has nothing to prove that he was here; neither have you."

"Then who did kill him?" the Judge demanded.

"I can't say yet," I replied, "but I have some ideas. The best thing for all of you to do is to go home and stay there until the police arrive. Will you do that and say no more about this?"

"I've got to stay here," Jerry announced. "I've given my word."

"Very well, stay here. But, Mary, please take the others and go home," I begged.

"Do it, darling," Jerry advised. "It's going to be all right. Trust Ethel and Abbie."

"We have work to do," I said with a nod to Abbie and Dave. "Remember, you can help most by being quiet."

"I never saw so many people so anxious to go to jail," Dave mumbled as we moved out onto the porch.

Sammy, one of our junior deputies, who had been sitting on the rail leading down to the float, slid from his perch and came trotting toward us.

"How are things aboard the *Starfish*?" I asked.

"Fine."

"Any one been ashore?"

"No, ma'am. All has been quiet. They haven't even looked at the 'you-know.'" His round eyes were full of our shared secret.

"Fine, Sammy. Keep up the watch."

"You betcha," he agreed with an impish wink.

"Where are the other boys?"

"They're looking for Mr. Taylor. He's missing. They're Boy Scouts. They know how to track people the way the Indians did."

"Really!"

"Yes, ma'am. They followed his trail along the shore. They'll find him, I betcha."

"Good, Sammy. We'll be back."

"Okay." He raced back to resume his watch.

"The Boy Scouts will win through for you yet," Dave teased.

"At least we know Graham didn't hit you on the head," I retorted.

"Or kill Spotty," he added.

"Which proves you were right in the first place. Graham may be running aliens into the country but he didn't kill Baldwin."

"You're sure of that? Don't forget the fifty thousand," he warned.

"I'm not. At the moment I'm more interested in what our Boy Scouts are doing."

"Lead on," he cried; "Abbie and I'll bring up the rear."

As we reached the road in back of the shed, a late afternoon sun broke through the clouds, tinting the sky with deep crimson.

"Red sky at night—" Dave started to quote and stopped to say, "I believe your Boy Scouts are there ahead of us."

Teddy and Mike were searching carefully along the edge of the road.

"What's doing?" Dave asked as we approached. The boys looked from Dave to me and refused to answer.

"It's all right. Mr. Walsh is a deputy too," Abbie assured them. "Sammy said you were trailing Mr. Taylor. Any luck?"

"We lost his trail after he came up from the shed," Teddy announced.

"Are you sure he was at the shed?" Dave asked, controlling the excitement in his voice.

"Sure, we followed him along the shore and up to the shed. There were a lot of tracks near the door. His came up here but we lost them. I guess we're not so hot."

"It's hard to follow a trail on a hard surface," Dave consoled. "The Indians couldn't do that themselves."

"We know what happened down by the shed, though," Teddy boasted. "There were three men down there."

For a moment I was seized with a terrible dread. Was there going to be a third murder? "Three?" I asked.

"Yes, ma'am. Two men were wearing sneakers and the third man was wearing hard shoes like Mr. Walsh's."

"I think we'd better take a look at things down by the shed," Dave said quickly.

"You and Abbie go with Teddy. Mike and I will try to pick up a trail along the road," I suggested.

Teddy scampered down the bank through the trees. Mike took up his interrupted searching. I stood at the road edge thinking. As Abbie and Dave went over the bank, I heard him say, "Nice kids."

"You like youngsters, don't you?" she asked.

"You bet. They're smart too. You can't fool 'em much."

"Too bad you didn't marry sooner, Dave, and have a nice family. You seem to understand boys."

"Better than women. I've met a swell girl but she's so bitter and tied up in knots inside that she can't see the forest for the trees."

"Like me?" Abbie asked warmly.

"Exactly like you, stubborn, contrary and all."

"You're too good to waste your thoughts on such a woman. There are plenty of fish in the sea."

"When you've seen the sun, Abbie, nothing else will do."

"That's a nice speech, Dave. I'll remember it."

"I'm glad to know your head is softer than that rock you call a heart."

"You're wrong, Dave. At this moment it's very soft and quite tender in spite of cold reason which tells me not to be a fool. If our deputy wasn't looking up at us with annoyed eyes demanding that we hurry, I believe I'd kiss that funny face of yours and believe the silly things you say."

He reached for her, but she eluded his grasp. He lost his balance, his foot slipped on some soft mud and down he went. He slid several feet before coming to a stop at the bole of a tree.

Abbie's laughter tinkled up to me, gay and warm.

"See what you do to me?" he said as he stood up and most unromantically scraped lumps of mud from the seat of his pants.

Their voices dwindled away. From far off there came a determined ringing of a bell. It had none of the solemn tones of a church bell. It seemed harsher and cheaper. I was wondering about it when Mike came back to me and announced, "That bell is for me. Sounds kinda mad too. I guess I'll catch it. I've got to go. Sorry." He cupped his hands and called, "Hey, Teddy, I gotta go home!"

"Okay. Me, too," Teddy's thin voice answered from below.

Mike trotted away down the road, a valiant little lad, his straight sturdy legs flashing as he increased his pace.

The red glow had faded from the sky. The long twilight had come. Wanting to give Abbie and Dave a little time to themselves, I strolled along the road taking up Mike's search where he had left off.

Some loose stones were the first things to attract my attention as they lay scattered over the pavement. Then I noticed the scarred bank. Some one had climbed the muddy slope. I could see the bruised leaves on a young sapling where the climber had grabbed hold to pull himself up to the bank's rim at the edge of the trees. Here, then, was the trail the boys had missed.

I made several attempts to follow the trail, but could not quite make it. The bank was too steep for me and the sapling too far out of my reach. My spirit was willing but my joints were weak. I felt hobbled as I tried to stretch my leg high enough to get a hold in that slippery mud. It was too much for an old lady. I hate to admit it, but my muscles are slowing down. I retraced my steps for several yards and found a spot where I could climb up onto the dirt ledge. I made my way cautiously along the bank to the sapling and then began some Boy Scouting of my own.

The tracks started up the wooded slope. I found myself regretting the waning light. I moved carefully, sometimes bent nearly double, to watch the footprints.

Have you ever been in the woods alone as darkness approached? I've been in a grove of trees in the heat of an afternoon and had the sudden snap of a twig startle me, but this was different. I was following a murderer's trail and it was growing dark rapidly, or so it seemed in my excitement. The uncanny silence was broken by the drip from the trees. Then there were scurrying noises that I didn't understand, little flickers of movement that seemed untraceable. Twigs snapped, sounding like the reports of guns. My skin grew sensitive to sound, then grew cold with each new unexplainable movement. I've often heard cold sweats described and I remembered thinking them rather inelegant expressions, but that is exactly the way I felt. I was suddenly shivery and uneasy.

I tried to be rational, telling myself that I was tired, that the sounds I heard all had reasonable explanations, that birds, field-mice, chipmunks, squirrels, excited by my presence were scurrying to cover. It was all true, but I didn't believe any of it as I grew tenser with tingling cold that raced up and down my spine.

By that time I felt eyes peering out at me from behind each tree. As I drove myself forward, I was in a nervous fever. I bit my lips to keep from crying out. I looked ahead and on each side of me. I fancied wildcats ready to pounce when I knew there were no wildcats within a hundred miles of me. I was determined to follow that trail as long as I could see, come what might. The tracks veered to the right, leading in the direction of the old sandpit. I was winded by the steady upward trend of the trail.

I paused to rest as I noticed the footprints led up a steeper than usual slope. Feeling a little more secure but still conscious of being watched, I started forward once more.

A sharp cracking sound made me look up. What I saw struck tenor into my heart. A huge boulder was bounding down the slope, headed straight for me. I thought it must have been loosened by the rain until I realized a second, and even a third, had started down.

For one moment I fancied myself crushed to the earth. I was in a relatively open spot free from shelter. The larger trees seemed miles away but they were my only salvation. I turned left and started to run. The rocks were almost on me when I was within a foot or two of the big trees. Gasping, frantic, I tried to increase my speed. My foot caught in a tangle of vine and I fell headlong. For one terrible moment I held my breath and then on hands and knees crawled forward as the first and largest of the rocks hurtled past me, leaving an eddy of cold wind behind it. The others followed. A smaller one smashed into the tree, which sheltered me. They thudded and crashed on down the slope. I waited until the woods had grown still again, solemnly, profoundly quiet.

I knew the general direction of the road which meant comparative safety. With cautious glances up the hill, I moved forward, always keeping a tree between me and that deadly slope.

I feared crossing an open space in the trees, for I fully expected to hear the zing of a bullet. Breathless, torn and bruised, dirty and hatless, I finally reached the safety of the road, and with dignity cast to the winds I ran as fast as my legs could carry me.

I paused once behind the shed to look up through the trees and my heart stood still. Jerry was there darting through the brush, moving hastily and furtively toward his own house.

CHAPTER SIXTEEN

IT WAS TWENTY MINUTES after seven when I stumbled up the stairs and stood panting for breath in the little kitchen. Dave and Abbie were preparing supper. They were so completely absorbed in each other that they failed to notice my disheveled condition. It was Pete, limping back from the front windows who asked "Where have you been, Ethel? In a mud fight?"

I offered no explanations I wanted to think before I told them what had happened. It was inconceivable that Jerry of all people had hurled those boulders down the hillside at me, yet he had been there and could have done it so easily. Why had he been prowling about on that hill when he was supposed to have been sitting at the Club more or less under arrest? One moment I told myself he wouldn't do a thing like that, and the next moment I knew perfectly well that you cannot predict what a person will do when they are motivated by fear and the consequences of their acts.

As I showered, I knew I'd have to have it out with Jerry immediately. There was only one point in his favor—the fact that nothing had been done to peril the lives of Dave and Abbie. Jerry, of all people on the island, knew the common knowledge held by the three of us.

They were very sweet when I finished telling them of my adventure in the woods.

"Are you sure you're all right?" Dave asked with real concern.

"He meant to kill you," Abbie said thoughtfully, a misty film over her eyes.

She was really fond of me. I glowed at the knowledge. I can think of no greater reward for a long life than genuine love and affection.

"You'd better sit tight, Ethel," Pete advised.

"We must all be careful," I cautioned. "We know too much for the murderer's comfort. He credits us with more clues than we seem to have. Don't go out alone, any of you, and whatever you do or wherever you are, for heaven's sake, be on your guard."

We were interrupted by a murmur of voices from below. Standing at the foot of the stairs, a group of people surrounded Archie Taylor. In the half-light he seemed dazed and helpless, gave me the impression of being buffeted by the excited group that hemmed him in.

Bill Baylis came up the stairs. He was excited and afraid. "You've got to do something!" he said between catches of breath. "That crowd is getting unreasonable, they'll be out of hand in no time. You know what mobs are!"

"But why?" Dave asked.

"We found him up beyond Art's house out on the ridge. He had a packet of bills in his pocket which he said he had found. He was down toward the rocks and the crowd thinks he had been hiding the money. "We couldn't find any more of the packets, but they still won't believe that he found the bills. They've been pretty rough with him and I'm afraid, Ethel. They're in a lynching mood. We can't have that happen. There are a lot of granters down there now and the excitement is boiling over. Do something, will you?"

I darted into the house and brought back the clothes I had been wearing earlier in the afternoon. With them over my arm, I followed Bill down the steps. Archie looked up at me, a plea for help in his eyes.

"What's going on?" I demanded.

"We've caught your murderer!" several voices shouted.

"That's fine. I hope you're right," I replied.

"He had the money on him!" some one cried, yanking Archie forward.

"I found it just beyond Art's house, Ethel," he protested.

"He's lying. He was hiding it!"

"Wait, wait!" I cried as a fist thudded into Archie's back. The courage of cowards in a crowd is a fearful and appalling thing. While Archie was a slight man and a rather meek one, I doubt if any of the men who mauled and shoved him about would have faced him alone in single combat.

"What's the good of waiting? We've been waiting all day!" some one growled up at me.

"That's right! We've got to take steps ourselves. We're all in danger now!" The voice was frenzied, had an incendiary quality about it. I was afraid of their mood as shouts greeted the remark.

"And do you have conclusive proof, any of you?" I demanded. "Who started this frenzy? Which one of you is trying to cover your own guilt by accusing this man?" They exchanged hurried suspicious glances. "We are not a law unto ourselves yet. The police are on their way here. Would you have them find us committing a great atrocity?"

"Then, why don't you tell us what you know?" a deep voice growled.

"I would if I knew anything to tell you. I'd tell you gladly. Not a half-hour ago the murderer tried to kill me! When did you find Archie?" I asked Bill.

"It was about seven o'clock," he replied.

"That's right," several voices agreed.

"And where was he?"

"Down on the point beyond Tobias' house poking about in the rocks."

"Then listen to this," I cried, and related my experience in the woods. "Don't you see," I ended, "that Archie couldn't have been in two places at once? The real murderer tried to kill me because he thinks I know too much. It was probably between five and ten minutes after seven that the rocks were loosened at the top of the hill. Archie was with you at that time."

"I told you I saw some one in the trees up in back of the Tobias house," a voice complained to Bill, but you wouldn't believe me."

"Who was it?" I asked quickly.

"I couldn't see clearly. It was like a shadow flickering through the trees.

I knew exactly what the man meant. Jerry had been darting from tree to tree when I spied him.

"That was your man," I announced with as much force as I could. "Archie didn't have the money. We know that he came as far as the shed door, then turned away." I looked directly at Archie. "Which way did you go?"

"I went back to the shore and followed the cove to a point opposite Art's house and climbed the hill from there."

"Why did you come up to the shed?" Dave asked.

"I had seen you on the shore ahead of me. I wanted to talk to you. When I got to the shed door over there, everything was quiet and still. I considered a moment. Then I heard a window raised or lowered. I changed my mind. That's all."

"And you saw no one?" Dave asked.

"Absolutely no one. I listened, expecting to hear you moving about, but there was no sound. I thought you had decided to take a nap."

"I did," Dave said grimly, "but the decision was made for me."

The crowd had grown sheepish. "Leave Archie here," I suggested. "We want to talk to him. Go home and have your suppers; by that time the police should be here."

They wandered off, fading into the deepening night.

When we were alone we went into the shed. Just beyond the safe one of the windows stood open. Archie had been right. The thief had gone that way.

"This rather proves that the thief and murderer are one," I said.

"Not necessarily," Dave objected. "How about the footprints the kids were trying to follow?" he asked.

I looked down at Archie's feet. He was wearing a pair of sneakers. "Did you walk up toward the road?"

"Yes, as far as the drive, then turned round and went back to the shore, as I told you."

"Then the trail you followed was left by the murderer," Abbie said. "Since he got away from here without being seen, what was he doing up near Art's, where he must have lost the money?"

"He went up there to kill the dog. He may have seen Archie, probably did. I don't know but I believe the arrival of Bill and those people undoubtedly saved your life, Archie."

"But I had seen no one!" Archie protested.

"But he didn't know that. You must have missed seeing him by seconds."

"Listen!" Pete cried. "Quiet!"

There was no mistake about it. From somewhere there came the steady throb of a motor. The next moment there was a flash of light as a beam swept across the entrance to the channel.

"It's the police at last!" Abbie cried with relief.

As we hurried down toward the Club I rather dreaded the things which were ahead of us. There was so much unfinished business, so many threads that petered out, too many things that led directly back to Jerry. He may have shoved the boulders down on me, which I doubted after I had had time to think about it, but he certainly had not killed Art's dog, and I didn't believe he had the money. That was the one thing in his favor. He had plenty of money of his own. And yet the crimes seemed to rest between Jerry and Graham; but Graham had not killed the dog either, because according to Sammy no one had left the *Starfish* during the time that Spotty must have been shot.

A homicide squad in charge of a man by the name of Warburton was at work when we arrived. There were a few scattered groups in the lounge, moving about and talking self-consciously because of the attendant policemen. Jerry, sitting alone in one of the large chairs near the fireplace, had difficulty managing a magazine because of the handcuffs on his wrists.

I marched in Jerry's direction, to be met physically by the strong arm of the law, which gently but forcibly held me back. "You can't talk to the prisoner," the policeman said.

"And who says I can't?" I demanded.

"I did." A clear strong voice carried across the room.

The policeman's arm went down and I proceeded toward Jerry. "What does this mean?" I asked.

Jerry looked up at me and smiled. "Don't get excited, Ethel. I submitted to arrest willingly, or at least this form of it. Warburton, here, was on a spot immediately upon his arrival. Nora and the Graces insisted upon my official arrest and since they seemed to be a representative committee, he didn't know what to do."

"Of all the fool things!" I stormed.

"You, I take it, are the famous Ethel Thomas," the clear voice said just behind me. "I'm Philip Warburton, in charge."

"Then take those things off him," I demanded.

Warburton laughed tolerantly. "He doesn't mind," he said, "and some of the ladies seem to feel more comfortable now that he is manacled."

"Ladies!" I sniffed.

"It's a safe term until one is sure," he said quietly with an amused chuckle behind the words.

I looked up at the man. He had a frank pair of dark eyes that looked directly at you when he spoke and his voice was most pleasant. A dark lock of hair had an intriguing habit of falling over his left eye, making him look more like a faun than a policeman. His last remark assured me that he had a sense of humor, for which I was later to be very thankful.

I introduced Abbie and Dave and said, "You've been listening to considerable misinformation or you wouldn't have done that." I pointed at Jerry and the manacles.

"We try to please all comers," he said. "What have you to tell us?"

"Plenty—for your ears alone," I added as I saw the scattered groups converging on us.

"Clear the room, Buck," he ordered quietly.

Abbie, Dave and I took turns telling the story.

As we talked, I realized anew that our time had been so crammed full of excitement from the moment Weeks had called at the shed that we none of us had had a chance to sit down and think things out. Dave, of course, had been doing some thinking on his own account, but he later confessed that most of his thoughts had been centered on Abbie. She had been as busy as I had and we really had not properly discussed the case at all.

That retelling of the day's activities to an intelligent and appreciative listener who interrupted only to ask apt questions, gave me a new perspective on the situation.

What we did was to give him a bare outline of the main events of the day's work. As we talked, little things crept into my mind, incidents that had happened, bits I had observed at the time but to which I had attached no importance, episodes which even then, in the recounting, had no place in the straight line of our story. Unimportant as they seemed in the telling, they became more and more significant to me.

At last I was beginning to get a picture of the problem. As each crooked bit fitted into place, the case began to take definite form and shape, the picture of the crime was emerging.

We told Warburton every important thing that had happened during the day, omitting nothing.

When we had, finished he said very gravely, "I gather from what you have said and more particularly from the things you have left unsaid, that you are firmly convinced that this Jerry Carter chap is not the murderer."

"He couldn't have done it," I stated flatly, my mind on the new theory which was developing.

"And while you are quite convinced that Graham has been running aliens into the country you are not sure about him as a murderer."

"Right," Dave agreed.

"And you don't seem to be too sure about this man Taylor, who probably hated Baldwin, had a quarrel with him yesterday afternoon, had the opportunity and was more or less in need of money."

"In other words," Abbie said dryly, "we've worked like dogs all day and have accomplished nothing."

"I wouldn't say that." Warburton turned to her with a smile. "You've accomplished a great deal. From all these facts, we must certainly ought to be able to find the murderer. What goes on behind those sharp eyes of yours, Miss Thomas?"

"An idea, nothing more, but if you're willing to cooperate I think it may work. I'd like to try something— put a plan in operation. It's not a policeman's method, but if you'll bear with me I think I can give you the answer to the riddle; that is, if you'll let me do it in my woman's way."

"Women have been running the world for a good many years, in one way or another. I don't see that we can lose anything. What do you want?"

"I'd like to take all the people concerned up to Baldwin's house."

"Just what people do you want?"

"I particularly want Archie Taylor, Graham, all of us, Weeks, Stella Ketcham and of course the people who live at the house."

"And do you want to let me in on your plans, Miss Thomas?"

"If you don't mind, I'd rather do it my way. You'd be going up there to question them, anyhow, wouldn't you?" He nodded. "And it wouldn't seem too irregular, would it, if you pretended to be carrying on the investigation, up there while your men were going through the routine work down here?"

"Not at all. I'll take a couple of the men with me. Where are these people you want?"

"Graham's coming through the door now—there—the big man. Dave, will you get Stella and Archie?"

"And how about Carter?" Warburton asked.

"I want him, of course. In fact, I want him handcuffed when you take him up there."

"But I thought you didn't approve of his arrest?"

"I didn't say anything about approving. I am merely asking you to keep him handcuffed."

"You might as well do as she asks," Dave grinned, "because she has a way of managing things."

As soon as Warburton agreed, I turned to Jerry and asked, "Could you, or any one else who understood how to do it, sink the *Albatross* easily?"

He was amazed at the question and considered a moment. "Yes. There are two ways. The packing around the propeller-shaft could be loosened, or there is a bung that could be knocked out if you knew where to find it."

"Good. Let's get going," I said to Warburton.

Jerry was a little skittish about going up the hill in the handcuffs, but gave in when I told him that I felt quite confident it would help us to find the real murderer.

We made quite a cavalcade as we started up the hill.

"How about the camp-followers?" Warburton asked.

"Let them trail along," I said. "After all, it's really their show."

We wound our way up the hill, flashlights gleaming in the darkness. "Looks like something out of the French Revolution," he commented as he paused once to look back.

"What are you up to?" Dave queried at my elbow.

"I'm not exactly sure, Dave. My little plan may miscarry. When we get to the house I want you, with the aid of one of Warburton's men, to keep all but the principals out of the living-room."

"How about our friends, The Three Graces?"

"Let 'em in. I'd like to see 'em squirm," I said with some anticipatory relish.

CHAPTER SEVENTEEN

WARBURTON WAS very, decent about helping me. When we were settled in the large living-room he made a few opening remarks explaining that I would go over certain phases of the murder so that all concerned in it would have a clear picture of what had happened. The porch was crowded with curious islanders who thronged at the windows wondering what was going on. Those in the room were somewhat nervous and fidgety, because Warburton emphasized the point that only those present were actively concerned in the actual crimes. There were shifting and speculative glances as they stole sly looks at one another.

While Warburton talked, I took Clara to one side to ask her if she had found any wet clothing anywhere in the house. Just as I had expected, she reported failure. As I stepped back into the center of the room he turned and said, "Now, Miss Thomas, the stage is yours."

I felt like a club woman about to make a speech on Garden Pests or something like that as I looked over my audience. They were a strange group. Mary's eyes were weighted with fear and dread as she tried not to look at the handcuffs on Jerry's wrists. The Judge actually squirmed nervously. Pete and Del were sitting on a love-seat. He gripped one of her hands tightly. Mrs. Dunn, her dark eyes more brooding than ever, watched Del and Pete. Stella had a new reason for living. She seemed intensely interested in the handsome Warburton and I must admit I couldn't blame her too much for that, he was a woman's man. Sidney stood near the fireplace watching Graham, who more than filled the Empire chair in which he sat. Dave and Abbie were together, leaning forward with the absorbed interest you see on the faces of theater lovers during that brief moment between the lowering of the lights and the rising of the curtain. The Three Graces righteously occupied a couch and had been making whispering speculations as they evidently commented on Jerry's rather tolerant and definitely brazen attitude. He most certainly was not playing the part of an arrested and practically condemned man.

"Will you kindly take those handcuffs off Mr. Carter?" I demanded as an opening speech.

Warburton had had no cues from me, but I must say he played his part well. He was properly hesitant, a frown puckering his brow, as he looked from me to Jerry.

"He is not the murderer," I insisted.

With a shrug that seemed to imply a reluctant willingness to humor me, he opened the manacles and dropped them into his pocket. I heard Mary give a sigh of relief.

"Can you name the real murderer, Miss Thomas?" Warburton asked.

"We'll come to that by the process of elimination. I have your permission to go ahead?" I asked.

He smiled warmly. I heard Nora Baylis sniff disgustedly.

When I announced, "Three people in this room have admitted they killed Baldwin," the entire group was more startled than I expected them to be. I could see a fine light of speculation and surprise in more than half the eyes as they waited for me to mention names.

"Three!" Warburton echoed the number.

"Yes, three. Unfortunately, however, none of the self-confessed murderers are guilty."

"How does she know?" I heard Nora's high tense whisper demand of Mrs. Deane.

"You are sure of that?" Warburton asked calmly.

"Yes. Because of information which Miss Abernathy, Mr. Walsh and I possess we know each of these admitted murderers was telling a lie to save some one they loved. If any of the three could definitely prove that they killed Baldwin you could close the case," I said to Warburton.

"A murderer doesn't usually try. He leaves that to the State," he smiled in reply.

"Then in this case the State must prove them innocent in order to get the real criminal. We have a great weight of damning and conflicting evidence. I think you'll find, Mr. Warburton, that both Baldwin and Tobias were killed with Jerry Carter's revolver, which was taken from the top of his duffle-bag yesterday while it sat at the head of the pier. Your ballistics experts will be able to prove that point. They will also undoubtedly prove that the gun used to kill Tobias' dog later in the day was of another caliber. I mention these facts because I know how black they may make the case against Jerry Carter if it is ever taken to court. I hope the case, however, never reaches the courts. I have heard it said that all criminals make a mistake. That may be true, but I wouldn't venture an opinion on that point. I would rather say that circumstances often spoil the best-laid plans. It is the unexpected event in this case which will, I hope, bring the criminal to justice.

"The most significant character, in this entire drama has been the dog, Spotty. Actually we are faced with three murders, two men and a devoted dog. The dog links the entire case into a strong whole. When the plan for Baldwin's death was made, there was no reason for the murderer to think of either Tobias or his dog, but the moment the murderer learned that Spotty was near the Club last night he became terrified because he knew, as every one on this island knows, that Spotty was never very far from his master at any time."

"Then you think the murderer saw the dog?" Warburton asked.

"I don't know. I'm inclined to think he learned of that later. There is another point which I think I can prove to your satisfaction, and is, I'm sure, important. The murderer was either naked at the time of the murders or wore only a pair of swimming trunks."

There was a gasp of surprise from Nora and her satellites which implied that I was not being quite nice.

Graham moved unexpectedly, making the chair creak under him.

"I know of one person who was in the water just prior to the murder, a person who probably had ample motive for the crime. What have you to say for yourself, Mr. Graham?"

There was a ripple of excited interest as he ignored me completely and spoke to Warburton, demanding, "Are you going to let a crack-brained old woman befuddle the issue in this case because she doesn't want her friend arrested for murder?"

"We'll wait and see what Miss Thomas has to say before we judge the quality of her mind," Warburton replied. "Better answer her question."

"I won't submit to it," Graham protested.

I saw his fists clench. He was ready to fight. "Don't excite yourself, Mr. Graham. Perhaps you can explain everything. You were in the water right after the *Starfish* arrived. Did you slip ashore to shoot Baldwin?"

"How could I have carried the gun?" he scoffed.

"You could have protected the gun in the same way you protected the money which you dropped astern of the *Starfish* just after your unsuccessful attempt to get away," I replied quickly.

"I don't know what you're talking about!" he shouted in quick denial.

"Oh, yes, you do! When you were quite sure you were not being watched you lowered a bundle under the stern of your boat. That bundle contained a lot of money, Mr. Graham, and we happen to know that fifty thousand dollars was stolen from Baldwin."

Graham was in a corner then and he knew it. He had to explain that money or be labeled as the most likely suspect after Jerry. He looked from me to Warburton as he considered for a. moment.

"All right. I did try to hide some money, because I knew what you and the police would think if you found that amount aboard my boat."

"That's a lot of money to carry around, Graham," Warburton said.

"You need a lot of money when you're living on a boat," he retorted.

I turned to Warburton. "If Graham didn't take the money from Baldwin, he was prepared to pay that amount to Baldwin this morning at breakfast."

"What?" Warburton gasped.

"You're crazy!" Graham shouted.

"Just a minute," I said. "Mr. Graham, if you can explain the fifty thousand dollars in any reasonable way we will be forced to withdraw the murder charge."

He glared at me sullenly.

"Do you mean to say that it is possible that one hundred thousand dollars is involved in this case?" Warburton demanded.

"It is quite possible," I replied. "I will help Mr. Graham refresh his memory. You brought four passengers with you last night, Mr. Graham. Why did Baldwin mention ten in the message he radioed to you?" I waited but he refused to answer my question "Didn't you owe Baldwin some money, wasn't there the possibility of a quarrel between you because you had failed to pay?"

"Pay for what?" Warburton demanded.

"For the illegal entry of aliens into this country," I replied. I hurried on to explain the records we had discovered relative to the arrival of the *Starfish* and her passengers who always went to the mainland.

"So you squealed, you dirty little rat!" Graham shouted.

He was out of his chair, on his feet and dashing toward Sidney, all in a split second.

Dave acted very quickly. If he had not, I don't know what would have happened. Dave's foot shot out, Graham tripped and crashed to the floor. Warburton's two men were on Graham the next instant. There was a brief struggle before they succeeded in getting handcuffs on him. He shook his manacled fists in my face and stormed,

"All right, old girl, I'll take the rap for the aliens if you can prove it, but you can't pin the murder on me because I didn't do it. If Carter's gun was stolen, how would I have got hold of it when I didn't arrive at the Harbor until nearly midnight? You're so smart, answer that one!"

"I merely said I believed Baldwin and Tobias had been killed with Carter's gun. I may be wrong," I reminded him.

"She is wrong! I didn't kill them!" He was desperate, afraid for his life as he cried to Warburton. "She's right about the aliens. That was a racket Baldwin and I had between us. That's why he came to Hidden Harbor, why he bought this swell house, why he wanted to marry the Verity girl because he felt the name of the Judge as a father-in-law would add to our safety. I did have fifty thousand dollars on board last night. It was to pay for the four people who came in and for some I owed Baldwin. When they told me about the missing money I naturally tried to protect myself. Why should I kill Baldwin? Why should I do anything which would spoil our business? If I wanted to kill him you don't suppose I'd do it here, do you, where it would he sure to get me in a mess as it has done?" he regretted dolefully.

Warburton turned to me, wondering what my next step would be.

"Did you leave the ship this afternoon after Miss Abernathy and I went aboard?" I asked.

"No."

"Had you discovered the loss of your money?"

"No."

"Why did you try to leave the Harbor this morning?"

"Because I thought if I could get out and bring help it would keep suspicion away from me and my reason for being at the Harbor."

It was a good reason and frankly given. It was what I expected. At my thoughtful silence he cried, "Why pick on me alone? Why not—"

"Just a minute, Mr. Graham. Let me do this," I interrupted.

The next moment, as I called Mrs. Dunn by name, I caught a gleam of understanding in his eyes. He was remembering what he had told me about her and Del. He was, I think, disappointed when I asked Mrs. Dunn for her house keys.

She was surprised, and of course had no idea what I had in mind. She handed the keys to me readily enough. "Which," I asked, "is the key to the wine vault?"

She ran over the bunch of keys and then, quite as if she didn't believe her eyes, went over them one by one carefully. "It isn't here," she said, truly puzzled.

"When was the last time you had it?"

"It was on the ring yesterday, I'm sure of that," she insisted.

"And so am I," I agreed. I turned to Warburton. "Would you like to make the arrest now or would you rather I proved my point first?"

There was a general murmur of surprise at my question.

"If you can," he said.

"I hope you will agree with me that the murder was planned to take advantage of Jerry's homecoming yesterday." He gave a slight nod. "When Jerry, in the excitement of his arrival, left his duffle at the head of the pier, he unwittingly gave the murderer an unexpected opportunity, to make the case even tighter against him. The gun which was left on top of the bag was an opportunity the murderer could not afford to miss. The taking of the gun may have been a mistake, but if it was, the murderer could not have known it at the moment. He was too obsessed with his plan, too delighted with the march of events which would keep suspicion from him and fasten the guilt on an innocent man.

"When the unexpected arrival of the *Starfish* made it necessary for Baldwin to transfer the party from the Club to this house, the murderer must have been delighted.

The tension between Baldwin and Jerry was bound to be increased. It was. Jerry learned the reason for Mary's sudden marriage to Baldwin. Mary also learned how Baldwin had tricked her. The Judge, too, knew of the situation. Those three people were truly outraged. The murderer must have chuckled with glee as he saw events shaping themselves to aid his plans. He knew then that there would be more than one possible suspect once Baldwin had been killed. The money, too, was important. Jerry and the Judge were the only people who were supposed to know of the fifty thousand dollars which Baldwin carried in his pocket.

The theft of the money was not part of the original plan. That, I believe came later. The murderer was on the porch of this house at the time Baldwin showed Jerry and the Judge the money. I cannot prove the point but I'm firmly convinced that the murderer saw the money through the library window."

"Who was on the porch at that time? Who is the murderer?" Warburton demanded eagerly.

Every person in the room leaned forward as they waited for my answer. The place was strangely quiet in the dull flickering light of the candles as I said, "Let me give you the case first as I see it. Let the facts and bits of evidence speak for themselves."

"She's stalling!" Graham grumbled.

"She doesn't know!" Nora whispered with satisfaction.

"Go on, Miss Thomas," Warburton suggested soberly.

There was a general fidgeting and a readjusting of positions as they looked from me to Mrs. Dunn, who was standing apart and truly bewildered because of the questions I had asked her.

"Mrs. Dunn's keys are a very important link in the story of the crime. The fact that one key is missing—the only key which would give the murderer an easy way of entering and leaving the house unobserved—narrows our suspects down to those people who were thoroughly familiar with the house and the wine vault."

"I do not have the key. I don't know what could have happened to it," Mrs. Dunn said, looking at me helplessly.

Del stood up and crossed to the mantel. She ran her fingers along the edge until she found what she was looking for. She turned to me and said, "Is this the key?"

I, in turn, handed it to Mrs. Dunn, who looked at it and said quietly, "That is the key."

Del faced us defiantly. For a fleeting moment I saw a look in Mrs. Dunn's eyes which seemed to plead for the girl to keep silent, but Del ignored that mute appeal. "She didn't kill him! She didn't leave the house last night. She begged me not to go out! She was with me when I returned. She had nothing to do with this murder." Dell crossed to Mrs. Dunn and put her arms protectingly about the older woman.

Del's statement about being out caused a stir. I saw no reason for an exposé of the Del-Mrs. Dunn situation and asked quickly, "How did you know the key was on the shelf?"

"I saw it there a short time ago when I reached up to get a candle."

"Have you any idea who put it there?"

Pete stood up and limped to a position beside Del. "You're not trying to pin this on Del, are you?" he demanded. "Because—"

I had to think quickly. There had been three confessions and I didn't want another false one just then. I ignored his question and said to Warburton, "May I borrow one of your men?"

At a signal from him one of the men stepped forward. Archie Taylor was startled as I called his name, tossed the key toward him, saying as he clutched it out of the air, "You know this house, Archie, since you built it for yourself. Take some candles and go down to the wine vault with this man and see what you can find."

As Archie and the policeman, hurricane-lamps in their hands, disappeared into the library, I continued, "Weeks came up here early this morning when it was still dark. He told the members of this household of the murder. He also told them he had seen Art Tobias' dog in the neighborhood of the Club shortly after twelve last night. Am I right, Weeks?"

"Yes, ma'am," Weeks agreed.

"That, then, was the first intimation the murderer had that his plans had miscarried. Tobias, because of the dog, became a menace to his safety. Tobias had to be silenced if silence was necessary. Weeks' statement sounded Tobias' death-warrant. Because he was killed we can be sure that his silence had to be assured. Can you imagine the murderer's feelings as he thought of the slip-up in his plans? Can you picture the fear and agony he endured wondering about Tobias and what he might have seen? Because she feared that the Judge might have killed Baldwin, Mary went out of this house this morning."

"That's not necessary!" Jerry cried in protest.

"I think it is," I replied crisply, "because it proves to my satisfaction that the second murder was committed between the time Weeks left here and our later arrival. It proves that Mary and the Judge had nothing to do with the second death and therefore did not kill Baldwin."

Jerry sank back with a sigh of relief.

"Could the murderer have gone from here to Tobias' house in the time you mention?" Warburton asked.

"Definitely. I don't know how much time elapsed, but it must have been at least an hour."

"It was longer than that," Del offered. "Wasn't it, Mary?"

"I don't know," Mary replied. "We went upstairs as soon as Weeks left. You tried to sleep, then came into my room and we talked for some time before we came down here to light the fire. It was cold upstairs," she explained to me.

"And the fire had been burning for some time before they came," Del added.

"Are you basing your theory on that time element?" Warburton asked, and I think from his tone he felt a little uneasy.

"Yes. That and other things. I am confident that the murderer was on the porch last night when Baldwin was showing the money to Jerry, and the Judge. That gave him a further incentive to kill Baldwin last night."

No one will ever know the relief I felt as I saw Archie and the policeman come out of the library, their hands full of things other than the lamps they carried. All eyes were on them as they moved forward to the couch and dropped a large manila envelope, the oiled silk which contained the money we had taken from the floor of the harbor at the rear of the *Starfish*, some rubber bathing-shoes, mud-covered sneakers and a pair of dark maroon tights. I had been watching the person I suspected to note the effect upon him. He was quicker than I expected him to be. Up to the moment the things were being deposited on the couch, he made no move which would make me sure that all my suspicions had been right. Under his unassuming manner he possessed a cold nerve and a will of iron I've never seen such self-control.

He made one quick swift move. "Stop him!" I cried, but my warning came too late. The library door slammed shut and a bolt was driven home. The next moment there was the dull report of a shot which told me that the mystery at Hidden Harbor was over.

"Not Sidney!" Del cried, and turned to sob into Mrs. Dunn's arms while Pete patted her reassuringly on the back.

"How did you know?" Warburton asked.

"He was on the porch last night when Baldwin and the others were in the library. He had the keys to the wine vault. I saw Mrs. Dunn give them to him when the guests arrived. He had been out in the rain last night because I quite accidentally put my hand on the couch where he had been sitting when we arrived and the upholstery was damp where his head had rested. When the girls came down here they made no mention of Sidney being with them."

"He joined us just a few minutes before you arrived," Mary said.

"Pretty flimsy evidence with which to catch the murderer," Warburton said.

"Oh, there were other things. When you examine his body you will notice a red welt on his hand. That, I think, was a scratch received from Spotty. Also this afternoon when I asked him if he had seen any one at the rear of the Club, he said, "No." We know he was there because Tommy Baylis hurt his leg when he fell over Sidney's bicycle. Sidney also denied knowing anything about the money we found and yet he was in the group when Tom told his mother what he had seen. Sidney also denied all knowledge of Baldwin's real business a connection with Graham. What his reason was I do not know any more than I know the real reason for the murder. It was probably a long hatred and avarice born at the sight of the fifty thousand dollars."

The policemen, who had gone round the house to get into the library, opened the door. "I think you had better leave now," Warburton suggested. "There is no further reason for your being here."

They tell me that romance has no place in a mystery story, but that amuses me no end. As a matter of fact, the climax to the strange happenings in so many ways reminded me of the end of an old-fashioned musical comedy. There were three weddings.

Abbie and Dave. They are settled in a New York apartment. Abbie is going on with her work as special investigator and there is talk of Dave's quitting the paper to take a hand in her business, which is growing out of all bounds.

Pete and Del are married and living in the Taylor place. Pete is in his seventh heaven. Del's money has made it possible for him to remodel the shed and he is now the owner of a fairly respectable yacht-building buiness.

Jerry and Mary were married quietly and left for southern waters on the refitted *Albatross*.

THE END

Resurrected Press Books in *The Chief Inspector Pointer Mystery* Series

MYSTERIES BY ANNE AUSTIN

Murder at Bridge

When an afternoon bridge party attended by some of Hamilton's leading citizens ends with the hostess being murdered in her boudoir, Special Investigator Dundee of the District Attorney's office is called in. But one of the attendees is guilty? There are plenty of suspects: the victim's former lover, her current suitor, the retired judge who is being blackmailed, the victim's maid who had been horribly disfigured accidentally by the murdered woman, or any of the women who's husbands had flirted with the victim. Or was she murdered by an outsider whose motive had nothing to do with the town of Hamilton. Find the answer in... **Murder at Bridge**

One Drop of Blood

When Dr. Koenig, head of Mayfield Sanitarium is murdered, the District Attorney's Special Investigator, "Bonnie" Dundee must go undercover to find the killer. Were any of the inmates of the asylum insane enough to have committed the crime? Or, was it one of the staff, motivated by jealousy? And what was is the secret in the murdered man's past. Find the answer in... **One Drop of Blood**

AVAILABLE FROM RESURRECTED PRESS!

GEMS OF MYSTERY
LOST JEWELS FROM A MORE ELEGANT AGE

Three wonderful tales of mystery from some of the best known writers of the period before the First World War -

A foggy London night, a Russian princess who steals jewels, a corpse; a mysterious murder, an opera singer, and stolen pearls; two young people who crash a masked ball only to find themselves caught up in a daring theft of jewels; these are the subjects of this collection of entertaining tales of love, jewels, and mystery. This collection includes:

- **In the Fog - by Richard Harding Davis's**

- **The Affair at the Hotel Semiramis - by A.E.W. Mason**

- **Hearts and Masks - Harold MacGrath**

AVAILABLE FROM RESURRECTED PRESS!

THE EDWARDIAN DETECTIVES
LITERARY SLEUTHS OF THE EDWARDIAN ERA

The exploits of the great Victorian Detectives, Poe's C. Auguste Dupin, Gaboriau's Lecoq, and most famously, Arthur Conan Doyle's Sherlock Holmes, are well known. But what of those fictional detectives that came after, those of the Edwardian Age? The period between the death of Queen Victoria and the First World War had been called the Golden Age of the detective short story, but how familiar is the modern reader with the sleuths of this era? And such an extraordinary group they were, including in their numbers an unassuming English priest, a blind man, a master of disguises, a lecturer in medical jurisprudence, a noble woman working for Scotland Yard, and a savant so brilliant he was known as "The Thinking Machine."

To introduce readers to these detectives, Resurrected Press has assembled a collection of stories featuring these and other remarkable sleuths in The Edwardian Detectives.

- The Case of Laker, Absconded by Arthur Morrison
- The Fenchurch Street Mystery by Baroness Orczy
- The Crime of the French Café by Nick Carter
- The Man with Nailed Shoes by R Austin Freeman
- The Blue Cross by G. K. Chesterton
- The Case of the Pocket Diary Found in the Snow by Augusta Groner
- The Ninescore Mystery by Baroness Orczy
- The Riddle of the Ninth Finger by Thomas W. Hanshew
- The Knight's Cross Signal Problem by Ernest Bramah

- The Problem of Cell 13 by Jacques Futrelle
- The Conundrum of the Golf Links by Percy James Brebner
- The Silkworms of Florence by Clifford Ashdown
- The Gateway of the Monster by William Hope Hodgson
- The Affair at the Semiramis Hotel by A. E. W. Mason
- The Affair of the Avalanche Bicycle & Tyre Co., LTD by Arthur Morrison

RESURRECTED PRESS CLASSIC
MYSTERY CATALOGUE

Journeys into Mystery
Travel and Mystery in a More Elegant Time

The Edwardian Detectives
Literary Sleuths of the Edwardian Era

Gems of Mystery
Lost Jewels from a More Elegant Age

E. C. Bentley
Trent's Last Case: The Woman in Black

Ernest Bramah
Max Carrados Resurrected:
The Detective Stories of Max Carrados

Agatha Christie
The Secret Adversary
The Mysterious Affair at Styles

Octavus Roy Cohen
Midnight

Freeman Wills Croft
The Ponson Case
The Pit Prop Syndicate

J. S. Fletcher
The Herapath Property
The Rayner-Slade Amalgamation
The Chestermarke Instinct
The Paradise Mystery
Dead Men's Money

The Middle of Things
Ravensdene Court
Scarhaven Keep
The Orange-Yellow Diamond
The Middle Temple Murder
The Tallyrand Maxim
The Borough Treasurer
In the Mayor's Parlour
The Saftey Pin

R. Austin Freeman
*The Mystery of 31 New Inn from the Dr. Thorndyke
Series*
*John Thorndyke's Cases from the Dr. Thorndyke
Series*
The Red Thumb Mark from The Dr. Thorndyke Series
The Eye of Osiris from The Dr. Thorndyke Series
A Silent Witness from the Dr. John Thorndyke Series
The Cat's Eye from the Dr. John Thorndyke Series
*Helen Vardon's Confession: A Dr. John Thorndyke
Story*
As a Thief in the Night: A Dr. John Thorndyke Story
*Mr. Pottermack's Oversight: A Dr. John Thorndyke
Story*
*Dr. Thorndyke Intervenes: A Dr. John Thorndyke
Story*
The Singing Bone: The Adventures of Dr. Thorndyke
The Stoneware Monkey: A Dr. John Thorndyke Story
*The Great Portrait Mystery, and Other Stories: A
Collection of Dr. John Thorndyke and Other Stories*
The Penrose Mystery: A Dr. John Thorndyke Story
The Uttermost Farthing: A Savant's Vendetta

Arthur Griffiths
The Passenger From Calais
The Rome Express

Fergus Hume
The Mystery of a Hansom Cab
The Green Mummy
The Silent House
The Secret Passage

Edgar Jepson
The Loudwater Mystery

A. E. W. Mason
At the Villa Rose

A. A. Milne
The Red House Mystery
Baroness Emma Orczy
The Old Man in the Corner

Edgar Allan Poe
The Detective Stories of Edgar Allan Poe

Arthur J. Rees
The Hampstead Mystery
The Shrieking Pit
The Hand In The Dark
The Moon Rock
The Mystery of the Downs

Mary Roberts Rinehart
Sight Unseen and The Confession

Dorothy L. Sayers
Whose Body?

Sir William Magnay
The Hunt Ball Mystery

Mabel and Paul Thorne
The Sheridan Road Mystery

Raoul Whitfield
Death in a Bowl

And much more!
Visit ResurrectedPress.com
for our complete catalogue

About Resurrected Press

A division of Intrepid Ink, LLC, Resurrected Press is dedicated to bringing high quality, vintage books back into publication. See our entire catalogue and find out more at www.ResurrectedPress.com.

About Intrepid Ink, LLC

Intrepid Ink, LLC provides full publishing services to authors of fiction and non-fiction books, eBooks and websites. From editing to formatting, from publishing to marketing, Intrepid Ink gets your creative works into the hands of the people who want to read them. Find out more at www.IntrepidInk.com.

www.ingramcontent.com/pod-product-compliance
Lightning Source LLC
Chambersburg PA
CBHW071303250626
47159CB00004B/1292